Trail of Tears

Also by Frances Patton Statham

Bright Sun, Dark Moon

Flame of New Orleans

Jasmine Moon

Daughters of the Summer Storm

Phoenix Rising

From Love's Ashes

On Wings of Fire

To Face the Sun

Mary Musgrove, Queen of Savannah

(Original Title: Call the River Home)

The Roswell Women

The Roswell Legacy

The Silk Train

Murder, al fresco

Mountain Legacy

Trail of Tears

Frances Patton Statham

Bocage Books

 Published in the United States by Bocage Books

ISBN: 978-0-9895007-1-5

(Previously ISBN: 0-449-90659-0)

Library of Congress Control Number: 2013917667

First Edition: Ballantine Books, February 1993

Second Edition: Bocage Books, November 2013

Cover design: Steve McAfee

10 9 8 7 6 5 4 3 2

Bocage Books

bocagebooks@mindspring.com

www.bocagebooks.com

Acknowledgments

Two of the most important people who gave me inspiration for this novel were a Cherokee medicine man, Chief Two Trees, and the Rev. Robert Bushyhead, a direct descendant of the Rev. Jesse Bushyhead, who led one of the detachments out west on the trail of tears.

I am grateful to them both for their sharing with me the oral traditions and some of the history not found in standard reference books.

And only in this second edition do I feel free to acknowledge also the benevolent unseen force that left gifts of feathers and small rocks on my breakfast table and caused a brief power outage three times in a row that deleted a particular page until I finally got the message: that the reference book I was using for a segment of the journey was incorrect. Once I turned to another reference, I had no further trouble.

I hope that this novel will give some insight into one of our more tragic legacies of the past, with the resolve that the past will not repeat itself.

Frances Patton Statham

"I will draw thorns from your feet.
We will walk the White Path of Life together;
Like a brother of my own blood, I will love you;
I will wipe tears from your eyes. When you are sad,
I will put your aching heart to rest."

Cherokee Traveler's Greeting

Trail of Tears

Chapter 1

The storm broke in full force, with lashing rain as cruel as wet leather whipping against the coach horses's flanks.

Laurel MacDonald, the coach's lone passenger, held on to the overhead rings to keep from being tossed to the floor.

Just ahead, jagged streaks of lightning and rumbling voices of thunder pierced the unnatural darkness of the wilderness trail, while less than a quarter mile to the south, three riders hurried to overtake the fleeing vehicle.

Aware of the danger surrounding her, Laurel listened to the coarse heaves of the exhausted horses and the soothing, hypnotic chant of the Cherokee driver, urging the animals to keep up their breakneck pace.

In the best of times the vast, lonely stretch of wilderness beyond the Chattahoochee was filled with a quiet beauty, with crystal waters trickling over polished stones and baby-feathered eaglets gliding awkwardly on the wind gusts that swept past their aeries. Only an occasional sound of an ax told of civilization's encroachment in the aged forest.

But all that was beginning to change. Overnight, lawless misfits had invaded the land, and today Laurel had been unfortunate enough to catch the attention of one of the outlaw bands. Her vivid exotic beauty—her lustrous, auburn hair, flawless silken skin, and topaz-colored eyes—could not be masked, even by the deliberately chosen drab brown traveling costume.

As she unconsciously fingered one of the gold nuggets she'd sewn into the hem of her petticoats, Laurel glanced back. One of the horsemen had come into view. "Two Feathers," she shouted. "They're gaining on us."

The coach gathered momentum downhill, splashed across a rocky stream, but then was forced to slow when the muddy trail turned sharply upward again.

At the top of the hill a tall loblolly pine stretched toward the sky, its branches forming a canopy over the narrow trail. Shortly before the coach reached the crest, a brilliant streak of lightning hit the pine, splitting it and sending it crashing to the ground. The horses shied in terror as the tree fell in front of them. With the road blocked, Laurel realized that she had lost the race to safety.

But she had not reckoned on the driver's actions. After Two Feathers had brought the horses under control, he jumped down and loosened the harness that yoked the two nervous bays to the coach.

Throwing a blanket across Cloud Maker's back, he said, "Quick, Laurel. Make a run for Dr. Podewell's medicine house."

"But what about you, Two Feathers?"

"I'll be all right. You're the one they're after." The Indian gave her a lift-up onto the horse.

Forgotten was the formal, ladylike seat taught her in the equestrian class at the LaGrange Female Academy. With her petticoats hitched up to her knees and her hands clutching the horse's mane, she rode astride, the howling storm obliterating any sound of what might be happening behind her.

When she was over halfway through the formidable, dark woods, a soaking wet Laurel allowed herself to look back again. One horseman was still following — close enough for her to see his features despite the rivulets of water falling from his slouched hat.

"Keep on, Cloud Maker," Laurel encouraged. "We don't have much farther to go."

White foam, blown by the wind, brushed past Laurel. She rode the horse over scattered tree limbs, through great puddles of water, and dervishes of wind-caught vines. Finally, in the distance, a log cabin, with smoke curling from its chimney, came into view.

The horseman, realizing that Laurel had slipped from his grasp, shouted after her, "Ya might think you've gotten away. But we'll git ya yet."

The string of threats and the man's blustering laugh vanished in the wailing wind.

* * *

"Land sakes, child, you're wetter than a settin' hen." Mrs. Podewell stood at the cabin door and watched Laurel, already on the porch, finish ringing the water from her skirt and petticoats. "What happened? And where's Two Feathers?"

"We had an accident. A tree's blocking the road, so he stayed with the coach."

"Well, come on in. The fire's all stoked up. You can dry your clothes while I finish cookin' the supper."

"I have to see to Cloud Maker first."

"Johnny can rub her down for you. And I'll get Will to take his ax and ride down the road to help Two Feathers."

Laurel hesitated. "He'd better take his musket, too, Mrs. Podewell. There're some unsavory characters around."

Tish Podewell touched the bulge in her apron pocket. "Humph. They're gettin' worse every day. Chappie makes me carry my pistol all the time—even to the outhouse.

"Johnny! Will!" she called to her sons. "Laurel's here."

The ten-year-old and his awkward teenage brother appeared almost immediately. When he saw her, the older Will's face lit up. "How are you, Laurel?"

"She'll tell you at supper," Tish interrupted. With quick instructions, she dispatched both her sons on their way and drew Laurel inside to the hearth. "Take off your wet clothes," the woman ordered. "You can wear one of my shifts while they're dryin'."

"I can wait for my trunk."

"There's no tellin' how long it'll be before your coach gets here. You hankering to be one of Chappie's patients, with the pneumonia?"

"Not if I can help it, Mrs. Podewell."

"Then hurry up and strip before Johnny comes back from the barn."

Tish Podewell made no allowances for Laurel's modesty. She stared curiously as the young woman removed her wet clothes. "Looks like you've changed from the skinny little girl you was several years ago. Filled out in all the right places—"

A few minutes later, with Tish's blue shawl tied around the linen shift, an anxious Laurel walked to the window. She saw no sign of the coach or Two Feathers.

Finally she turned back to Mrs. Podewell, busy with her cooking chores. "What can I do to help?"

"You can set the table. I don't know whether Chappie will get back tonight or not, since all the Bothwell babies take their own good time gettin' into this world. But put down six plates, just in case."

Familiar with the rustic log cabin, its sleeping loft above the large keeping room, and the brick cooking hearth where the aroma of possum stew, sweet potatoes, and corn bread wafted through the room, Laurel walked over to the cupboard in the corner.

She took down the chipped enamelware plates, so different from her own family's Wedgwood china. And then she reached into the drawer for the few pewter knives and spoons. By the time she'd placed them all on the rough-hewn pine trestle table, a cheerful Johnny returned from the barn.

"Cloud Maker's been rubbed down proper, and she's eatin' her oats," he announced, gazing hungrily toward the hearth.

"Thank you, Johnny."

The faint sound of a musket firing caused Laurel to rush toward the door.

"Sounds like Will's gun," Tish commented, still stirring the cooking pot.

"Let me go and see, Ma," Johnny said, edging closer to the hearth.

"No, son. I need a man in the house with Laurel and me," Tish replied, softening her refusal. Feeling the sudden gust of wind from the outside sweeping through the cabin and threatening to put out the cooking fire, she said, "Close the door, Laurel. The wind and rain's blowin' in."

Once her attention returned to the hearth, the woman was not quick enough to ward off the boy's attack on the skillet of corn bread, kept warm in the ashes. "Mind your manners, Johnny," she scolded, swatting at his hand. But he had already stuffed a large piece of bread into his mouth.

A few minutes later, the wind suddenly ceased. An eerie blackness crept through the cabin, forcing Tish to lay down her long-handled ladle and light the wick in the oil lamp. Once the crystal globe was in place, she carried the lamp across the room and placed it on the trestle table, where the other two occupants of the cabin were already seated.

Joining them, Tish frowned at the silence now surrounding them. "I don't like it," she finally said. "When it gets too quiet out here, something bad always happens."

"The last storm we had took the roof off the barn," Johnny informed Laurel. "And blew the rooster in the well."

"Hush, Johnny, and listen."

Soon the rain and wind started afresh. With a dull thud something fell onto the roof, causing soot to fall onto the hearth. Then, from the barn, Cloud Maker snorted a loud protest, followed by a sudden, loud-pitched squeal from one of the pigs.

Tish rose from her chair. Reaching one hand into her apron pocket, she motioned for Johnny and Laurel to remain quiet while she tiptoed toward the barred door.

Seconds stretched into minutes, with lesser sounds swallowed up by the wind. Then the barely distinguishable creak of the wooden steps and the scraping of feet across the porch indicated that someone was about.

Laurel had heard no carriage come into the yard. Would Will be coming back alone? No, she told herself. Not unless something had happened to Two Feathers.

As they all watched, the handle of the door began to twist slightly. "Who's there?" Tish challenged.

A deep voice called out, "It's me—Chappie. Open the door, wife. It's worse'n hell out here."

Chapman Podewell was a bear of a man, with a grizzly beard to match. He'd deliberately chosen to live on the edge of civilization, for he didn't like other men telling him what he could or couldn't do. His freedom to come and go as he pleased and his friendship with the Indians, who could help him with his healing herbs and plants, were more important to him than all the amenities of a settled town. The wilderness life he'd chosen was healthier for his family, too.

When Tish unbarred the door for her husband, he gave himself a great shake, sending droplets of water across the porch.

"Did you see Will?" Tish inquired.

"Yes. He and Two Feathers'll be here in a few minutes."

The worried lines vanished from her forehead. "Then you know that Laurel's come."

He nodded in her direction. "The Bothwell baby, too. Another boy."

Later that evening, after Two Feathers and Will had arrived with her trunk intact despite the outlaws, Laurel sat at supper with the Podewell family while Two Feathers chose to take his plate to the barn.

For four years Laurel had traveled safely back and forth through this wilderness—in the fall to the academy, and then back home when the term was over. On each occasion Two Feathers had driven her, and they'd always stopped at the Podewells' medicine house to spend the night.

In the silence that accompanied the first part of the meal, Laurel tried to keep her mind on the food, as the others were doing, rather than on the next day. But she was grateful when Tish got up to replenish her hungry husband's plate, her action signaling that conversation could now begin.

"I was tellin' Laurel earlier," Tish remarked, "that it's a shame her last trip has to be spoilt by such a bad storm."

A stricken Will gazed at Laurel. "You mean, this is the last time I'll ever get to see you?"

Staring disgustedly at his older brother, Johnny said, "Don't you know? Laurel's graduated. She's too old to go to school anymore."

"I won't be going back to the academy next fall," Laurel admitted to Will. "Johnny's right about that. But it doesn't mean I won't ever come this way again."

"You get your teaching diploma?" Chappie inquired.

"Yes." Her voice was filled with pride as she announced, "And the Reverend Worcester's offered me a job at the mission school in New Echota."

When the meal was over, Laurel helped Tish to clean up.

It was a chore that she enjoyed, for at home, the servants always attended to it.

Late that night, when the last lamp had been blown out and the two boys had climbed the ladder to the sleeping loft, Laurel lay on her pallet by the hearth. She was fully clothed, for Two Feathers had warned her to be ready to slip out quietly at a moment's notice.

It seemed that she had no more than gotten to sleep when she heard someone whispering her name. She sat up quickly. "Is it time to leave?"

"No. It's still the middle of the night. But I just had to talk with you, Laurel."

"Will, go back to bed. You'll wake your parents."

"No. Pa's a sound sleeper. And if we whisper, we won't wake up Ma, either."

Brushing the hair out of her eyes, a sleepy Laurel said, "Then hurry and say what you've got to say."

"I love you, Laurel."

"Will..."

"No, I didn't mean to blurt it out like that. But ever since supper tonight, I've been thinkin' about it. I've loved you from the first time I ever saw you four years ago, and I want to marry you, Laurel."

"You know I would never move away from my people."

"Yes, I know that." Will's earnest young voice continued, "So I've decided that three months from now, when I turn eighteen, I'll sign up for the land lottery. There's plenty of good farmland in the valley not far from your folks. I know I couldn't give you everything you have now—at least not right away, but—"

His voice began to get louder with his eagerness, and Laurel reached out to put her hand over his mouth. "I think your parents are stirring. You'd better go back to bed."

"But you haven't given me an answer."

She hesitated. "Will, I like you. I like you a lot. But I'm not ready to settle down. Can't we just be friends?"

A disappointed Will reached out and took her hand. "If that's what you want. But you won't forget what we talked about, will you?"

"Of course not."

"And you'll write to me this fall from New Echota?"

"Yes."

"Thank you, Laurel." Will leaned over and quickly kissed a surprised Laurel on her lips. Then he fled across the room and climbed the ladder to the loft.

Several hours before dawn, as the Podewell family still slept, Laurel MacDonald was awakened again—this time by Two Feathers. On the hearth she left a nugget of gold for Tish. With a small portion of dried venison and two pieces of leftover corn bread wrapped in a napkin, she slipped from the cabin and, being careful to listen for the door bar falling back into place, she began the second phase of her journey along the wilderness trail.

Chapter 2

With the blue haze of the Cohutta Mountains spreading like silent fog and settling into the rich, fertile valley of the north Georgia hills, Alex MacDonald of the Cherokee Nation left his gold mine and headed in the direction of his two-story wood-frame house. His wife, Trudie, he knew, would be busy preparing for their daughter's homecoming.

It was not a good time to be away from home, either for Laurel or for himself, because of the sudden invasion of outsiders into the Nation. But it was because of these invaders that young Night Hawk had sent word to him. Someone had discovered the MacDonald mine and was systematically taking as much gold as he could find.

Alex was gratified that the invaders had not found the main shaft. They had merely panned the nuggets and tracings that continuously washed into the nearby creek. But it was only a matter of time before they discovered the rich veins of ore inside the earth. When they did, Alex stood to lose much of his wealth. But for the moment at least, the hidden opening had not been discovered.

In companionable silence Alex and Night Hawk rode their horses south. Approaching the valley, they passed a few rude, dirt-floor cabins where white squatters had elected to settle.

Looking at the proud young chieftain riding beside him, Alex said, "I'm glad that Laurel will be getting back to the Nation for good. I've worried about her this past year, with such animosity directed against our people."

"Her fair skin has served to protect her body in the white man's world," Night Hawk assured him. "But there was nothing to protect her heart from embracing the white man's ways."

"I don't think we have anything to fear from that. She has always been proud that she's a Cherokee."

"She has been away from her people for a long time," Night Hawk countered.

"It was necessary, for her education. But you must be patient for a while longer, Night Hawk. A year or so at Worcester's school, and then she will be ready to settle down."

Night Hawk nodded. "But she must accept me of her own free will, not because of my friendship with you. I would not have it any other way."

* * *

By noon the two men had finally reached the muddy street of the Carter settlement, where a general store, a post office, and a boardinghouse faced the blacksmith's shop and livery stable on the other side.

"Looks like we're not the only ones arriving," Alex remarked.

"Surveyors," Night Hawk said, with a disparaging voice, noting their equipment visible from one of the wagons.

With their horses taken care of, Alex and Night Hawk crossed the street and made for Miss Ellie's boardinghouse, where the proprietress was serving the noonday meal.

"You're in luck, Alex," the plump, middle-aged Ellie called out, seeing the two men entering the dining room. "Fried squirrel and all the turnip greens you can eat. And Daisy here's fixed apple pies for dessert. Real sugar, too."

Ellie turned to her pretty but slightly retarded daughter, who was standing at the open door to the kitchen. "Well, come on, Daisy. Don't just stand there gawking. You seen Mr. Alex and Night Hawk a dozen times. Say howdy to 'em and then go fix 'em a plate."

A shy Daisy giggled and nodded before disappearing into the kitchen.

"I'm surprised to see you this time of year, Alex," Ellie remarked. "Hope everything's all right with you."

"As well as can be expected, with all the strange goings-on."

"I know what you mean. Times are changin'. And not for the better."

Daisy soon returned with plates heaped high with food. She stationed herself near the kitchen door—attending to her mother's two customers until they had finished. Then she rushed to remove their empty plates.

"Are you ready now for your pie?" she asked.

Night Hawk and Alex both nodded, and Daisy disappeared back into the kitchen.

While the two men waited for their dessert, three clean-shaven and reasonably well-dressed outlaws left the general store, run by Ellie's husband, Jake, and began to follow their noses down the muddy track to the boardinghouse.

Several days earlier Vincent, the leader, had shot two surveyors and stolen their wagon. It had seemed like a good idea at the time, so they might travel throughout the Nation without arousing suspicion. But so far the wagon and equipment had merely slowed them down.

"God, I'm bored with this wilderness," Vincent commented, angry that good fortune had eluded him.

Les responded with a teasing suggestion. "A nice romp

with a whore would sweeten you up, I vow."

The younger Billy merely listened without joining in.

"Little chance. The only females I've seen around here are does."

"It'd be mighty convenient if you happened on an Indian girl in the woods."

"Yeah. Especially since she couldn't testify against me, whatever I did to her."

The conversation halted at the open door of the boardinghouse.

Seeing the strangers standing there, a pleased Ellie, already calculating the unexpected windfall of three more customers, greeted them with a broad smile. "Gentlemen, come in. Guess you'll be wantin' a meal, will you?"

Vincent nodded just as Daisy returned from the kitchen with two large pieces of apple pie. But he stopped when he saw where she was taking them. "Sorry, ma'am. But we don't eat in the same room with savages. Come on, Les. Billy."

"Wait a minute," a flustered Ellie called out.

Aware of the sudden tension in the room, Alex casually stood up and put his money on the table. "We have a long ride ahead of us, Night Hawk. Why don't we take our pie and head on out?"

"Good idea."

"See you on the next trip, Ellie," Alex said, turning his back to the three men and walking through the kitchen to avoid any confrontation.

"Thank you, Alex. Night Hawk," Ellie whispered. "And I'm sorry—"

"We understand."

A few minutes later, the three outlaws began their meal. Daisy openly stared at them, for she had seldom seen any young men so handsome— especially the dark-haired one. But she did not shirk her duties.

Trained by Ellie, she brought fresh, hot biscuits as soon as they'd finished their first round. And when the younger one drained his mug of milk, she immediately brought another pitcher to the table.

With Ellie out of sight, Vincent seized his opportunity. He patted Daisy as she leaned over to pour the milk, but when she turned suddenly to stare at him, his eyes were innocent. "You're a pretty little thing," he said. "What's your name?"

For a moment she was silent.

"What's the matter? Cat got your tongue?" he teased.

"Daisy."

"How old are you, Daisy?"

"I'm not sure. Fourteen. Maybe fifteen. But I could ask my mama."

"Don't trouble her," he responded quickly. "Old enough, I expect," he said, smiling at her.

He was so nice and friendly. Maybe she had only imagined that he had touched her.

"You have a boyfriend?"

"Not yet," she answered, with a giggle. "But I got a best friend—Louise. Everybody calls her Lulu. Mama said I could go and visit her when I finish washin' up the dishes."

"How would you like to go for a ride instead?"

"I don't think my mama..."

"Haven't you ever done anything without asking your mama?"

"Once—but I got in a heap of trouble."

Vincent winked at his two friends and raised his voice when he saw Ellie returning. "I declare, this is the best meal I've had all week. Makes me want to stay a few days longer before heading back to Milledgeville."

"I have some extra beds upstairs what aren't let. That is, if you need a place to stay," Ellie said, trying not to sound too eager. "And Daisy makes some mouth-watering pancakes at breakfast time."

"Are the Indians staying here, too?"

"No," Ellie was quick to admit. And then ashamed of her reaction, she felt obligated to defend them. "You got the wrong idea about those two men. They're both rich Cherokee chieftains—with lots of property. Educated, too. Night Hawk went to the Moravian school at Spring Place, and Alex's daughter, Laurel, is at that fancy school in LaGrange. I only wish my Daisy—"

"Tell you what," Vincent interrupted. "We still have a little surveying to do this afternoon. If we decide to stay around, we'll be back well before sundown. That'll give you enough time, won't it?"

"That'll be just fine."

Vincent lingered, waiting for Ellie to disappear so he could get a word alone with Daisy. "You're sure you can't go for a ride?"

"I can't," Daisy answered.

"Then how about meeting me at the footbridge when you've finished your chores? I have a present to give you, for being so nice."

Her cornflower-blue eyes lit up. "What is it?"

"I can't tell. It's a secret. Not a word to your mama."

"But it's all right if I take it to Lulu's to show her?"

"Sure."

At the livery stable Vincent caught up with Les and Billy. "Well, she's going to meet me at the creek."

Les laughed. "The girl's not very bright, is she?"

Vincent matched his laugh. "Maybe not. But she'll know a whole lot more once she's been with me."

"You think she'll be willing to learn?"

"If I have any trouble with her, that fine lace shift I took off the clothesline in the valley yesterday should be enough to convince her."

Billy spoke for the first time since they'd left the boardinghouse. "You shouldn't be plannin' such mischief, Vincent."

He was already sorry that he'd come along with the two men.

Vincent and Les looked at each other and shook their heads. "What are we going to do with him?"

"Maybe give him a taste once we're through with her?"

They both laughed as Billy's face turned red at their lewd suggestion. Tousling his shaggy blond hair, Vincent said, "Go on, boy, and get the wagon."

With her chores done for the afternoon, Daisy went to her room to freshen up. She felt a surge of excitement as she poured water into the basin to wash her face. She always felt this way when her mother let her visit Lulu. But there was another reason, too. She was going to be given a present—just like the time Papa came home from his long trip. And whatever it was, she could share it with her friend.

By the time her mother appeared upstairs to rebraid her hair, Daisy was already dressed in her new calico.

"Now don't stay all afternoon at Lulu's," Ellie cautioned her daughter. "I still need you to help me with supper."

"All right, Mama."

"And be careful of your dress. Try to keep the mud off the hem."

"Yes, Mama."

Ellie sighed as she watched her daughter leave the house. What a pity that Daisy was slow. Ellie couldn't help but feel that awful fall from the wagon was responsible. She'd been such a smart little thing before the accident. Yet not being able to read and write would not be held against Daisy, since most of the people in the valley couldn't either. And she certainly didn't look different. Her long golden hair was finer than the silk tassels in the cornfield, and she still had such sweet ways.

Ellie brightened. Maybe Daisy would find some kind-hearted man who'd be willing to marry her.

Not far from the footbridge, Vincent tethered his horse and found a spot behind a tree where he could watch for Daisy. He chewed on a blade of grass and swatted at a bluetail fly that kept buzzing about his head.

For a half hour he waited. And all that time he saw only one person crossing the bridge—a young boy with his rabbit trap. He was becoming impatient when he finally spotted her in the distance. Her bonnet hid her face, but he could tell from her walk and the swing of the basket she was carrying that it was Daisy.

As she approached the footbridge Vincent left his hiding place. "I thought maybe you wouldn't be coming," he said, greeting her. "Thought maybe I'd have to give the present to someone else."

"That wouldn't be fair," Daisy said, the distress showing in her face. "You said you'd give it to me."

"And so I will." He smiled and reached out to take her hand.

"Where is it?"

"Not far. I left it down in the woods so nobody could steal it."

For a moment Daisy hesitated. But the lure of the present and Vincent's smile were too overpowering. She did not resist when he led her away from the bridge to the thicket in the distance.

From the small opening in the dense thicket Daisy saw the most beautiful sight she'd ever seen. Draped across a blanket on the ground lay a white lace shift decorated with pink ribbons. She put down her basket and quickly climbed inside to retrieve the present. But as she began to back out she bumped into Vincent, who was directly behind her.

"Do you like it?" He was now so close that she could feel his breath on her neck.

"Oh, yes. It's beautiful. Thank you."

When he still blocked her way, she frowned. "I have to

go to Lulu's now."

"Not yet. You'll have to pay me first."

"Pay you? But I don't have any money."

"Then what *do* you have?"

"The cookies in the basket. Maybe Lulu won't mind if you eat one."

"I'd rather have something else."

Before Daisy knew it, Vincent was on top of her, his hands holding her face as he covered her lips with his.

"No."

"Be quiet, Daisy. A bargain's a bargain."

"But I didn't—"

Daisy didn't understand what was happening. She only knew that the man's hands were hurting her. She began to fight, until she heard her dress suddenly tear. Her mother would be so angry at her for not taking better care of her new calico. So in an attempt to protect it, she stopped struggling.

Like a small animal at the mercy of a predator, she whimpered while the onslaught continued. With her skirt over her head, Vincent began to push something hard and warm against her leg, moving upward until he found a place to his liking, judging from the sounds that came from his throat. The pain as he gained entrance to her body caused Daisy to cry out, but it didn't stop him.

On and on he continued, deeper and deeper, with a frenzied rhythm to match the terrible noises, until his entire body shuddered and then lay like a dead man upon her. Terrified, she tried to free herself.

"Be still," he ordered. "I'm not through with you yet." Resting on top of her for a while, the man had begun his attack again when from the other side of the thicket a voice called to him, "Vincent, it's my turn. Don't be so greedy."

As Vincent finally removed his weight from her, Daisy whimpered, "Can I go now? Please?"

"No. You have to be nice to Les."

"But I don't want the present anymore. I want to go home."

The second man avoided looking into Daisy's hurt eyes. "Now that Vincent's had his way, guess I don't have to be so careful."

Words that she had never heard before accompanied the second man's actions. She felt his fingernails digging into her neck and tearing at her breasts, while he, too, invaded her body. She drifted in and out of consciousness, the only way she could blot out the terrible nightmare. Finally, when she opened her eyes again, she was alone.

Daisy began to cry, tears streaming down her cheeks. Clutching at the blanket, she felt the ribbons of the lace shift entwine about her fingers. In horror, she seized the ribbons and tore them from the lace, at last throwing the hated present as far from her as she could. Then, on all fours, she began to crawl out of the thicket.

Billy was waiting on the other side. When he saw her, he drew in his breath. "Oh, my God, Daisy. You look like you tangled with a wildcat."

"Leave me be," she cried.

Seeing how frightened she was, he said, "I'm not gonna hurt you. I stayed behind to help you."

"I want to go home," she wailed. "I want my mama."

"You need to get cleaned up before you go back to the settlement. Here, I'll take you down to the creek, where you can wash the blood off. Wish I had some salve for the scratches on your neck and face." He was gentle, carrying her to the water's edge, where she sat and mended her body and dress as well as she could.

Twenty minutes later, as the sun began to reach the treetops, Billy accompanied Daisy to the footbridge. He handed her crushed bonnet to her. "I'm sorry this happened to you, Daisy."

He watched her stumble across the bridge and disappear toward the settlement. Then he hitched his horse to the wagon and moved out to catch up with the other two outlaws.

At the boardinghouse, Ellie had already aired out the extra room in case the men came back. The supper was cooked and waiting in the warm oven, but there was still no sign of Daisy.

For the third time a worried Ellie walked to the open door to take another look down the muddy lane. In relief, she finally spied her daughter coming home. But her relief vanished when she saw how unsteady the girl was on her feet.

Ellie left the boardinghouse and hurried to meet her. The closer she got, the more alarmed she became. "Daisy, darlin'. What happened to you?"

Daisy had no words to describe what had occurred. She tried to remember what Billy had said. "Wildcat," she finally mumbled, and promptly fell into her mother's arms.

Chapter 3

Along the wilderness trail Laurel and Two Feathers kept up a steady pace. In the darkness before first light, each tree, each bush became a source of uneasiness, harboring dangers that made themselves known only by fleeting sounds and vaporous shadows against the waning moon.

With each mile Laurel's sense of outrage grew. Who were these lawless men to force her to flee before them like a fox to its den? They had robbed her of the sense of wonder and majesty of the forest, and replaced it with an alien feeling. But she would refuse to name this new feeling; for in showing honor by bestowing a name upon it, she would somehow be summoning it to her side, to stay. Instead, her attention returned to the road ahead.

The previous evening's rainstorm had left muddy furrows and derelict branches of trees scattered along the trail. But the rain had stopped. Soon now the sun would be breaking through, and its warming rays could begin to heal the ruts in the wilderness road.

From the east the first sign of the sun began to emerge. Slowly, in and out of the trees and darkness, hints of light, captured by a hanging vine, a fluttering leaf, moved uncertainly at first, until the sun finally burst upon the horizon in blood-red splendor.

With this first light of a new day Laurel breathed a sigh of relief. The forest no longer appeared so formidable.

Yet, as Laurel relaxed, Two Feathers became even more alert. It was now one mile to the ferry, its approach bordered by open, treeless terrain, visible on all sides.

As if aware of the Indian's thoughts, Laurel whispered, "I hope the ferryman has his raft on this side of the river."

"Yes," Two Feathers replied. "There is little place to hide, if we have to wait."

Farther behind, the three horsemen followed the muddy tracks made by Laurel's coach.

"I told you we shoulda got an earlier start," Skeeter, the youngest one, complained.

"Calm down, boy," his uncle scolded. "She's not that far ahead, and we got plenty of time to catch up with her before she gets into the Nation."

"Yeah," Roy, Skeeter's brother, agreed. "But it's gonna take somethin' to steal her away from that old Indian, short of killin' him."

"But we can't do that. Else who'd take the ransom note to her daddy?"

Skeeter grinned. "And bring back all that gold."

"That's right. The Scruggs family is gonna be stinkin' rich soon."

"You aimin' to let her go after we get the money?"

Jude glanced at his older nephew, "Now, what do *you* think, Roy?"

The signal bell reverberating along the river gained Jude's attention. "Hell, sounds like she's already at the ferry. Let's go, boys, and pray that Nate, the ferryman, ain't on this side of the river."

The three set off in a gallop, with mud flying from the

hooves of the horses. A few minutes later the pine and hickory trees began to dwindle as Jude and his nephews neared the bottom land, where Nate's spring crop of corn was now knee-high.

"There she is," Skeeter said, gloating. "And Nate's in the middle of the river. We've got 'er."

"Not yet, boy." Jude, seeing the ferryman pole the raft along the swift-moving current toward the closer bank, lifted his hand to halt the other two.

"Why're we stoppin', Uncle?" Roy asked.

"We can't let Nate see us. Better for us to go downstream and ford the river so's we can already be waitin' for her on the other side."

"You always *was* a sly one," Skeeter complimented.

"Got to be," Jude replied, "if you're gonna make somethin' of yourself in this hard world."

Jude veered his horse through the woods, with the other two following. Peering down the long vista, he could barely make out Laurel's coach as it rolled onto the ferry raft. Invisible at that distance was the overhead rope that kept the raft from being swept downstream by the current. But the song of the ferryman echoed in his ears.

Finally, at water's edge, the three horses struggled to gain a foothold on the opposite bank. With much slipping and sliding, the riders maneuvered their mounts onto the land, toward a dense clump of willow trees.

"We'll stop here and rest the horses," Jude said. "Then we'll be off to catch up with that little Indian girl soon as she crosses."

A half hour later, with Laurel's coach and horses as cargo, Nate poled the ferry to the other side. He cast the chains from the raft, as usual, and hitched them to the iron rings attached to the wooden pilings. Then Cloud Maker and Sundance, obeying the driver's sharp whistle and shout, plunged across the planks and pulled the rolling vehicle onto the north bank of the river.

In a steady pace the coach traveled the winding trail toward the distant mountains. A bird trilled its mid-morning song from a treetop, the only sound besides that of the coach horses.

Catching an occasional glimpse of the coach as the road twisted and bent and then straightened again, the three horsemen traveled, with Jude waiting for an appropriate time to make his move.

"All right, boys. Go!" he shouted, brandishing his pistol and digging his bony knees into his horse's flanks.

Roy and Skeeter, whom Jude had taken in after his brother, the boys' father, had been killed in a brawl, had their instructions—to cut off the coach from the side and front while Jude approached from the rear. Roy burst from the woods first, his sudden movement causing the coach horses to rear in fright.

Within seconds Roy and Skeeter had grabbed the horses' harness, bringing them to a stop.

Riding up from behind. Jude called out, "Get down, Indian. Unless you're hankerin' to be a dead man."

"What is this? Why are you stopping us?"

In disbelief, Jude stared at the stranger—a bearded young white man, dressed in buckskin. What was this man doing driving the MacDonald coach? Where was the Indian? Unable to comprehend what had happened, Jude dismounted, grabbed at the door of the coach and opened it.

But it was not Laurel who gazed at him in terror. A young woman, her belly distended with child, began to wail. "I *told* you, Horace, this was too good to be true. We should have kept our own wagon and mules."

"Don't harm my wife, mister," Horace begged. "She's gonna have a baby any minute. Besides, we didn't know the coach was stolen. That Indian said—"

"Shut up!" Jude ordered.

His head ached. All his plans, and the Indian had outsmarted him. But not for long. "Skeeter! Roy! We got to get back to the ferry!"

The puzzled couple, still trembling with fear, watched as the three horsemen disappeared down the trail.

Up ahead, Laurel and Two Feathers continued their rough ride in the wagon pulled by two sway-backed old mules.

"Do you think the woman will be all right?" Laurel asked.

Two Feathers nodded. "Better for her to be in a well-sprung coach, in her condition."

"I hope she makes it to Miss Ellie's before having the baby."

"It'll be close," Two Feathers admitted.

For the rest of the day they traveled, stopping only long enough to water the mules and eat the bread and venison brought from the medicine house. They kept a sharp lookout for Jude and his two nephews.

That night, no fire gave away their hiding place. Their supper consisted of the largesse of the forest—pine nuts, sorrel, assorted berries, and saxifrage. While Laurel slept in the wagon, hidden under a canopy of pine boughs, Two Feathers slept near the mules, in an equally hidden spot off the trail.

By the next day, Two Feathers was aware that the three men had picked up their trail again. But he and Laurel were now within the boundary of the Nation, and so the danger was considerably lessened. In another hour or so, he would deliver Laurel safely to her doorstep, then go over to the white settlement to swap the vehicles and animals and retrieve the trunk.

With every passing mile Laurel's eagerness to reach home increased. She acknowledged each familiar tree, each remembered turn of the road while her eyes watched for the gate that would announce the beginning of her family's property.

When it came into sight, a sense of pride welled up in her heart.

"I'll get out here, Two Feathers, and walk the rest of the way."

The Indian stopped the wagon to let her down, but he followed slowly at a distance, just in case. It would not do for him to turn his back at the last minute, since the property was vast, with cornfields and orchards, pastures filled with cattle, and acres of vegetables growing in the fertile soil. The three horsemen might still be hoping to take her before she reached the house.

Laurel was glad to be out of the uncomfortable wagon. Relishing the familiar smells of the earth, the plants, and all living things around her, she reached down and, asking permission, she plucked a sweet-scented wildflower. Holding it up to her nose, she took in a deep breath of appreciation before threading the lavender flower into the lace collar of her dress.

Feeling a sense of joy, she began to run along the winding road, with the cool mountain breeze brushing against her face.

She waved to the servants leaving the fields for the day. They smiled and waved back at the daughter of the household, who appeared so happy to be at home again.

"Mother! Father!" she shouted. "I'm home."

Trudie and Alex, sitting on the porch of the two-story clapboard house, with its tall, fieldstone chimneys, heard their daughter's voice. Only a moment before, Trudie had stared down the road, hoping to catch a glimpse of the carriage.

The family reunion took place in the brush-swept yard, bordered by mountain laurels, for which their daughter had been named.

Trudie MacDonald, an aging, sloe-eyed beauty with delicate bones and a regal bearing despite her small stature, reached out and gathered her daughter in her arms. Alex, equally happy to see his daughter, was slightly more formal. "Welcome home, Du-su-ka," he said, speaking in Cherokee.

But then, in a puzzled manner, he inquired, "Where is Two Feathers? And where is the carriage?"

Laurel's eyes clouded, and she spoke in a hesitant voice. "We had a little trouble. But everything's fine now. The carriage and horses are at the settlement. Two Feathers has gone over to get them."

The sudden moos coming from the barn diverted Alex's attention. Frowning, he said, "Sounds as if something's wrong with the milk cows."

He began to walk rapidly toward the barn, with Trudie and Laurel following. As he rounded the bend in the road Alex suddenly stopped at the sight of three white men coming out of his barn.

The men, whom Laurel recognized as the ones who had followed her all the way home, were leading three of Alex's milk cows toward their horses, which were tied to the fence.

In righteous anger Laurel gazed toward the men and then back to her father. But Alex merely stood still and watched.

"Father, they're stealing our cows," she said. "Aren't you going to stop them?"

A sadness marred Alex's face. "Be quiet, Laurel. There is nothing I can do."

"You can get your gun and shoot them."

Her mother intervened. "You evidently haven't heard of the new laws, Laurel," she said.

"What laws? There's no Cherokee law that says it's all right to steal."

"Georgia has passed certain laws that—"

"But we're a sovereign nation, not subject to *any* state's laws."

"Do you want to see your father hanged?"

"Of course not."

"Then come back to the house with me and forget what you've seen."

Trudie placed her hand on her daughter's shoulder and began to guide her away. "Cousin John Ross has called a council meeting at New Echota. But in the meantime he has advised us to do nothing when challenged by the white man. For the good of the Nation, we must all follow his advice."

Laurel's homecoming had turned bitter. Heartsick, she took one last look at the vanishing horsemen with the protesting cows tugging at their ropes. Then she turned her back and walked toward the house with her mother.

Chapter 4

"I'm not takin' in any boarders this week," Ellie explained to the man standing at her door. "Maybe Wandra Honeycut, three miles down the road, will have room for you."

An exhausted Horace Martin stood his ground as Ellie attempted to close the door in his face. "Please," he begged. "My wife can't make it that far. The baby's comin' any minute."

"Horace," a woman's voice screamed from the carriage. "I need you."

The young man's eyes silently pleaded his cause and Ellie finally relented. "All right. Bring her in. But you'll have to take care of her yourself. I got problems of my own."

She watched Horace rush to the carriage and remove his wife. Seeing the condition she was in, Ellie shouted for the stable boy across the street.

When he appeared almost immediately, Ellie said, "Unhitch these fine horses, Ned. And take good care of them."

"There's an Indian who's supposed to be comin' for them soon," Horace explained. "For the carriage, too. He'll be bringin' my own wagon and mules."

"Yes, sir."

Following Ellie inside the boarding house, Horace carried his wife up the narrow stairs to a bedroom that faced the street. Ellie would have preferred moving the woman farther down the hall, since the bedroom was directly across from Daisy's room. But it was the only one with the bed already made up.

Yet, if the woman screamed in pain, it probably would not bother Daisy. For two days she had been oblivious to every noise, as if she were somewhere far away. Hard as Ellie had tried, she couldn't get her daughter to speak a word beyond the initial ones when she found her.

Ellie looked down at the young woman, hardly a year older than Daisy, and then back to her nervous husband. "This her first baby?"

"Yes."

She might have known it. With no doctor within miles, she would be the one bringing the puling infant into the world. The hand-wringing husband would be no help at all.

"I'll come back with some hot water and linen. Just as soon as I check on my own child."

"I'm mighty grateful to you."

"Don't thank me yet. I expect it's gonna be a long night, and I'll have to charge you a midwife's fee, too."

Ellie left the room, and on her way downstairs to the kitchen, she opened her daughter's bedroom door to take a peek inside. The girl was still asleep, so Ellie carefully closed the door again and proceeded down the flight of stairs.

When she reached the kitchen, Ellie's hungry husband, Jake Dodge, was arriving for supper.

"How's Daisy?" he asked immediately.

"Same as yesterday."

"Well, Augie thinks he got the wildcat that attacked her.

Had its carcass in the back of his wagon. He said it wasn't foamin' at the mouth or anything when he shot it this morning."

When he didn't get the expected response, Jake said, "I thought you'd be relieved, Ellie, knowin' our Daisy won't go mad."

"If it *was* a wildcat."

"What do you mean by that? I thought she told you."

Ellie decided to keep her suspicions to herself. It wouldn't do any good to alarm Jake. " 'Course she did. And I'm pleased that Augie shot the creature. It's just that my mind is on that poor boarder upstairs—havin' her first baby and all."

At his questioning look she added, "I know what you're thinkin'. But how could I shut the door on the two, seein' the shape the woman was in?"

Jake shook his head. "The woman be damned. You never *could* shut the door on an extra dollar or two, could you?"

"That's not fair, Jake. I need the money."

"No, you don't. I make more than enough in the store for us, Ellie."

"But I got to have a dowry for Daisy. How else are we goin' to get some man to marry her?"

"I'd just as soon she'd stay here with us."

"Well, that's neither here nor there. I got to heat up some water and get back upstairs. If I send the husband to the kitchen, you think you could dish up some supper for both of you?"

"I reckon."

During the night the painful cries of Bess Martin spread throughout the house, causing a nervous and slightly drunk Horace, seated with Jake by the cold hearth downstairs, to tighten his grip on the mug in his hand.

Upstairs, across the hall, the same cries also penetrated Daisy's room. She sat up and listened. Then she began to whimper and cry, too, as she remembered the terrible thing that had happened to her in the thicket. But looking around her for the first time in two days, she realized that she was safe in her own room.

She stopped crying, but the noise on the other side of the hall continued. Still feeling frightened, she got out of bed and began to search for her mother. Ellie was not in her own room. Neither was her papa.

The light coming from under the door drew her toward the other bedroom. "Mama?" she called as she pushed open the door that stood slightly ajar.

She saw the red-haired woman in the bed and then her mother at her side, holding something tiny in a white linen wrapping.

"Daisy, darlin', go back to bed."

"Mama, what's wrong?"

"Nothin', pet. This woman's just had her baby—a pretty little boy."

Daisy's eyes lit up. "Let me see, Mama."

Ellie pushed back the wrapping so that Daisy could get a better look at the squirming infant with blondish-red fuzz on his head.

"Oh, let me hold him. I'll be careful. I promise."

Delighted that Daisy had come to herself, Ellie said, "All right. Sit down in the chair. You can hold him while I go downstairs to get the father."

"Is *she* dead?" Daisy inquired, looking at the small, still figure in the bed, with her ashen face and red hair still wet with perspiration.

"No, but she's mighty weak. It'll be up to the good Lord whether she lasts the night or not."

When Horace arrived, he rushed to his wife's side and took her limp hand. "Bess? Bess? Are you feelin' all right?"

When Bess didn't answer, Ellie replied for her. " 'Course she's not feelin' all right. She's lost a lot of blood. I couldn't do much about that. But she's given you a fine son."

It was then that Horace spied Daisy sitting in the shadows and cooing to his son as she rocked him. But when he reached out to take the child, she recoiled.

"Give him his son, darlin'." Ellie instructed.

Reluctantly her daughter did so.

For the next week Bess lingered, too sick to nurse or take care of her child. With Horace at his dying wife's bedside, it was Daisy who took charge of the baby. And it was Daisy who held him at the funeral on a windy afternoon, with the steady breeze blowing down the hillside, while Jake spoke a few Christian words over the grave. Ned, the stable boy, Jack, the blacksmith, and his wife Cora, were the only other mourners, hastily gathered for the occasion by Ellie.

"It's a terrible bad situation," Ellie commented to the grieving Horace after the others had come back to pay their respects, eaten the victuals she'd prepared, and gone their way again. "A man alone, and with a baby to raise." She cast her eyes toward Daisy, sitting by the hearth and feeding the baby with the skin teat stretched over the milk bottle.

"You think I could board him here until I got settled?" Horace asked. "I'd come back for him later."

"Say yes, Mama," Daisy urged. "I like taking care of little Billy."

"Wait a minute. His papa is the one to name him, Daisy. Not you," Jake chastened.

"I've been too upset even to *think* about a name for the little chap." Horace's eyes suddenly softened. "Guess Billy's good enough. My grandpa's name was William."

With Billy left in Daisy's care, Horace Martin claimed his wagon and mules that Two Feathers had left. Inside the wagon were the gold-mining equipment and grubstake that he'd purchased from Jake's store.

Watching him pull out of the Carter settlement, Ellie sighed. "I just hope he won't forget to come back."

Jake, standing at her side, replied, "Might not be such a bad idea for him to disappear altogether."

"Why do you say that?"

"Just look at our daughter. She's so wrapped up in that baby, it'll take some real pryin' to get him loose from her arms."

Several months later, as the sun began to sink beyond the horizon, a tired and dusty Horace reappeared in the Carter settlement. Before announcing his arrival at the boarding-house, he took a bath in the blacksmith's shed and shaved off his beard. Then he walked across the street and knocked at the door.

"Well, young fellow, I'm surprised to see you back," Jake said. "Come on in. Ellie, look who's here."

Busy clearing off the kitchen table, Ellie nodded at the handsome young man. "Hardly recognized you without the beard. Have you had your supper?"

"No, ma'am."

"Then sit down and enjoy some leftovers. Daisy just went upstairs to put little Billy to bed. I'll call her to bring him down."

"Not yet, Miss Ellie. First I got somethin' important to say to you and Jake."

Horace seemed in no hurry to begin. He sat at the table and in silence began to eat the pork chop, a large slab of bread slathered in butter, and peach preserves.

Jake, seeing that he was nervous, casually said, "You find any gold up in the hills?"

"No. Wasn't that lucky. And it was mighty hard work."

"Too bad."

"Lonely , too, I hear," Ellie commented.

Horace nodded and took a big swallow of buttermilk. "But I got me a good job lined up for the fall. I'm goin' to be the overseer for Chief Joe Vann up near Spring Place."

"He's a rich one," Ellie said. "Will he be payin' you well?"

"Not only that. He'll be givin' me a nice house to live in, too." He cleared his throat. "Bein' up in the mountains gave me time to think. I need a wife, now that Bess is gone—someone like Daisy, to take care of my son, and to do the cookin'."

Ellie placed her hand over her heart to stop an eager fluttering.

"I know it's powerful soon, but this is a hard wilderness, and a man needs as much help as he can get."

"That's for sure," Ellie agreed.

"It was a terrible shame about Daisy's accident—how it knocked out some of the sense in her head. But I reckon she's got enough left to do the chores."

Ellie couldn't resist another comment. "And she's awful pretty, too."

Jake merely listened.

"I'd like your permission to marry her, if you think she'd have me. But we'd need to stay here with you until it's time to go to Spring Place."

With Ellie nudging his side, Jake grudgingly said, "I was thinkin' of hirin' on some extra help in the store. If Daisy says yes, then you could have the job—until it's time to move on. 'Course, if it's agreeable to Daisy."

Horace smiled. "Then it's all right with you if I speak to your daughter?"

Ellie hesitated. "Let me talk to her first, before you say anything. When you're finished eating, go on up and get reacquainted with your son. Leave Daisy to me."

As soon as he'd disappeared, Jake said, "Is this what you want for her, Ellie?"

"Yes. It's what I been prayin' for every day."

"But they'll have to wait a suitable time."

"No!" Ellie's voice was unusually sharp. "The sooner the better."

"With his first wife hardly cold in the ground? People will talk."

"People will talk even more if we wait."

"What do you mean?"

"Don't ask questions, Jake. Just send for the circuit preacher as quick as possible—before Horace Martin changes his mind."

"No tellin' where he is, Ellie. It might take weeks before I can track him down."

"Well, start on it today, Jake," Ellie said. Already her mind was busy planning Daisy's wedding dress.

In the end, it was the Reverend Samuel Worcester from New Echota who was persuaded to perform the wedding ceremony uniting Daisy and Horace.

The only thing that Daisy understood beforehand was that in marrying Horace, she would get to keep little Billy for her own. The rest of the things her mother had told her about being a wife had no meaning at all.

Chapter 5

Excitement filled the air as Laurel approached New Echota, capital of the Cherokee Nation. Once again, Two Feathers drove the family coach, and once again, Laurel's trunk was lashed to the back.

The exquisite days of summer had served to ease the memory of her earlier homecoming, replacing the sorrow and anger with an unusual joy and a feeling of camaraderie with her parents, her cousins, and her elders.

Now, with the passing of summer, Laurel realized that she was entering a new phase of her life. Her childhood had been packed away as surely as the clothes she had outgrown. But she knew she'd never outgrow the sense of awe she always felt when she entered the capital.

The town was laid out in one hundred one-acre town lots, its central square approached by a street sixty feet wide, with all the others ten feet less in width.

Coaches and horses were everywhere, wagons with supplies and provisions lining the streets, the activity signaling that the town was getting ready for the upcoming council meeting, when chiefs, judges, and elected representatives from the various clans would gather from the Carolinas, Georgia, Alabama, and Tennessee. Later in the week her own father would be coming.

"Two Feathers, look," she said, spying a tall, turbaned man walking across the green. "Isn't that Sequoyah? I thought he was still out west."

"Perhaps he came back with the Reverend Bushyhead for the meeting."

"Yes. That must be so."

Sequoyah was a source of pride for all Cherokees; for he was the one who had earlier invented an alphabet, making it possible for them to read in their own language.

"I know Elias Boudinot will be happy to see him," Laurel commented, referring to the editor of the Cherokee newspaper. "As well as the others," she added.

The coach carefully wound its way past the log taverns, the courthouse and council house, the stores and trading posts, past the homes of the year-round residents. When the newspaper office, where the *Cherokee Phoenix* was printed, came into sight, Laurel saw the turbaned man disappear inside.

"Oh, Two Feathers. That *is* Sequoyah," she affirmed. "You must tell Father as soon as you get home."

Two Feathers smiled at the excited Laurel's comment. "I hope your pupils will be as enthusiastic as you are."

A serious note crept into her voice. "When I'm teaching them the alphabet, I shall also teach them about Sequoyah."

They rode the rest of the way in silence, until the white-washed two-story mission school appeared in the distance. Set apart from the village by a private winding lane and a wide expanse of green, the house was surrounded by ancient oaks, orchards of peach and apple, a well, and all the outbuildings—corncribs and storage barns—used to house the harvest of the fields.

Two porches ran the length of the house, with an outside staircase connecting the lower porch to the upper. For in addition to being a schoolmaster and a missionary, the Reverend Samuel Worcester was the officially appointed postmaster for New Echota, with the public post office on the second floor.

After the coach had drawn up and stopped at the door, Vervia Worcester, the reverend's wife, sitting in a rocker on the front porch, rose to greet its occupants.

"Good afternoon, Laurel. Two Feathers," she said, nodding to one and then the other.

"Hello, Mrs. Worcester," Laurel called out.

The woman was thin and plain-dressed, with her graying hair pulled severely back from her face and twisted in a small knot on the top of her head.

"Samuel will be sorry he wasn't here to welcome you. He was called away to the Carter settlement. But he'll be back tomorrow."

"I heard that Daisy Dodge is getting married. He must be performing the ceremony."

Vervia nodded without smiling and returned her attention to Two Feathers, who had begun to loosen the trunk from its place at the back of the coach.

"It might be easier for you to use the outside stairs," the woman suggested. "We'll meet you on the upstairs porch. Come with me, Laurel."

Laurel followed the woman inside, through the parlor and up the narrow inside stairs.

"You'll be sleeping in one of the bedrooms adjacent to the mail room," Vervia explained. "And you'll be sharing quarters with two of the boarding students. I'm sorry that I couldn't give you a room to yourself."

"I don't mind, Mrs. Worcester."

"Yes. Well, it can't be helped. Samuel has more students than usual, and we've even boarded some of them with local families."

A half hour later, Laurel was alone. She opened her trunk and began to sort through its contents, choosing the few dresses she would place in the corner linen press. Since she would be sharing it as well, the majority of her possessions would have to remain in her trunk at the foot of her bed. But she was a teacher. That was the important thing—not the amount of space she had been given. Anyway, if she felt too cramped, she could always go outside.

When Laurel had finished her unpacking, she walked past the mail room to the deserted porch, where she stood, feeling the steady breeze fanned by the limbs of the tall oaks. Even from the higher vantage point she could see nothing of the capital. The avenue of trees effectively cut the house off from the rest of the town.

But as she stood drinking in the view, she saw a telltale trail of dust and heard the dull thud of horses' hooves pounding the sandy lane to the mission.

Down below in the kitchen, Mrs. Worcester heard the same noise. Peering from the side window, she recognized young Edward Farraday, the stagecoach driver. Quickly she wiped the flour from her hands and was on the porch by the time he halted his horses.

"You made good time, Edward."

"Afternoon, Mrs. Worcester," he replied, hopping down and tying the double reins to the hitching post. "The roads were dry, and I didn't linger long at the Vann trading post."

There was something about Edward Farraday that bothered Vervia. He was far too handsome for his own good, with his maleness affecting most of the females who came in contact with him. How different he was from Samuel, a true man of the cloth. Even she had to struggle against being drawn to Edward. Because of this her voice was a little harsher when she spoke to him.

"As soon as you've watered the horses, you may come into the kitchen for something to eat and drink."

What he wanted more than anything was a good mug of

rum, which he could get at the tavern. He was ready to decline her invitation when he looked up and saw Laurel, her hands on the upstairs banister. He had never seen anyone so beautiful. He stared openly until Laurel quickly turned and disappeared inside.

"Edward?"

"Uh, thank you, ma'am. That's mighty kind of you."

When he unhitched the horses and led them to the trough, Edward began to wonder who the young woman was. He'd never seen her before. Her white blouse and long black skirt indicated she might be a teacher, but then she hardly looked old enough. Maybe she was one of the older students. But no, she wouldn't be dressed like that if she were a student.

Edward drew several buckets of water from the well and poured them into the trough. When the horses had drunk their fill, he drew another bucket for himself, drinking from the tin dipper and then splashing some liquid over his face to wash off the dust of the road. Quickly he smoothed back his brown hair and then took the route into the kitchen at the back of the house.

He sat at the table and stared at the fresh milk and cookies that Vervia put before him. He waited expectantly for Laurel to appear, but as the minutes passed and she didn't come, he casually asked, "Have the students started arriving yet, Mrs. Worcester?"

"Why, no. They won't be coming for another two days."

"But when I drove up, I saw someone standing on the upstairs porch."

Mrs. Worcester smiled for the first time. "Oh, that's the new teacher. She's getting settled in. More milk, Edward?"

"No, ma'am. Thank you kindly," he added. "Guess I'd better be bringing in the mailbags."

"Elias Boudinot has a stack of pamphlets and the *Cherokee Phoenix* that he's anxious to get out as soon as possible. I'd better send Laurel to his office to let him know you're here."

"Laurel? Is that the new teacher's name?"

"Yes. Laurel MacDonald."

Trying to keep the eagerness out of his voice, he said, "Maybe Miss MacDonald would like to ride over in the stagecoach. I could bring back the packages—"

"No, Edward. There's no need to put yourself out. Elias can bring them over himself, as he usually does."

"Oh, I wouldn't be putting myself out."

"Edward, Laurel is a Cherokee chieftain's daughter. She's not for you."

At her plain words Edward ducked his head in embarrassment, but he couldn't stop from saying what was on his mind. "I only wanted to be introduced to her, Mrs. Worcester."

Vervia did not soften her resolve. "I'm sorry, Edward, but there wouldn't be any point to it. Samuel has accepted her as a teacher until she's old enough to marry Night Hawk."

The news was like a sudden stab in his gut. A disappointed Edward pushed his tall frame from the table and stood. "Thank you for the refreshment. I'll bring in the mailbags now."

Over at the Carter settlement Samuel stood in the large dining room of Ellie's boardinghouse and waited to perform the marriage ceremony uniting Daisy and Horace.

Ellie had outdone herself, dividing the room in half, with the crude wooden tables pushed together at the back and all the chairs arranged in rows, like pews in a church. The old fieldstone mantel was covered with greenery and candles, and in the gaping cavern of the fireplace she'd put a large vase of Black-eyed Susans.

She had also invited the entire settlement, with Lulu as bridesmaid, Ned the stable boy to stand up with Horace, and wheezy old Matthias to blow a tune on his harmonica.

Twisting against his heavily starched collar, Jake said, "I don't understand why you had to go to so much trouble, Ellie. Why couldn't it have been just you and me and the preacher? Daisy and Horace wouldn't have minded."

"It's good for business, Jake. When Tilda Mae sees the fancy weddin' cake, she's gonna want me to bake one just like it for Lulu when she gets hitched. And there'll be others, too, when the word gets 'round.

"Besides, it won't hurt *your* business none when the people see the fine bolt of cloth you got for Daisy's dress."

Her argument effectively shut off any further grumbling. He had to come up with the wages to pay Horace now, an additional expense. So he needed to start selling more at the store.

Ellie and Jake took their places on the front row of chairs, with Ellie holding the sleeping Billy. She'd had a terrrible time with Daisy, persuading her that a bride couldn't walk down the aisle with a baby in her arms.

Then Matthias began playing his harmonica, and all the people in the room became quiet, craning their necks toward the door. Ned was the first to enter. With unwavering eyes he walked straight toward the fireplace, keeping his back to the people and stopping in front of Samuel.

The dark-haired and dimpled Lulu came next, in her pale yellow gown, with a nosegay of wildflowers held close to her breast. She walked slowly, savoring every moment that all eyes were on her. It took her twice as long to reach the fireplace as it had taken Ned. Once she had arrived, she turned slightly so she could watch for Daisy and Horace.

Horace was dressed in a suit borrowed from the store, with his face clean-shaven except for his drooping mustache. Beside him walked Daisy in the pale blue silk that Ellie had made for her. She also wore a smart wide-brimmed hat of matching color, with a short veil that partially covered her face. She held a larger nosegay of the same flowers Lulu held. Gazing at her, Ellie couldn't help but feel a measure of pride. Her daughter was so beautiful.

It didn't take long for the "dearly beloveds" spoken by the preacher. At the signal Daisy smiled and said, "I do." She hardly waited for the completion of the service before she turned to reclaim the still-sleeping Billy from her mother's arms and return to the place beside Horace.

Immediately the second service began—the baptism of little Billy, in his long white gown. For Daisy, this was the service that had the most meaning. She'd had to go through with the first one before she could become little Billy's mother. Now no one would ever be able to take him away from her.

"This is truly a day of joy," Samuel concluded. "Amen, and the Lord be praised!"

Mathias's harmonica changed to a more lilting tune, and with the arrival of food, drink, and the tall iced wedding cake on the back tables, the scraping of chairs against the wooden-planked flooring indicated the eagerness of the guests to sample it all.

"Miss Ellie, you've outdone yourself," Lulu's father exclaimed, his mouth half-full.

"Just doin' my best for my child," she answered. "You and Tilda Mae will do the very same thing, Obadiah, when Lulu's found herself a fine husband."

Ellie glanced toward Tilda Mae, who was still looking a little green. Knowing she'd planted the challenge, Ellie moved on to attend to her other guests.

An hour later only one person was ready to leave. Jake and Ellie followed Samuel to his waiting carriage at the door. "Wish you could stay longer, Reverend."

"Thank you both, but with the new school year starting soon, I need to get back to New Echota tonight."

The two stood for a moment and watched the carriage disappear. "There goes a brave missionary," Jake confided. "Not many are willin' to risk prison after the government told 'em to get out of the Nation."

Ellie shivered. "A ghost just walked across my grave when you said that, Jake. Let's go back inside and forget the Indians. This is our daughter's day of happiness."

Chapter 6

In the halls of the Georgia capitol at Milledgeville, Governor George Gilmer paced up and down in anger. He had received a "bucket," one of those anonymous, slanderous letters designed to ruin a man's political career.

The past twenty-five years had been bitter ones in Georgia politics, with opposing factions resorting to eye gouging, hair pulling, and duels. But the buckets were the most insidious tactic of all. Too cowardly to sign their names, the perpetrators could not be tracked down and dealt with.

Gilmer glanced again at the crumpled sheet of paper. Indian lover, indeed! He had been accused of a lot of things, but never that. Hadn't he signed into law that made all bills enacted by the Cherokees null and void? And hadn't he issued an edict stating that all Cherokee lands, including the gold mines, now belonged to Georgia, and that all Indians would have to cease operating these mines?

What he had not reckoned on was the United States stepping in to deal with all the riffraff that had headed at once for the goldfields, bringing with them a vicious frontier life, with murder and drunken brawls. But the federal government had overreached its authority. It was up to the *state* to maintain law and order.

He had another bone to pick with Jackson, too, over states' rights. Georgia had already declared that no treaties could be made with the Indians, because they were uncivilized. But here, President Jackon had just negotiated the Treaty of Dancing Rabbit Creek with three of the Choctaw chiefs. True, he had to bribe them into signing their land away for land in the west. But it would be next to impossible for that to happen with the Cherokees. Their damned newspaper kept them too well informed, along with their head chief, John Ross. The only way they could be persuaded to leave was to remove them by force.

In the quiet afternoon shadows Gilmer stared up at the recently hung portrait of the Marquis de Lafayette, who had undertaken a nostalgic trip to America, marking the places where he had fought nearly fifty years earlier. Remembering the state visit of the French nobleman, when the Georgia assembly chamber had been lit with a thousand candles for the elegant ball in his honor, Gilmer felt a sense of inadequacy. His predecessors, Troup and Forsyth, had been right at home with the marquis, for they were aristocrats—a little eccentric, but still educated men, with degrees from Princeton College.

"Well, Mr. Lafayette," Gilmer said aloud, as if the nobleman could hear him, "I wasn't so lucky when it came to education. My tutor was a cruel vagabond sailor, who got his exercise by whipping us on cold days. I hated his guts, just like I hate the guts of the man who sent me this bucket."

"Did you say something, Governor Gilmer?"

Embarrassed at being caught talking to a portrait, the governor quickly turned to face his male secretary. "I was drafting a reply to this letter. That is, whenever I find out the name of the bastard who sent it."

"Oh, sir, I'm so sorry you saw that. We've tried to intercept all the buckets."

"You mean there've been others?"

"Just a few. But I understand Senator Troup gets even more."

That knowledge caused Gilmer's frown to lessen.

"I have the proclamation to President Jackson ready for your signature, sir."

"Good. I'll be in my office in a few moments."

Later that afternoon the proclamation was sent—demanding that Jackson implement the Indians' removal from Georgia—by force, if necessary.

* * *

In Washington, Andrew Jackson had his own agenda concerning the Cherokees. He needed no reminder by Gilmer. He was just as anxious to get the matter settled once and for all.

Forgotten were the Cherokee warriors who had fought beside him against the Creeks a few years earlier. Also forgotten was the U.S. treaty guaranteeing the Indians protection in their homeland.

"Eaton," he called out to his secretary of war, waiting to see him. "Come in here."

"Yes, Mr. President?"

The middle-aged cabinet member had a soft spot in his heart for Jackson. Everyone else in society-conscious Washington had followed Floride Calhoun's example, ostracizing Eaton's wife because she had been a barmaid before he married her. But not Andy.

"I want you to appoint someone to attend the Cherokee's council meeting in October. You have a good man in mind?"

Eaton thought for a moment. "How about John Lowery?"

Jackson nodded. "He's not easily intimidated, I hear.

With the message he'll carry from me, he'll *have* to be firm."

"Shall I contact him then? To see if he can go?"

"Yes. And if he can, then give him this message. I want him to inform the Cherokees that Georgia is coming in to survey every inch of land in time for the lottery. And that treaty or no treaty, there's not a damned thing the U.S is going to do to stop it.

"And he's to report directly back to me what the chiefs have to say about *that*."

At New Echota, a happy Laurel led her students to the empty courthouse, used by Worcester as a classroom at certain times of the year.

"Take your places on the benches, please," she said, and watched the assortment of excited boys and girls choosing their seats.

Then, trying not to show her own excitement and awe, Laurel held on to her long skirt and walked up the railed steps to the platform where the chief justice always sat when court was in session.

Her hand ran along the smooth edges of the rostrum while she waited for the group to become quiet. Tatsu'hwă, or Redbird, the seven-year-old who shared her room, smiled shyly at her. Her classmate, little Kama □mă, was far too busy gazing at one thing and then the other, such as the flitting of the yellow butterflies in the meadow outside.

"Today is a special one," Laurel began, "for you are getting to see where our government carries on its official business.

"This building is used for a specific purpose. Can you guess what it is?"

Laurel waited as a few hands went up. "Deer Stalker," she said, nodding to one of the boys.

"It's the supreme court," he answered.

"Yes. And what does that mean?"

Tatsu'hwă's hand went up and Laurel nodded. "Yes, Redbird?"

"It means that when the people aren't satisfied with what the district court says, they can have the case brought here, for appeal."

"Very good."

"Our papa told her that," Black Moccasin grumbled.

"But she remembered. That's the important thing," Laurel pointed out.

Just then a crow flew through an open window, perched himself on the judge's chair, and began to caw, to the amusement of the students.

With the flapping of her slate, Laurel shooed the bird out and continued her lesson, unflustered. "In several weeks another building will be used—the council house—for the annual meeting. Does anyone know the name of the council president?"

"Major John Ridge."

"Correct. And the speaker of the council?"

"Going Snake."

The sound of a vehicle coming at great speed drew the children's attention. From the corner of her eye Laurel saw that it was the stagecoach, bringing the mailbags to the post office. It was equally difficult for her to keep her mind on the lesson, knowing that the handsome Edward Farraday had arrived. It was strange, but she still had not met him. If she didn't know better, she might suspect that Vervia Worcester was deliberately keeping them apart.

A few minutes later the unmistakeable sound of the wheels along the lane indicated that the coach was returning.

When the vehicle reached the courthouse, it slowed down, as if to stop. But then the schoolbell rang at the mission house, causing the driver to speed up again and disappear from sight.

Within moments the courthouse was empty. Laurel straightened the benches, closed the windows, and then locked the door. Most of the children had rushed to the playing field, where the Reverend Worcester was waiting for them. But Redbird and Kama'mă, the little butterfly, had remained behind, choosing to walk with Laurel back to the mission house.

"Don't you want to go and play with the others?" Laurel asked.

"Not today," Redbird replied. "I want to see if I have a letter from my mother."

"Yes. With the mailcoach coming, I expect we'll all hear from our families," Laurel said.

"Except for Kama'mă."

"Why do you say that?"

Kama'mă puffed her face out like a frog. "Tatsu'hwă, you promised you wouldn't tell on me."

"I haven't."

Laurel glanced from one to the other. "But you can tell *me*, Kama'mă. What's wrong?"

Kama'mă glared at Redbird before confessing, "I didn't finish writing my letter last week, the way I was supposed to."

"No. She stuffed it in her trunk and forgot about it."

"You see. She's telling on me."

Laurel sighed. There seemed to be no secrets in the small, cramped room. "Maybe you can find the letter and finish it once we reach the house. I'm sure your parents would enjoy hearing about your visit to the court today, Kama'mă."

"If Tatsu'hwă doesn't make too much noise."

"Well, *I* plan to snore away until supper," Laurel said. "I'm tired."

Both girls giggled. "You don't snore, Miss MacDonald," they piped in unison.

"Good. I'm glad to hear that."

With the slight unpleasantness forgotten, the three walked onto the porch, climbed the outside stairs, and pushed open the door to their room.

On each of the beds there were letters. Laurel had two—one from her mother, Trudie, and the other from Will Podewell.

Kama'mă held up her own letter for Redbird to see. "I got a letter after all."

"But I got *two*, like Miss MacDonald," Redbird replied.

Laurel, knowing that the two girls got along quite well when she was not around, took her letters and walked outside to a bench under one of the tall, old oaks.

She opened her mother's letter first and read the usual news about the farm, the servants, and her father. Then, in the last paragraph, Trudie MacDonald wrote: "Cousin Quatie is ill again, so I will go to stay with her at Coosa while Cousin John comes to New Echota. It was your father's idea. I think he is uneasy for me to be here alone, in light of what has been happening all around us."

Folding the letter, Laurel sat for a moment, staring toward the distant green, where the children were still laughing and playing. But in a split second she saw them crying and running in fear, with soldiers chasing them down.

What was happening to her? Laurel blinked her eyes several times until the scene returned to normal. But the disturbing vision had imprinted itself on her mind.

Her hands still shook when she finally picked up Will's letter and tore it open. Searching the page for some clue to her sense of impending disaster, she skimmed over the awkward avowals of love until she found what she had feared. "Governor Gilmer has called up the state militia. Now that I'm eighteen, I'll have to serve. So I'll be getting to Cherokee country a lot sooner than I counted on. But that's all right with me. Folks around here say that soldiers get the best pick in the land lottery."

"Oh, Father," Laurel cried, "come to New Echota soon. You and Cousin John, Night Hawk, and Major Ridge—all of you have to stop these people from taking our homes from us."

Chapter 7

Traveling toward New Echota in time for the council meeting, Principal Chief John Ross, better known in the Nation as Gu'wisguwi′, crossed the ferry near Spring Place and urged his tired horses toward the palatial red-brick mansion of his kinsman, Chief Joseph Vann.

John was a small, slender man, more Scottish than Cherokee in his ancestry; yet his matriarchal line had guaranteed him that heritage, too, just as his marrying Quatie assured his children's Indian heritage.

Another heritage was also important in his life—that of knowledge and learning. His father, Daniel, a prominent and wealthy mercantile trader, had seen to it that he and his brothers, Lewis and Andrew, had been surrounded by books all their lives and had hired a tutor for them until they had been old enough to go away to school.

John's unusual skills had served him well as aide to Chief Pathkiller and Associate Chief Hicks in Cherokee treaties and negotiations with the U.S. government. Taken under Hicks' wing, John had been groomed to become the eventual head of the Nation. Refusing political bribes, offered so freely by government agents, John was held in high esteem by his

Cherokee kinsmen. And after Pathkiller and Hicks had died within two weeks of each other, he had been elected to a four-year term as principal chief, to guide the Nation during these perilous days.

Coming directly from Washington, John was as tired as his horses. For the past fifty miles he had been traveling on the old federal post road, the wilderness highway built through the Cherokee land, connecting Nashville to Augusta. But it was so imperative for him to reach New Echota before the council meeting began, that he could stop only long enough for his horses to rest.

There was not even time to go home to see about his wife Quatie, pregnant with their sixth child.

He'd missed his family greatly during these past four months. The only one he'd seen was his daughter Jane, a student at the Moravian Female Academy in Salem. And that visit had been altogether too brief.

As John rounded the curve in the post road he watched for the three-storied Federal-style house high on the hill to come into view.

The sudden dazzling sunbursts mirrored in the leaded windowpanes caused him to shade his eyes with his hand. This was the reason for the house's name—Diamond Hill—given to it by Joe Vann's father, James, who had built it in 1804.

But in the end, if Ross were not successful in his petitions to the U.S. Supreme Court against the forceable removal of his people, then this house—surrounded by several thousand acres, eight hundred of which were under cultivation—and its orchards, barns, corncribs, smokehouses, and foundries, were as much in jeopardy to the Georgia land lottery as his own properties.

"Tsan-usdi´, welcome!" a hearty voice called out, using the childhood family name for John Ross. "You're just in time to break bread with us."

"It's good to see you, Joseph," John replied, with the glimmer of a smile at the sight of his cousin.

The horses were whisked away to the barn to be rubbed down and fed while a travel-worn John gave himself up to the ministrations of the servants. Upstairs, a tin tub was soon filled with bathwater and a fresh change of clothes laid out. By the time he reappeared downstairs, no trace of his English-cut coat or cravat, suitable for an emissary to Washington, remained. Instead he was dressed in Indian style, in a colorful turban with a clay pipe at his side.

"Ha! I see you have left the white man's clothes behind," Joseph teased, indicating an empty seat at the end of the dining table.

"It's not necessary now that I'm in the Nation," John replied.

Ordinarily, a number of friends, including the Moravian missionary, whose school was funded by Joseph, would have been seated around the long trestle table set with pewter goblets and Wedgwood china. Outsiders, too, were always welcome—important government officials, presidents, and an occasional foreign gentleman touring the country in disguise, such as the dauphin of France, whom his father had entertained, or the Marquis de Lafayette, whom Joseph, himself, had welcomed. But today, there were only Joseph's wife, Jenny, and children—and John.

The familial table made for much freer conversation. But although Joseph was eager to hear the outcome of the Washington trip, he would have to wait until later. Any subject that might destroy the digestion was taboo. And from John's demeanor, Joseph knew there was no cause for celebration.

Determined to bring a smile to his serious cousin's face before the meal was done, he turned to his two small children. "If you want to hear a good story, you must ask Cousin John to tell you about the time he saved Kalsatee on the Arkansas River."

"Oh, Cousin John," the daughter pleaded. "Please tell us."

John looked at the eager faces of both children. Turning back to the little girl, he said, "Only if you promise to play a piece on the pianoforte for me later."

"She promises," little Joe affirmed enthusiastically, to the laughter of his mother and father.

"It happened about eighteen years ago," John began, "when I was but twenty years old. Some of the Cherokee had been persuaded to move west, and Agent Meigs asked me to visit their settlement on the Arkansas River."

"Did they give up their land willingly, Cousin?" the boy asked, too shy to look directly into John's eyes.

"No. But that is another story." He continued with the narrative. "Since they had no agent, we were taking a boat load of supplies owed them—homespun and beaver traps, butcher knives and calico. It was December, and the cold winds threatened to overturn the ancient, flat-bottomed boat in the middle of the river. So right before we arrived in Huntsville, I bought a keelboat."

"What happened to the flat-bottomed boat?" the little girl asked.

"As soon as John Spears, Kalsatee, and Peter Esquebell, my Spanish-speaking servant, had helped me transfer the goods to the keelboat, the old boat gave a groan and slowly sank.

"We continued our uneasy journey, with a group of white men on horseback following us along the bank for some miles. Finally, where the Tennessee and Ohio rivers join, they finally caught up with us and forced us to stop.

" '*Do you have any Indians on board*?' one shouted. '*If you do, we're gonna kill 'em, like we did the three we caught on the river yesterday.*' "

John looked at the Vann children, hanging on his every word. "You must remember that at the time white bounty hunters were paid for each Indian scalp they brought in. So what was I to do? If I answered, 'Yes, we have some Indians,' then there would have been a terrible battle and my peaceful mission would have ended in failure."

"So what *did* you do?"

"I was evidently in no danger from them. But the others were—especially Kalsatee, the only full-blood, whom they were eyeing the most.

" 'My companions are Spanish,' I said."

" *'I don't believe you,'* the leader growled, lifting his musket.

"In a low voice, I urged Peter to begin speaking Spanish to them at once. He smiled, nodded his head, and began. *Buenos dias, señores.* Then in a whirlpool of words, he spat out every Spanish word he knew. The men scratched their heads, and while they were still deciding what to do, I got underway again. They climbed back on their horses and finally galloped away. But knowing that a closer look at Kalsatee would not be good, I got him off the boat and made arrangements for him to meet us later at Fort Massac."

"The men are probably still waiting for Kalsatee at the next ferry," Joseph added while his children clapped their hands in delight at John's story.

But young Joseph's face became quite solemn as he addressed his elder cousin, "To me, the story says that it is good to be able to speak another language."

"Yes. That is why you must work hard in school," John said, taking a last bite of dessert before leaving the table.

Later, after a brief, private conversation, Joseph stood on the steps to see John off. "I'll be leaving within the hour, too, Tsan-usdi´," he said as the two clasped hands.

"Until tomorrow," John replied.

To the strains of a Mozart sonata coming from the parlor, John climbed into his waiting carriage, and the rested horses turned their heads toward New Echota, capital of the Cherokee Nation.

John had been on the road for about twenty minutes when the familiar mail coach approached, heading north. As the two vehicles passed, John and Edward Farraday waved and went their respective ways.

* * *

For a number of evenings at the MacDonald house, Laurel's parents, Trudie and Alex, had discussed the best way for Trudie and her black servant, Tansee, to travel to Head of Coosa, the Ross property at the juncture of the Etowah and Oostanula rivers, where they flowed together to form the Coosa, twenty miles below New Echota.

"We can't afford for Two Feathers to be away at the same time we both are," Trudie had argued. "So why don't you ride with Tansee and me as far as the turnoff to New Echota, and then we'll go the rest of the journey alone."

"But that's over twenty miles," he'd protested.

"The road will be filled most of the time with other people going to the council meeting. What could possibly happen to us with so many of our friends about?"

Alex, recognizing the strength of her argument, finally relented. "Do you want me to come for you when the meeting is over?"

"No. You'll need to get back home. Besides, I don't know how long I'll stay. Especially if Quatie's baby comes before Cousin John finishes the Nation's business."

"I'll speak to him. I'm sure that he'd be more than willing to furnish a driver for you."

And so, on that morning the MacDonalds prepared to leave.

While Two Feathers helped finish loading the carriage,

Alex said to him, "I'd appreciate it if you'd keep a sharp eye on the property while we're away. If any rogues come around, scare them off, but don't shoot."

"I will be vigilant, Ina′li," Two Feathers responded.

Trudie seated herself beside Alex on the carriage box, relegating Tansee to the inside of the carriage so she could watch over the pies, ham, and other food that they had spent the last two days preparing.

With Cloud Maker and Sundance harnessed together in front, and Alex's horse and Laurel's pony, Thistle, trotting behind, the carriage left the yard and rolled along the lane bordered on each side by the cultivated fields, abundant with harvest.

A chill was in the air, a subtle reminder by the wind blowing over the mountains that winter was eager to appear. But the trees on the slopes and hills were still green, with the exception of the poplars, whose leaves had already turned a cadmium yellow from the first frost.

Trudie and Alex traveled in comfortable silence. While Tansee's mind was on the safety of the pies threatened by the occasional bumps in the road, the married couple was more attuned to the majesty of their surroundings. Old legends of the land, told by the elders, filtered in and out of their thoughts.

It had been so long ago that no one knew from where the first Cherokees had come. Around the sacred fires the holy men had spoken of their ancestors emerging from the caves in the hills, to take possession of the land that the Great Spirit had allotted them.

At noon they stopped along the roadside to eat, and later that day, at the fork in the road, Alex turned the horses' reins over to his wife and unhitched his own horse and Thistle from the back of the carriage.

"I know Laurel will be happy to have her pony," Trudie

said as he mounted his horse. "And don't forget to give her my message."

Alex nodded. "Tell Quatie I wish for her a safe delivery of the child."

For some reason he could not fathom, Alex was loath to see his wife disappear. "Tansee," he said, "go and sit with your mistress on the box."

"Yes, sir."

"But the pies, Alex," his wife protested.

"They can take their own chances. You're more important than the pies."

"The horses are not apt to get out of control—"

"No. But Tansee can hold the parasol to shade you from the afternoon sun."

The black woman looked from one to the other, waiting to see which would win, before moving from the inside of the carriage.

Trudie laughed. "Well, come on, Tansee. Climb up here with me so that Chief Alex won't be late for his committee meeting."

Alex had not voiced the real reason for his request. But Trudie had understood. From a distance, big Tansee, dressed in her huge old gray coat and hat, would appear a much more formidable foe than the small woman at her side.

Once the carriage had gotten underway again, Alex urged his horse to a gallop. With the pony keeping pace, Alex raced toward the capital—and his daughter Laurel.

Chapter 8

Along a dusty road from the west, Night Hawk galloped at breakneck pace. His friend, Jumping Rabbit, was a short distance behind.

"Wait for me, Tskĭ-lĭ ´," Jumping Rabbit called out. "I'm choking on your dust."

Night Hawk laughed as he changed to a canter. Jumping Rabbit had never been able to keep up with him, even when they were boys at the Moravian school. Now that he had grown plumper, Jumping Rabbit was even less of a challenge, except when they played the ball game of a´ne´tsâ.

Finally catching up with Night Hawk, Jumping Rabbit said, "I know how eager you are to see Laurel, but you needn't be so hard on our horses."

"I appreciate your concern for the animals," Night Hawk replied, his dark eyes twinkling.

"I'm also concerned for *you*, my friend."

"Why?"

"Because you've been too reticent about your intentions. Have you thought that while you're waiting for Laurel to grow up she may promise herself to someone else?"

"But Ina´li knows how I feel."

"It might be better if you told Laurel how you feel. And soon."

"Surely there's no hurry."

"You actually believe that?" Jumping Rabbit's voice took on a more disturbing tone. "Many chieftains will be at this meeting. When they see how beautiful and intelligent she is, they will not be nearly so caring of your feelings as I am."

Night Hawk mulled over his friend's advice. A few minutes later he said, "What did you mean, Jumping Rabbit, about caring for my feelings?"

Jumping Rabbit smiled. "Do you think that I'm blind to Laurel? If it were not for my friendship with you, I would have spoken to her, myself, long ago."

Jumping Rabbit's surprising admission decided Night Hawk. He knew he could not afford to wait any longer. At the first opportunity he would seek out Laurel and talk with her.

Trudie and Tansee had been traveling steadily ever since Alex had left them at the fork in the road. From the position of the sun Trudie knew that they were less than five miles from Quatie's house. Nothing untoward had happened. The few travelers they had met on the way were of her own people—some strangers, others of nodding acquaintance.

Then, when the carriage emerged from a heavy grove of trees into a more open terrain, Tansee suddenly pointed to a squad of Georgia militia on the road ahead. "Look, mistress."

"What is it?" Trudie asked, searching for her spectacles.

"Soldiers. Looks like they got somebody chained to the back of the wagon."

"Probably some of the lawbreakers they've caught," Trudie said. Once she'd found her glasses, she peered at the two white prisoners in the distance. She watched as one fell and then was impatiently prodded with the butt of a musket.

"Whatever they've done, it seems inhuman to treat their

own people that way."

"I'm scared," Tansee said. "Let's stop for a while and let them get on down the road."

Driving the military wagon, Will Podewell felt sick. He didn't relish this first assignment with the militia.

"Speed up the mules, Podewell," the captain barked. "We got to get these prisoners to circuit court by tomorrow mornin'."

"We could make better time, sir, if you put the prisoners in the back of the wagon."

"Don't be insubordinate, Private," the captain yelled. "They broke the law, and they sure as hell aint' goin' to ride in comfort."

"Yes, sir."

But the mules refused to speed up. They were tired, and no amount of persuasion on Will's part could force them. Seeing this, the captain finally relented. "All right. Hold up. We'll give the mules a short rest."

Seeing the military convoy stopping by the side of the road, Trudie was dismayed. She watched as the soldiers dismounted and tied their horses to the nearby trees. But once they disappeared into the brush beyond, leaving only the driver of the wagon with the prisoners, Trudie felt better.

"We'll drive by slowly. That way, Tansee, we should not attract undue attention."

Trudie's plans completely disintegrated when she recognized one of the prisoners. She stopped the horses and turned over the reins to Tansee before jumping to the ground and running toward the man.

Seeing the Reverend Samuel Worcester's neck encircled by an iron collar, Trudie was aghast.

"What have they done to you?" she asked.

"They've arrested me. But it's all a mistake."

"No mistake, madam," one of the soldiers said, reappearing from the bushes. "He has no permission from the state of Georgia to remain in the Indian Nation."

"But I'm a postmaster at New Echota. That's a *federal* appointment, so I'm not subject to your fraudulent state law."

"You're a missionary to the savages," the soldier said, addressing Samuel. "That puts you under the jurisdiction of the state. Ain't no fault but your own, since you decided not to pay attention to the warning."

The soldier turned back to Trudie. "Drive on, madam. This affair doesn't concern you."

Trudie forced herself to smile. "Perhaps you're right. But in the name of Christian charity, I'd like your permission to give these men some water to drink. They both look so thirsty."

The soldier grudgingly nodded, and Trudie rushed back to the carriage for the container of water and some food.

Without looking at Samuel, she administered the watering can to the first prisoner, Elizur Butler. Then, moving on to Samuel, she whispered, "Where are they taking you?"

"To Gainesville."

"But that's over fifty miles. Are the soldiers going to make you walk the entire way?"

"If they do, the Lord will give us strength."

"What can I do, Samuel?"

"Get word to my wife and Elias Boudinot."

"What about the school?"

"Laurel can handle it until I'm released. She's a capable teacher."

"All right, they've had enough water," the soldier said, waving Trudie from the prisoners.

Hurriedly she handed the nearly empty container to

Tansee, climbed onto the carriage box, and within a few minutes had disappeared down the road.

Will, setting the mules in the direction of Gainesville, was remarkably quiet. He had never seen the woman before, but he had recognized the horses, Cloud Maker and Sundance, and the MacDonald carriage. He was glad that Laurel's mother had no inkling of his identity—and equally glad that the soldiers had not suspected that Mrs. MacDonald was Cherokee.

By the time Trudie and Tansee arrived at the Ross plantation house on the Coosa River, the day had ended, taking with it the warmth of the sun. Smoke from one of the red-brick chimneys curled upward in a lazy spiral to meet the cold mist coming in from the river.

At first, the two-story clapboard house appeared deserted. But then, through a slight clearing in the mist, Trudie could see the flickering oil lamps, set in the windows as a welcoming sign.

Within moments of hearing the carriage, a pregnant Quatie, with her young son Silas beside her, was on the porch.

Trudie did not wait for the traditional greeting. "Quatie," she called out, "I need a fresh horse and a rider. Samuel Worcester's been arrested by the militia."

Quatie clapped her hands and a servant soon appeared. "Tsi′skwa," she said. "Get Swiftfoot from the stables. You'll have to ride him to New Echota with a message tonight."

Seeing the manner in which Quatie was holding her swollen stomach, Trudie realized that she had arrived none too soon. "Please go back into the house, Quatie. Tansee and I will take care of things."

Quatie did not protest.

* * *

The Indian rider kept to a steady pace, urging Swiftfoot,

the best stallion in the Rosses' stables, toward the capital. In little more than an hour he had arrived at the busy, noisy tavern.

"I bring a message to Elias Boudinot," Tsi′shwa announced at the entrance. "Could someone direct me to his house?"

His voice was drowned by the laughter of old friends who had not seen each other in a year's time. Realizing that no one was paying the least attention, he finally walked to the nearest table, where Night Hawk and his friends had just finished their evening meal.

Annoyed at being interrupted in the middle of a story, Night Hawk glared at the man.

"I come from the Ross house with a message from Chief MacDonald's wife. I must find Elias Boudinot."

"I'll walk with you to his house," Night Hawk said, getting up from the table.

"Aren't you going to finish your story?" Jumping Rabbit asked.

"Later."

It did not take long to get to the Boudinot house. The message alarmed Elias. "I was afraid something like this would happen. I'll have to go and tell Mrs. Worcester immediately. It's good that she's not alone."

"Who's with her?" Night Hawk asked.

"John Ross and Alex MacDonald. They're having dinner there tonight."

Knowing that Laurel would more than likely be there too, Night Hawk decided to accompany Elias while Tsi′skwa walked back to the tavern.

At the mission house Vervia had waited as long as possible before serving the evening meal. It was not like Samuel to be late, especially when he knew they were having guests. He was extremely eager to hear about John Ross's trip to Washington.

"We'll go ahead and eat," she finally said. "Laurel, you may tell Round Tree to begin serving." She then led her guests into the dining room.

Halfway through the meal, the familiar creak of the second porch step signaled someone's approach. Hearing the sound, Vervia smiled and said, "That must be Samuel now."

But within moments, as a knock sounded on the door, her face grew grave again. Samuel would not have knocked.

"I'll go and see who it is," Laurel offered, picking up one of the lamps.

The meager light from the lamp did little to pierce the darkness beyond the front door. "Yes? Who is it?"

While Night Hawk remained in the shadows, Elias stepped forward. "It's Elias, Laurel. May I come in?"

"Of course. Father and Cousin John will be happy to see you." She opened the door wider.

"I'm afraid not. Your mother has sent some bad news."

"It's not about Quatie, is it?"

"No. The message is for Mrs. Worcester. Why don't you remain on the porch with Night Hawk while I speak privately with her."

"But she may need me—"

"I'll call you if she does."

"She's in the dining room."

As Elias disappeared inside, Laurel placed the lamp on the table and stepped onto the porch.

"Laurel?"

"Night Hawk?" She rushed toward the dimly lit figure. "Do you know what's wrong? Has something happened to the Reverend Worcester?"

"He's—"

A woman's cry interrupted him. And then Alex's voice called out, "Laurel, we need you. Mrs. Worcester is having one of her heart spells."

A disappointed Night Hawk watched Laurel vanish inside the house. There was no need to remain. He would have to wait for a more appropriate time to talk with Laurel.

Slowly be began to walk back to the tavern where his friends were waiting for him.

For five hours Trudie had sat by Quatie's bed. The pains were coming at regular intervals now, and Trudie knew that before dawn a new Ross child would more than likely be entering the world.

"I'm so glad you're here," Quatie said, biting her lip.

"I know you would much rather have John with you."

"I don't mind. Really, I don't. He has such tremendous responsibilities—" She stopped speaking as another pain washed over her. A few minutes later she continued. "But he's been gone so long this time that poor little Silas won't recognize him when he comes home."

"Yet, one day Silas will be very proud of him."

"Yes. The new baby, too."

The birth should have been easier. And Quatie should have conserved her strength. Yet Trudie understood the woman's need to speak of her husband,

Toward morning, the baby was born—another son. His strong lungs announced his arrival. Soon afterward, the entire household went to sleep.

On the day of his son's birth John Ross attended the council meeting at New Echota. It was a serious time, with life-threatening questions taken up by the representatives. With their every action monitored by the federal agent, and the arrest of the missionary on their minds, the assembly felt the pall that covered them like an unlucky omen.

To the meadow, sweet with flowers and wild grass, Laurel, with the responsibility of the mission school on her young shoulders, had brought her wards. There, the students sat and listened to the voices through the open windows of the white clapboard council house.

"The land in the west is poor and grows nothing," the Reverend Bushyhead advised the council. "This is the reason I have undertaken the long and dangerous trip from Arkansas—to warn you that the government has not been honest with us. I beg of you not to sign the treaty. It would be far better for the rest of you to remain here, where the Great Spirit has given you abundance."

"But in the end, will we not be driven off this land?" Laurel recognized Elias Boudinot's voice. "So why not accept the inevitable and make a new life elsewhere?"

"For how long, Elias?" John Ross asked the editor of the *Cherokee Phoenix*. "Our people accepted each previous treaty in good faith, believing the promises that we would not be asked to give up any more of our land and that we could live in peace in perpetuity.Yet when the white men grew greedy again, they broke the treaties and even held back the money reimbursing us for the previous land.

"Now, if we cannot follow Samuel Worcester's example and take a stand against our forceable removal, regardless of the cost to us, then one day we will have lost our entire heritage, and even the name of our people will be erased from the earth."

Laurel looked at the children, their serious faces indicating their struggle to understand the momentous discussion. This would be a day of remembrance for them. But it would not be good for them to become too anxious. "Come, students," she said, smiling. "It's time for play. Black Moccasin, you may go and get the ball and bat."

The children began to run toward the ball field. A few minutes later, as the game began, their thoughts were on winning the game—nothing else.

Chapter 9

At the Carter settlement, an unhappy Horace Martin took his time closing up the store. His father-in-law, Jake, had been gone all day, hunting for bear. It was just as well that he hadn't been around when the letter from Chief Vann was delivered.

Horace felt he'd been unlucky ever since he'd left the piney woods of the Carolina low country with his pregnant first wife, Bess. Nothing had worked out for him—not the search for gold, not his marriage to Daisy. But until that afternoon he hadn't realized how much he'd been counting on leaving the settlement and the Dodges.

He stared down at the letter in his hands and began to read it for the sixth time, as if by some miracle the words would change. "I'm extremely sorry, Mr. Martin, but I won't be able to hire you as overseer. Word has come to me that Georgia has recently passed a new law making it a crime for an Indian to hire a white man...."

What was he going to do? He was there on sufferance as Daisy's husband. But in actuality, she was no wife. Each time he'd tried to get near her, she'd acted so skittish. With Ellie and Jake in the next room, there hadn't been much he could do about it, except be patient until they were in a house of their own.

If Ellie Dodge found out that the marriage hadn't been consummated, Horace's position would be even more tenuous than ever. If she also discovered he'd lost the overseer's job, she might even decide to annul the marriage and kick him out altogether.

There was only one thing left for him to do. Consummate the marriage as quickly as possible, before word got out that he had no job. With a grim resolve, Horace tore up the letter, dropped the pieces into the potbellied stove, and lit a match.

Then he placed the cover over the cheese to keep the rats away, turned the sign to "closed," and locked the door behind him.

By the time he reached the boardinghouse, Daisy had finished feeding little Billy and was upstairs putting him to bed.

"Has your pa gotten back from hunting?" Horace asked.

Daisy shook her head. "Mama's not back, either. She went to the sewing bee at Tilda Mae's. Said if she wasn't back when you got home for me to go ahead and fix your supper."

"I'm not in any hurry." He walked over to the cradle and stood beside Daisy. "Little Billy has made you happy, hasn't he?" It was not so much a question as a comment.

"Yes. I love him," she replied, replacing the afghan over the sleepy baby.

"When he grows a little older, he's goin' to be mighty lonesome, unless he has somebody to play with."

"But *I'll* play with him," Daisy said, puzzled.

"I was talkin' about another child—a little brother or sister."

"Well, I don't know where we could get one."

"We could *make* one, Daisy."

"You mean, like the rag doll Mama made me when I was a little girl?"

"A lot better than that. Maybe a doll baby like you, with blue eyes and corntassel hair." Horace reached out and caressed her hair while she stared at him uncomprehendingly. "Come to bed, Daisy. And I'll show you how."

"Wait, let me get Mama's sewing kit first."

In exasperation, Horace watched her disappear. But it took only a few moments before she was back, delving into the basket and pulling out needles, thread, and scissors.

"Put them on the nightstand, Daisy. We won't need them right away." He motioned for her to come and sit beside him on the bed.

Horace was gentle but determined. He made a game of his seduction at first, with Daisy not suspecting what he had in mind.

But once the seduction had reached the point where Horace had fallen on top of her, a horrified Daisy, remembering what had happened to her in the woods, rebelled.

"No," she screamed, and began to push him away.

"It's all right, Daisy. This is the way to make a baby."

She had trusted Horace, but he had tricked her. He was acting exactly like the two men who had hurt her. And neither her mama nor her papa was at home to rescue her.

When she suddenly went limp, Horace whispered, "That's more like it, Daisy."

But all the time her right hand was slowly reaching toward the nightstand. Her fingers finally closed around the scissors. When she used them, Horace didn't know what had hit him. He was far too busy consummating the marriage.

By the time Ellie got home from Tilda Mae's, it was dark. She took off her cloak and hung it on a nail near the door. In the backyard, Jake was busy stripping the carcass of the brown bear he'd killed. Watching his every move was old Runy, his hunting dog. Ellie could hear Jake whistling to himself as he worked.

"My, that's a mighty fine bear," she said, standing in the back doorway.

Jake turned around to acknowledge Ellie and then went back to work with his knife. "More'n six feet tall," he said with pride in his voice. "And just look at the fur. You can tell it's goin' to be a cold winter in these mountains."

"You aimin' on sellin' it?"

"No. I thought I'd give the skin to Daisy and Horace as a goin'-away present."

"Well, don't let me keep you. As soon as you're finished, I'll have your supper ready."

Ellie closed the door and went into the kitchen. The house was strangely silent, and the fire on the hearth had gone out. She frowned in displeasure, for her daughter was usually more responsible than that.

She took the lighted lamp from the kitchen table and carried it up the stairs. "Daisy," she called. "Where are you?"

There was no response.

"Horace?"

There was still no answer.

As Ellie walked past her own bedroom, with its door ajar, she stooped to pick up a spool of thread in the hallway.

Seeing no light coming from the other bedroom, she knocked lightly so as not to wake little Billy. "Daisy? Are you in there?"

Finally Ellie pushed the door open. When she saw the bulge under the covers, she smiled. Daisy and Horace must have gone to sleep together. Ellie walked closer, hating that she had to waken her daughter, but she needed help downstairs.

The large red stain on the blue-and-white patterned quilt was the first indication that something was wrong. Still holding the lamp in her hands, she tentatively pulled back the cover.

A half-naked Horace lay spread-eagled on his stomach, with the handles of the sewing scissors protruding from his back.

Ellie put her hand to her mouth to keep from screaming. Frantically she began to search for Daisy, afraid that she would be found in the same condition. Had the culprit killed little Billy, too?

She ran to the cradle. The baby was gone. And hard as Ellie looked, she could find no trace of Daisy either.

Then she began to follow the trail of bloody handprints—to the drawer where the baby clothes were kept, and then to the hiding place where Daisy kept her special treasures, like the little pink quartz rock and the eagle feather that weren't worth anything except to her daughter. They were gone, too. It finally dawned on her what must have happened. Daisy had killed Horace and taken little Billy to hide somewhere.

Deep within, Ellie felt she, herself, was to blame. If the authorities found out what her daughter had done, they would either hang Daisy or put her away.

No, she would never let that happen. With a grim resolve, she closed the bedroom door and walked downstairs to fetch Jake.

"I'm almost finished, Ellie. Just a few minutes more—"

"No, Jake," she whispered. "You got to come *now.* It's a matter of life and death."

He put down his knife, wiped his hands on his buckskin shirt, and followed his wife.

"My God, it's Horace," he croaked, when she pulled the covers back. "Is he dead?"

"Yes. And Daisy's not anywhere around, Jake. I feel sure she did it and then ran away."

"Now calm down, Ellie. Somebody else might have done it—"

"No. You don't know everything's that's happened. I think it was a man who hurt Daisy before—and not a wildcat. If Horace started doin' the same thing...Don't you see, Jake? For *her* sake we got to get rid of the body."

"But Ned, and Obadiah, and Cora. Won't they all think it mighty strange for Horace to disappear overnight? They're bound to ask a lot of questions."

"Everybody knew he was leavin' soon. We'll just say that he got word to come a little earlier."

Within twenty minutes Ellie and Jake had wrapped the body in the bloodstained quilt and brought Horace downstairs. The only thing they could do was to bury him in the backyard, next to the barn. But Jake would have to work in the dark. He could not afford for his neighbors to suspect what he was doing.

Jake and Ellie had no more than gotten the body out of the house when there was a knock on the door to the street.

"We won't answer it," Ellie whispered.

But the knock was persistent, and then a male voice began to call. "Jake? Jake?"

"He's comin' through the kitchen!" Jake said.

"Quick!" Ellie cried. "Throw the bearskin over Horace."

"I thought you must still be outside," Ned said, pushing open the backdoor. "Heard you'd killed a granddaddy of a bear and I come to take a look, if it's all right."

Jake swallowed hard and tried to keep his voice steady. "Well, there he is. A big one, ain't he?"

"Sure is." Ned started to draw closer to see the animal better, but Jake's hound began to growl and show his teeth, forcing the young man to step back.

Jake laughed. "Old Runy here's staked out his territory. Thinks you want to steal his share."

Having been bitten by Runy before, Ned was in no mood

for it to happen again. He remained where he was. "What does Horace think about it?"

Ellie's warning look caused Jake to think hard before he spoke. "He didn't get to see it before he left. But I expect he'll be impressed. I'm goin' to give the skin to him and Daisy as a housewarmin' present."

"What do you mean? They've already gone?"

"Yes," Ellie replied. "This afternoon. It was hard to see them go."

"Well, I knew that letter that came for him at the store this mornin' must be awful important."

Far into the night the swishing of the scrub brush kept Jake awake as Ellie tried to remove all traces of blood from the bedroom floor and the stairs.

Toward morning, when she finally climbed into bed, Jake said, "Did you get it all?"

"I think so."

A little later, as Ellie's body still trembled, Jake touched her arm to reassure her. "Everything will turn out all right, Ellie. Daisy won't go far. And she'll come home when she's not frightened anymore.

"At least she had the good sense to take the goat with her, so little Billy won't go hungry," he added.

"But what are we goin' to tell Chief Vann?" Ellie asked. "He'll start makin' inquiries when Horace doesn't show up when he's supposed to."

"We've got plenty of time to think about that. The hardest part for us both is to act natural tomorrow, like nothin' unusual has happened."

With almost no sleep, Jake and Ellie got up at the regular time. Ellie's eyes were still puffy, but he didn't comment about them.

Immediately after breakfast Jake left for the store. He

leaned over and kissed Ellie good-bye—something he hadn't done for a long time. "I'll be back for lunch," he said, and then hurried out the door.

The morning was a frosty one, and as he blew on his hands to warm them Jake couldn't help but think about Daisy and wonder where she had spent the night.

A great sadness welled up inside him, but he felt no remorse over what he and Ellie had done. He would do anything to protect his own flesh and blood. But unlocking the store, Jake decided he needed a few more minutes to himself before facing the people in the settlement. So he relocked the door behind him and went to the potbellied stove to make a fire.

With several sticks of pine kindling in his hand, he opened the lid. There, he saw small pieces of paper, charred at the edges. Was this the letter that Horace had gotten the day before? If so, why had he tried to burn it? Curious, Jake reached in and pulled out as many pieces as he could, fitting them together like a puzzle on the counter.

Much of the message had been burned beyond reading, but from the little that was left Jake realized that he and Ellie had no cause to worry when Horace didn't show up at Spring Place.

Knowing that Ellie would be as relieved as he, he debated about going back home immediately to tell her. But then Tilda Mae was knocking at the door, demanding to be let inside.

"Hold your horses, Tilda Mae," he called out.

Hurriedly he scooped up the remnants of the letter and stuffed them back into the stove, placing the kindling on top. Striking a match, he started the fire. The hiss of the flames, licking at the resin in the wood, accompanied his walk to the door.

""What brings you here so bright and early, Tilda Mae?"

"Well, you're certainly sounding mighty chipper in light of

what's happened."

Casually Jake walked over to the cheese and secretly swiped at the rat before Tilda Mae could see. "What are you talkin' about?"

"I just left my horse and buggy over at the livery stable. Ned tells me that Horace got a letter yesterday, and he and Daisy up and vanished without as much as a by-your-leave."

"Yes. Well, you know how it is when a job's waitin' for you."

"I expect Ellie was mighty sad to see Daisy go."

Jake nodded. "That she was. Maybe you could go over and cheer her up a little. Have a cup of tea with her or something."

"That's a good idea. I know if it was my Lulu, I'd be cryin' buckets of tears."

Jake leaned over and said confidentially, "I'd appreciate it if you pretended not to notice that Ellie's been doin' the same."

"You can count on me, Jake." She handed him her list and then rushed from the store.

Chapter 10

For the past several weeks Two Feathers had made a habit of riding along the entire boundary of the MacDonalds' property, checking on the condition of the fences and the fall crops. He had not been at his own cabin over the ridge all during this time.

That morning, as he began riding from east to west, he decided to stop off at his house for a few minutes to retrieve another clay pipe; for his favorite one had broken the day before.

It was not as if he really needed to check on anything. He had no family left. His wife and children were dead. And he had moved the animals that could not fend for themselves over to the MacDonalds' on the same morning Trudie and Alex had left.

Approaching his house, in an isolated area bordered by a flowing creek and dense woods that separated his property from the MacDonalds', he suddenly stopped his horse and began to listen. The faint tinkling of a bell was coming from his barn. Had a squatter moved in while he had been away?

Warily, Two Feathers dismounted, tied his horse's reins to a tree, and began to reconnoiter toward the barn, being careful to remain hidden from view.

A hopeful nanny goat, her udders uncomfortably full, gazed up at the human who had just slipped into the barn and was staring at her through the wooden slats of the stall. "*Maa,*" she bellowed, moving her head from side to side, setting off the bell again.

With a soothing tone, Two Feathers spoke to the goat and then left the barn to continue his investigation closer to the house.

Taking his time, he walked past the corncrib, the smokehouse, and the brick-and-wood well house in the backyard, where he crouched, listening for the slightest noise coming from inside the cabin. He remained there for several minutes, watching and waiting. No smoke curled from the chimney; no one left the house to go and milk the goat.

Finally Two Feathers stepped onto the back stoop and tried the door. It had not been barred. He pushed it open and walked inside, his hand on his knife.

The cry of a baby alerted him that someone was in the bedroom. So squatters *had* come. Two Feathers was not afraid to confront the man, who, without permission, had evidently moved his family into his house. Resolutely he walked to the threshold of the bedroom.

"You are trespassing," he began, and then stopped to stare.

The young woman on the bed looked more animal than human. Her long yellow hair was matted with leaves and burrs, and what was left of her dress seemed to be caked in dried blood. Two Feathers had seen the same, wild-eyed look before—in cornered animals waiting to be slaughtered. A quick gaze at the baby beside her showed the child was no better off than the mother, that neither one had received any care for some time.

"Where is your husband?"

Without a sound coming from her throat, she remained

in the same cowering position, her arms around the baby.

"Don't be afraid. I won't harm you."

Throughout his questioning, she remained silent, like the favored ones whose minds had been touched. If that were so, and she had been deserted, then the Great Spirit required him to protect her, since He had sent her to his house.

Within a half hour Two Feathers had milked the goat and started a fire to make corn gruel for the half-starved mother and her baby.

"Do you have other clothes?" he asked. He did not expect an answer, and got none.

Later, when he left to go back to the MacDonalds', Two Feathers had heated enough water for the woman to bathe the infant and herself, and had laid out clean clothes that had long ago belonged to his own wife and child.

Throughout the day, as he supervised the MacDonalds' servants and kept a careful watch against intruders, he continued to puzzle over the occupants in his own house beyond the ridge.

At New Echota, the agent of Jackson relayed the president's message—that he would do nothing to stop the state of Georgia from surveying every inch of land in the Cherokee Nation for the upcoming land lottery.

A small minority, mainly the family and kin of Oo-Watie, provided a dissenting vote to the vote of the majority concerning their course of action. But John Ross, principal chief, knew that the Cherokee constitution rendered them powerless to negotiate with the U.S. government. Only those chosen directly by the entire representative body could sign treaties. By Cherokee law, it would be considered treason, with the penalty of death, for any unauthorized person to sign away any land.

John Ross still maintained the hope that, through the

lawyer hired to represent them in Washington, the official delegation would be able to seek legal redress. And he cautioned everyone to stand firm.

Night Hawk was tired of the long hours of oratory. He was also frustrated that he'd been unable to spend any time with Laurel.

As he gazed out the open door of the council house, he saw Laurel walking along the lane, several heavy books in her arms. With the important business of the council already dealt with and the business meeting finally coming to an end, Night Hawk decided to slip out.

"Where are you going?" Jumping Rabbit whispered.

Seeing Chief Joseph Vann frowning at the interruption, Night Hawk merely shook his head and left. "Laurel, wait," he called, rushing to catch up with her.

At his approach she said, "Is the meeting over for the day?"

"No. But I've grown tired of sitting. Will you walk with me for a while?"

"Let me take the books back to the mission first."

He reached over for them. "I'll carry them. If you get too near the school, you'll be deluged with children, and I'll lose the chance to have you all to myself for a few minutes." He turned quickly in the opposite direction.

"I have to stay within sight, Night Hawk," she protested.

"You wouldn't have to if you were with the man you're going to marry."

Laurel laughed. "But I'm not. I'm with my father's friend. Yet I have to be careful of appearances."

"Then come and sit here under this tree. Everyone walking back and forth along the lane will be able to see us."

He took his coat and spread it on the mossy bank. She sat down, with the books beside her.

"Jumping Rabbit has told me that I've been remiss."

"Oh? What about?"

He casually sat down near her. "About not speaking to you sooner, to let you know how I feel about you."

Laurel became uncomfortable. Remembering Will Podewell, she said, "I hope this is not going to be an avowal of love, Night Hawk. I'm certainly not ready for that."

Night Hawk frowned. "My own mother was married when she was sixteen."

"But I don't plan to marry for at least another five years."

Night Hawk reached out and began to slide his hand along the length of her palm. He smiled at her reaction. "You will not be able to wait that long. Your response tells me that you are already a woman, with womanly feelings."

She quickly drew her hand into her lap. "Perhaps I am, but the mission school needs me, especially with circumstances as they are."

"I understand that Worcester will be released soon. But I'm a patient man, Laurel. I've waited for three years to speak with you. I can afford to wait another year, until you come to me of your own free will."

"You will get tired of waiting, Night Hawk," she warned.

He stared at her, seeking to understand what she was telling him. Did she have her eye on another—perhaps even a white man—for her husband? Had her years away from her people changed her heart?

The mail coach approached and raced down the lane. Observing Laurel closely, Night Hawk knew his worst fear had just been confirmed. He stood up and, in a cold voice, said, "Perhaps you are right. Come, I will walk with you back to the mission."

At Coosa, Trudie was still worried about Quatie. It had been two weeks since her son had been born, but she was still weak and unable to stay up for long periods of time.

"John will be home soon," Trudie reassured her. "I know

you'll feel better when he's home."

"Yes. But I'll hate to see you and Tansee go. You've both been such good company for me, as well as wonderful help."

Close to her breast, Quatie held the letter from her husband. John was not fluent in writing Cherokee, so he had written in English, a language she could not read at all. Although she could have asked Trudie to translate, she preferred not to. It was sufficient that John knew she had borne another son and had responded to her message.

* * *

At the end of the month John Ross sent word that the council meeting had ended and he would be returning to his family for a brief time before leaving for Washington again. So with Tsi′skwa as driver, Trudie and Tansee left Head of Coosa and began their journey home.

In the month's time, winter had invaded the hills. Along the tallest peaks in the distance, layers of snow forecast the fate of the valleys.

Tansee shivered and hid her hands in the baggy sleeves of her huge old gray coat. Trudie seemed oblivious of the cold as she pored over the latest issue of the *Cherokee Phoenix.*

When they had been on their way for some time, Trudie removed her spectacles and leaned her head out the window. "Tsi′skwa," she called out, "I've decided to stop by New Echota to see my daughter. Don't miss the turnoff."

Tansee's brown eyes showed her amusement. "I knew you wouldn't be able to go past without checkin' on 'er."

"I'd like to see the Reverend Worcester, too. I'm so glad he's been released from jail—at least for now."

At the capital, life had returned to near normal. Gone were the delegates, the noise, and the horses crowding the lanes. The taverns were nearly empty, except for the regular patrons, and the council house had been turned over to Samuel to use again, along with the courthouse.

By the time the MacDonald coach arrived, the sky had already assumed a winter palette of orange, purple, and yellow, the brilliance of the colors making up for the shortness of the day.

"Mother, what a surprise!" a delighted Laurel cried as she rushed toward the carriage. "Father didn't tell me you were coming."

The carriage stopped near the porch of the mission house, and with the help of Tansee an impatient Trudie climbed down. "He didn't know, Laurel."

"No," Tansee said. "She only made up her mind about a mile from the turnoff."

"Tansee, it's good to see you, too. Did you bring any of your apple pies?"

"I might be able to find one in the basket."

"Maybe we can have it for supper."

"We can't be staying that long, Laurel," Trudie said. "Only long enough for the horses to be watered."

But Samuel, coming from the field with a basket of winter corn, was insistent when he recognized the visitor in his yard. "You must come in, Mrs. MacDonald, and share our hospitality. It's far too cold for you to be traveling farther tonight."

"Yes, Mother. Do stay," Laurel begged. "You can leave early in the morning."

"I would not want to be any trouble—"

Samuel said, "I daresay we have nothing that will taste as wonderful as the food and water you gave Elizur and me on the road, but the least Vervia and I can do is show our gratitude."

In the end, Trudie was persuaded. With Tansee and Tsi′skwa taken care of for the night as well, Laurel's mother shared the evening meal with her daughter and Samuel and

Vervia Worcester.

"You should have been here for the council meeting," Laurel said. "It was so exciting. But I can't believe how quiet the capital is now that they've all gone."

"Did you see Night Hawk?" Trudie asked. She and Vervia silently looked at each other for a moment.

"Yes. Briefly." Then Laurel, with Night Hawk forgotten, recounted her visit with Sequoyah. Once she had finished and the adults were all looking at her in silence, an embarrassed Laurel said, "I'm sorry. I didn't mean to monopolize the conversation."

"I'm afraid she mesmerizes her students equally well," Samuel said, smiling. "They adore her."

Once the meal was over, the conversation took on a more serious note, despite Samuel's efforts to hide his distress.

"Yes, Mrs. MacDonald. Elizur signed the oath, but I chose not to do so."

"What will happen now?" Trudie asked.

"The authorities are determined to get all missionaries out of the Nation so that the outside world will not know the terrible crimes being planned.

"As for myself, I cannot help but believe the government will strip me of my position as postmaster so the way will be clear to arrest me again."

Vervia, shuddering at his words, said, "I think we will be more comfortable by the fire."

She took the lamp and began to walk into the parlor. The others followed.

As Samuel put another log on the waning fire, he added. "I have told Vervia that she must pack and go back to her family in Connecticut."

"When will you leave?" a surprised Trudie asked.

Seeing the stubborn jut of his wife's jaw, Samuel answered for her. "Next week."

That night, with Kama´mă and Redbird on a rare visit to their families, Laurel shared the upstairs bedroom with her mother.

It was past midnight before they stopped talking and went to sleep. For some reason it had been important for Trudie to share old family stories with her daughter.The snow seen on the distant peaks that afternoon, the sad howling of the wind, like a wolf caught in a trap, and the conversation with Samuel had served to remind her of the fragility of the Cherokees' future.

Chapter 11

As soon as Alex MacDonald returned home from the council meeting, Two Feathers drove his cattle back to his own property. He half expected the woman to be gone. Instead, she was sitting by the cold hearth, rocking her child.

She had combed her yellow hair and put on fresh clothes—the calico, with the homespun red shawl about her shoulders and the moccasins on her feet. The baby had also been attended to, and lay asleep in the woman's arms.

No apples or bread remained in the wooden platter on the kitchen table. But beside it stood a small bucket of fresh milk, indicating that she had milked the goat for the baby's sustenance.

"Are you feeling better today?"

Two Feathers' words went without acknowledgment. In truth he expected no reply. Her only reaction was to half rise from the chair, as if to hide from him. But Two Feathers, speaking in the same, soothing voice he used to talk with the animals, said, "You are safe here. Be content, Agitsi′."

With that, she sat back down and began rocking the baby again.

The Cherokee brought seasoned logs in and remade the

fire. Then, as soon as he had the kettle steaming and the bread baking, he went outside to the smokehouse to cut some meat.

That night, after he'd buried the bloodied dress, he went to the barn. He fleetingly thought of the warmth of the fire and his clay pipe lying on the mantelpiece. But then he wrapped his blanket around him and went to sleep on the straw.

Months passed in the hills and valleys of the Cherokee Nation. These were troubling times for all, with each new season seeing the erosion of the people's dreams.

No one came for Daisy, whom Two Feathers merely called "woman" or Agitsi′. But Samuel Worcester was not so lucky. He was arrested again, as he knew he would be, and sentenced to four years at hard labor. It didn't matter that the U.S. Supreme Court ruled that he'd been unfairly imprisoned. Both President Jackson and the state of Georgia merely ignored the ruling.

Then the event that the Cherokees dreaded most occurred. Even as John Ross and his official delegates were in Washington, seeking to be seen and to have the earlier treaties honored, surveyors came, marking their papers with hostile symbols designed to obliterate their ancient civilization.

During that time on Two Feathers' isolated little farm, no one came except Tansee, the MacDonalds' black servant. And that had been because he'd needed a midwife at the birth of Agitsi′'s second child.

"What have you been hidin', old man?" Tansee asked, staring down at the pregnant woman on the bed.

Swearing her to secrecy, Two Feathers replied, "She was sent by the Great Spirit."

"You mean she's touched in the head?" Not waiting for Two Feathers to reply, she added, "Looks like you could be a mite touched yourself, giving a white woman shelter. Who is she?"

"In truth, I don't know who she is or where she came from. I only know she looked half-dead when I found her." He did not mention the bloodied dress. Whatever story it harbored had been buried with it.

The young woman on the bed began to cry in pain, prompting Tansee to remove her gray coat and sit down beside her. Two Feathers then left the house, taking the small, red-haired toddler with him.

Now remembering the birth of the dark-haired boy child, Two Feathers rested by the creek later one afternoon. With inner eyes, he watched the movement upon the water—the black spirit shadow, soaring and circling, calling to him and telling him of deeds on the other side of the mountain.

It was not necessary to look upward to the sky; for the eagle and its shadow cried the same cry—of pain and sorrow.

It now became a crime to meet and conduct the Nation's business in the state of Georgia. And so John Ross had no recourse but to move the seat of government beyond the state line to Red Clay, Tennessee.

The federal government became equally punitive, withholding the annual annuities owed the Nation in an effort to force the representatives to sign the removal treaty.

"Without the annuities, the Nation is broke, John," his brother Andrew complained. "What are you going to do?"

"Joseph and several others will give us enough money to run on for a while," John replied, not mentioning his own generous contribution. "When that money runs out, we could go on a subscription journey. We have many friends throughout the United States who would be willing to help in our cause."

But Andrew was thinking of the secret meeting he'd attended with the Ridge faction, the men who had been impeached by the council and who were no longer a part of the governing body. He had not yet decided whether to join them against his brother. If he signed the unauthorized treaty behind John's back, he would be taking an awful risk. For he was well aware of the ancient blood law, with the penalty of death for anyone who ceded public lands without the express consent of the Nation. But the government had not only promised payment to each individual who signed, but special favors as well.

Fearing that John's legal delaying tactics could only result in their losing both the land and the money, Andrew finally made up his mind. "It's better to be paid *something* for the land," he said to himself. And he knew he wasn't alone. Elias Boudinot, Ridge's cousin, felt the same way.

In the mission house at New Echota, Laurel awoke with a sense of uneasiness. All through the night, her sleep had been interrupted. Fragments of the previous evening's conversation with Elias had drifted in and out of her consciousness.

Elias had been unhappy ever since he had resigned as editor of the *Cherokee Phoenix.* He now spent most of his time corresponding with newspapers and writing pamphlets setting forth his views. "Have you heard the news, Laurel?" he'd inquired. "A peddler came through this afternoon, saying that prominent chieftains and their familes are mysteriously vanishing overnight from their homes."

"But that's impossible. How could they disappear, Elias, without someone's knowing?"

"Have you heard from your own parents lately?"

"No. But I haven't written, either. With Samuel gone, I've had the responsibility of the school, the lessons, the children—"

"When was the last time you had a letter?"

She thought hard and, in surprise, answered, "At least three weeks. You don't suppose that something's happened to them, too, do you?"

"I pray not."

Shortly before dawn Lauel left her bed and began dressing. She would ask two of her helpers to watch over the children for the day while she went home to check on her parents. As soon as she was dressed, Laurel tiptoed from the room so she wouldn't wake Redbird and Kama′mă.

She was glad that her father had brought her pony, Thistle, to her. Fleet of foot, the pony would make the trip much faster than if she took a carriage. Riding him, she would have no trouble getting back to New Echota long before the day ended.

With the helpers promising to be vigilant, Laurel left the mission house and the town.

Beyond the road that she took, the land was incredibly beautiful, with its red clay soil and lush plants that held the secrets of life. Mountain laurel and amaranth, honeysuckle and leafcup clothed the trails and woodlands.

Laurel did not take time to enjoy their beauty. Her eyes remained on the road. Thistle's hooves scattered the dust as she urged the animal faster and faster toward home. Except for one small gray fox, no creature crossed her path.

Several hours later she reached the gate to the MacDonald property. Only then did she allow herself to look around. Nothing seemed amiss. She continued to ride down the lane, observing the newly planted crops, the animals grazing in the fenced meadows. By the time she came within sight of the barn, she began to relax.

The familiar sounds of chickens clucking and pigs squealing in delight as they rolled around in the mud caused her to smile. Chagrinned, Laurel took herself to task. Nothing was wrong. She had allowed the conversation with

Elias to spook her, like the ghostly stories that Two Feathers spun around the hearth on a cold winter's evening.

But then, as she wheeled her pony into the brush-swept yard, Laurel saw a stranger, a freckle-faced young woman a year or so younger than she, standing on the porch of her house. She was dressed in the blue French calico that Tansee had made for Laurel's sixteenth birthday.

Laurel and the young woman stared at each oither. But it was Laurel who broke the silence. "What are you doing wearing my dress? Where are the MacDonalds?"

A look of fright passed over the young woman on the porch. "Pa, ya better come quick."

Immediately a middle-aged white man ran out of the house with his musket. Pointing it straight at Laurel, he said, "Git off my property, Indian gal."

His words made Laurel furious. "You're the one who's trespassing. This is MacDonald property."

The man continued to point the gun at her. "Ain't no more. Got it fair and square, I did, in the lottery." His face took on a meaner look as he threatened, "If I catch ya sneakin' around here again, I'll fill ya full of shot." He waved his musket in the direction of the road. "Go on now."

Struggling to understand the nightmare in which she was caught, Laurel stood her ground and said, "Please, can you tell me where my parents are?"

"How should I know? Might be halfway to Arkansas by now." He scratched at his stubbled chin in a calculating manner. "How come ya ain't with 'em?"

"I..." Laurel stopped, sensing danger. Giving no explanation, she quickly said, "I'll be going now."

"Not so fast!" He again pointed the musket at her. "Looks like ya mighta stole somethin' from me."

"I beg your pardon?"

"That there pony. Ya like the pony, Rebecky?" he asked, turning to his daughter.

Her eyes lit up. "Yes, Pa."

"Then it's yours."

"No! You took everything else. But Thistle is mine!"

"If I says it's mine, the law says it's mine. Go git your pony, Rebecky."

His daughter walked to Thistle and reached for his bridle. "Ya heard my pa. Git off," she ordered Laurel.

Laurel looked back at the armed man. Slowly she dismounted and, whispering a sad farewell in Cherokee to her beloved Thistle, she turned to walk down the lane. Behind her she heard the whinny of her pony, protesting at being left behind.

"Ouch, he bit me!" the new owner cried. "Pa, come and help me put this devil in the barn."

At the gate Laurel finally stopped to brush away her tears and take one last look down the avenue of trees. The only home she'd ever known was hers no longer. And her parents had disappeared without a trace. She debated over seeking out Two Feathers. But if her parents had vanished, he probably had vanished at the same time. Otherwise, he would have sent word to her.

As Laurel set out for New Echota a sense of loss and desolation overcame her.

* * *

While Will Podewell marched with Colonel Bishop and the rest of his band of Georgia militia toward Spring Place, Edward Farraday crossed the river ferry a few miles to the north.

If he was lucky, Edward would be invited to eat at the Vann table as fresh horses were being harnessed to the mail coach.

He'd never had such a coachful of letters before. Chief Vann always received his fair share, but today the bulk of the mail was addressed to the new editor of the *Cherokee Phoenix.* His recent newspaper editorials had certainly brought a response from the outside world.

Besides a good, home-cooked meal, Edward was looking forward to his overnight visit farther south, at New Echota. Lately he'd whiled away the lonely hours of riding through the wilderness by thinking of Laurel MacDonald. He'd never forget the first time he'd seen her up close and talked with her. She was even more beautiful than he'd imagined. But he'd had to wait a long time—until Vervia had packed up and gone home to Connecticut—before Samuel had introduced them.

Now, with Samuel gone too, he was free to speak with her as often as he liked—that is, when she wasn't busy with the school. He'd even received official permission to change his schedule, spending the night in the tavern at New Echota, rather than at the Vann trading post. Without a postmaster to help him, it made sense for him to spend more time there.

Soon after Edward had arrived at Diamond Hill, Spencer Riley, who was staying the week with the Vanns as a non-paying boarder, left his third-floor bedroom and began to walk down the two flights of stairs to the parlor.

Conducting business in the Nation, he had not bothered to get an official pass. But he knew he would not get kicked out of the Nation by the government; for he had no particular love for the Indians. In fact, it riled him to see some so rich, with all their property and possessions. It wasn't fair, when white men like him had to scrimp and scrounge for every penny, and still not get anywhere.

He took special note of the quality of the wood, the carvings of the Cherokee rose on the stairs, and the lavish furnishings in all the rooms. But he knew something Chief Vann probably didn't know. Soon his violin, his silver pipe, and all his other possessions would be confiscated, and he would be just another poor old Indian in chains, waiting to be shipped to the no-man's-land out west.

"That's mighty pretty music, Chief," Spencer said, standing in the doorway of the front parlor.

"Come in, Spencer. You know Edward Farraday?"

"Can't say as I do."

"I drive the mail coach on the federal post road," Edward said.

Spence laughed. "Well, I expect a fellow as goodlookin' as you has a lot of little loveys waitin' all down the road."

Edward laughed, too. But he was not amused—merely embarrassed.

With the ringing of a bell announcing the meal, Joe put down his violin. Edward and Spencer followed him into the hall and to the dining room, where the trestle table gleamed with pewter and fine china.

Joe Vann's wife, Jenny, presided over the meal. Seated near her were their two youngest children. And to her right was the Moravian schoolmaster from down the road.

For some reason, Edward had taken an instant dislike to Mr. Riley. Watching him, he wondered why Chief Joe had allowed the man to stay in his home, when he could have sent him to the tavern, instead.

"My, that certainly is fine-lookin' china, Mrs. Vann," Spencer said, eyeing the feather-tipped porcelain in the corner hutch. "Saw some like it in another house one time. Is it Spode?"

"No, Mr. Riley. It's Wedgwood," Jenny replied. "It's been in the Vann family for several generations."

Joe smiled. "President Madison once ate from that china."

"Must have cost a pretty penny."

Jenny frowned and changed the subject, speaking to the schoolmaster.

They continued their meal, with the conversation punctuated by Riley's impertinent questions. He seemed to be interested in the worth of everything he saw in the dining room.

Colonel Bishop, riding from the east, gave orders for his men to rest. He took out his spyglass and looked in the direction of Diamond Hill. Like the finest prize of all, it stood unprotected against the blue sky.

It didn't matter that Joe Vann had somehow found out about the new Georgia law and rescinded his hiring of the white overseer. The fact that he had done it at all now gave official excuse for his house and all his property to be confiscated by the state. That was why the law had been passed in the first place.

Yet, staring at the magnificent brick mansion with its sturdy white columns and pediments, Bishop decided that it would not go into the land lottery. He would claim it instead, for his own family.

"Corporal Podewell," he called. "Take your men and quietly surround the house. I don't want this rich Indian to escape."

"Yes, sir."

Inside the dining room, Jenny had just given the servant the signal to serve dessert. But seeing the expression on her husband's face, she said, "What's wrong, Joseph?"

"I don't know."

All conversation ceased as Joe got up from the table and looked out the window. Soldiers were everywhere he looked, guarding all exits from the house.

Turning back to his wife, he said in a quiet voice, "The soldiers have come. Take the children to the cellar."

Edward Farraday watched a frightened woman gather her two small children and disappear from the dining room just as a rifle butt sounded against the front door.

Then an intimidating voice shouted, "Vann, this is Colonel Bishop. Your house is surrounded. In the name of the state of Georgia, I order you to open this door."

Chapter 12

Spencer Riley was always ready to profit from another person's troubles. And it seemed to him that Joseph Vann's imminent arrest was tailor-made for him to gain a considerable fortune. All week he had coveted everything in the house. Now, if he played his cards right, the entire property could be his.

"Chief, let me go to the door instead, and see what the colonel wants."

"There's little doubt, Spencer. He's come to arrest me." A resigned Joe began to walk toward the front hall.

"Wait. Why don't you let me at least try to persuade him otherwise?"

"Yes, Joseph," the schoolmaster, Saltzer, agreed. "It could do no harm for Mr. Riley to talk with him."

Spencer looked at Edward, as if seeking a unanimous decision, but Edward remained silent.

At the sound of the second impatient rap on the door, Joe nodded for Spencer to go ahead.

The boarder did not open the door. Instead, he stood on the other side and called out, "Colonel Bishop, I'm Spencer

Riley. Will you please state your business here?"

"I have orders to arrest Joseph Vann. But just who in the hell are you?"

"Why, I'm the new owner of Diamond Hill. I moved in last week."

A furious Bishop said, "I don't know what trick you're trying to pull, Riley, but I'm claiming this property for myself. If you don't open the door, I'll break it down."

"We'll just see about that, Bishop. Possession is nine tenths of the law, and *I'm* the one in possession. If you want the house, you'll have to burn me out first."

Spencer was so involved with hanging on to the property that he had completely forgotten about Joseph, Edward, and the schoolmaster, Saltzer.

"Corporal Podewell," Bishop yelled, "find a log to use as a battering ram."

"Yes, sir."

Hearing the colonel's order, Spencer left the front hallway and raced up the two flights of stairs to retrieve his pistol. But then he changed his mind about coming down again. He would barricade himself instead on the third floor.

The sound of heavy furniture scraping across the hardwood planking overhead indicated that Riley was intent on making it extremely difficult for Bishop to dislodge him.

Downstairs, a distressed Aaron Saltzer said, "Joseph, what are you going to do?"

"In truth, I can do nothing, except wait and see which man wins. If I resist, my family might be killed, too."

The bombardment against the front door began, with an initial heavy blow. Then a shot rang out from upstairs, followed by an oath from one of the soldiers below.

"You hear that? They're actually having a battle over the house," Edward said in disbelief.

Joseph looked from Edward to Saltzer. "You'd both better go. It's not safe for you here now."

"We can't leave you to the mercy of the soldiers," Saltzer protested.

"Besides," Edward said, "if we open one of the doors to get out, the soldiers will swarm inside."

Seeing that the two had no intention of leaving, Joseph turned to the schoolmaster. "Then, Mr. Saltzer, I'd appreciate it if you would join my family in the cellar."

As soon as the man had left, Joseph looked intently at Edward, as if trying to make up his mind about him. "Edward Farraday," he finally said, "are you a friend of the Cherokee?"

"You know I am, Chief Vann."

"Then come with me. You must ride to New Echota as fast as possible. It's too late for me. But others might be saved, if they're warned in time."

For Edward, the most important one at the capital was Laurel. But surely she would be safe from the soldiers—she and the children. They wouldn't force them out of the mission house.

While the stalemate between Bishop and Riley continued, Edward followed Joseph back into the dining room and watched as the chief pushed aside the corner hutch containing the Wedgwood porcelain. Hidden behind it was a set of steps leading downward.

"The tunnel will take you to the river near the trading post. You should have no trouble doubling back and getting your coach. Hurry, Edward, and warn everyone at New Echota."

Joseph took a lamp from the side table, lit it, and handed it to Edward. Behind him, Edward heard the hutch sliding back into place, leaving him in almost total darkness.

Heeding Chief Vann's advice, Edward drove his mail coach at a relentless pace. It was good that the horses were fresh; for he had no intention of stopping for anybody or anything.

The wind had gotten stronger, and so he pulled the collar of his coat closer to his face to ward off the chill. With his brown eyes staring straight ahead at the road, he urged the horses even faster.

He had been traveling for about twenty minutes when he caught a glimpse of someone standing on a hill and waving.

"Edward! Edward! Stop!"

Recognizing Laurel, he reacted quickly, pulling at the horses' reins. But the coach was going too fast to stop immediately. The vehicle continued down the road, past the hill. By the time Edward had slowed the horses to a trot, turned the coach around, and returned, Laurel had reached the road.

"Oh, Edward, I was so afraid you hadn't seen me."

"What are you doing out here, Laurel? And why are you on foot?"

As he helped her onto the box beside him, she answered, "They took my pony."

"Who?"

"The strangers in my house." Her voice showed her distress. "Something has happened to my parents, Edward. I can't find them."

Remembering what had occurred at the Vann house, he hesitated to alarm her further. What if the same thing had happened to her own parents? He would have to tell her soon enough about the soldiers. "It's started, Laurel. You know all those forts and stockades that I saw going up north of here?"

"Yes?"

"Well, I think that they were built to hold your people prisoner until they could ship them out west."

"Do you think my parents could be in one of the stockades?"

"I don't know. But I'll try to find out for you."

He began to tell her what had happened at the Vann

house. Hearing it, Laurel became even more upset.

"But you and the schoolchildren won't have anything to worry about," he assured her. "It's the others at New Echota we'll have to warn."

At New Echota, the news of Bishop's men invading the Nation had caused alarm to everyone except Elias Boudinot. He had been privately assured by the new governor, Lumpkin, that his property, as well as the property of the few others willing to sign the removal treaty, would be immune to seizure.

For the next three days the residents watched and waited for the Georgia militia. But the soldiers were still involved in breaching the Vann house and ousting Spencer Riley.

It had turned unseasonably cold, with the soldiers on guard building campfires for warmth. The storehouses had been divested of meat and staples, so no one was going hungry.

By the third morning Will Podewell awoke to the smell of coffee brewing in the open. Trying to sort out his jumbled dreams about Laurel MacDonald, he wrapped his government-issue blanket around him and walked to a small fire, where one of the privates was tending a tin can that hung on a pronged stick over the fire.

"Did you think the lottery was goin' to be anything like this, Podewell, when you signed up?" the young soldier asked.

Will hesitated, remembering the land lot he'd drawn several weeks before. He was just beginning to realize what the term,"land, with improvements" meant. "Improvements" meant it was already a man's home, with cultivated fields, barns, and orchards.

"No, Elliott," he replied, pouring coffee into his tin cup. Feeling guilty that he was going to be benefiting from another man's labor, he did the only thing he could to feel better. He lashed out at the Cherokee Nation. "But the Indians should have moved on instead of bein' so stubborn about it. After all, when Georgia ceded their land all the way to the Pacific Ocean to the federal government thirty-odd years ago, the United States promised to remove the Indians."

"But Lieutenant Waylon said the United States had also signed a treaty with the *Indians* at the same time—that they would never be forced off their land," Elliott argued.

"Well, this is progress," Will replied. "We can't help it if a few people get caught in the way."

Glad that his own father couldn't hear what he'd said, Will quickly gulped down the rest of his coffee and left the campfire. Being with Bishop all these weeks had caused him to see things differently. He now knew, with certainty, that his love for Laurel was doomed.

The bombardment of the house began again, with Will in the forefront. Riley, evidently low on ammunition, did not shoot at them. And the strong front door finally gave way to the battering ram.

"Get Vann first. Then we'll attend to that bastard, Riley."

With a shout, the soldiers rushed inside.

Down in the cellar Joseph heard the sound of feet above. He now knew that the house was not inviolate. "Come, Jenny," he said, "it's time to leave."

Opening the hinged iron gate to the secret passageway that connected to the tunnel, the Vann family fled only a moment before the soldiers arrived in the cellar.

"He's not down here," one of the soldiers shouted.

"Then continue the search," Bishop ordered. "He couldn't have gotten out. He's still hiding somewhere in the house."

When Vann could not be found, Bishop vented his entire wrath on the man barricaded on the third floor. "Podewell, bring in a log from the fire and throw it on the stairs. If Riley wants to be burned out, then by God, I'll accommodate him."

"It's an awful fine house, sir," Will said, hesitating.

"Did you hear me, Podewell? I've given you an order."

"Yes, sir."

A few minutes later the log, placed strategically on the stairs, began to burn, sending a layer of smoke upward.

"The house is burning down around you, Riley," the colonel exaggerated. "You're trapped." Talking even louder, to make sure the man could hear him, he said, "Corporal, give orders for the men to pull out."

"Yes, sir."

Spencer had always been afraid of being burned alive. Frantically he began to remove his barricade. As the smoke seeped under the door, he started to cough. Once he had cleared the door, he wrapped a sheet around him, and brandishing his pistol, he made a run for it.

At the landing Spencer saw that the log had been thrown on the stairs. It was burning fiercely. The flames licked at his ankles as he jumped over it. But the shot that hit him in the arm caused him to miss his footing. He tumbled the rest of the way to the bottom of the stairs, where he banged his head on the final tread.

"I thought the smoke would get you out," Bishop said, calmly looking down at the man he'd just shot.

Then, with their commanding officer's signal, two soldiers rushed up the stairs with several buckets of water to put out the fire. As they dragged the smoldering log out of the house, Colonel Bishop surveyed the damage. He was gratified that only a small segment of the staircase in his house had been charred.

With Bishop's men on the march, the families, who'd been alerted, kept an uneasy watch. During that time Laurel continued the search for her parents, writing letters to all her relatives, with the hope that Alex and Trudie had sought refuge with one of them. While she waited anxiously for replies, Edward inquired at the forts and stockades, but with no luck.

Then, one afternoon, Laurel's letter to Quatie Ross was returned, unopened.

Chapter 13

For the past several months Principal Chief John Ross and the officially elected delegates had been in Washington. This time they had met with a few sympathetic congressmen, and an unsympathetic secretary of war.

Yet, for the Cherokees, the use of war to settle differences had long ago been given up for the council of good minds working together. It was through legal procedures and the courts that their memorials and grievances were to be heard.

But it seemed that the very men that John needed to see had turned their backs on him. This was something new, for at many previous sessions of Congress, John had been present, representing the wishes and hopes of his people, with all doors open to him. In his years of negotiations he had been received by each president, from Monroe onward. But this time the presidential office door had been closed in his face.

Then word came that Vice-President Van Buren would see him. With that promise John began to have a glimmer of hope that something could be worked out, even though Jackson was still in office.

He was even willing to concede a large part of the Nation if the Cherokees could keep one small portion of their sacred land. For if they were forced west, John foresaw nothing but devastation and perhaps the total annihilation of the Cherokees.

But even that small hope vanished when he saw that Van Buren had also invited Senator Troup, the former governor of Georgia, who was on the removal committee. Each made it clear that he would be satisfied with nothing less than the ceding of the entire Cherokee lands—in Georgia, Tennessee, Alabama, and the Carolinas.

Now, riding his horse homeward, John was overwhelmed by a sense of melancholy and failure. The journey had been long, and all he wanted was to be with Quatie and his children, and to spend the night in his own bed. That was why he kept going, urging his animal a few more miles.

He thought of his young sons, Silas and little George Washington, named for the president his people most admired. Washington had been fair with the Cherokees—not like Jackson, who had used them to fight against the Creeks and then deserted them, with promises as dead as the possum that lay in the road.

"We'll be home soon," John whispered to his tired horse.

Overhead the sky was filled with stars and a new moon cast its shadow on the pristine hills. As John passed a grove of trees near his fields, an owl hooted and the leaves sang with the wind.

Inhaling the smell of freshly turned earth, John was pleased that the overseer had already prepared the land for the new spring crops, even though they would have to wait until the danger of frost was over before planting.

With so much of his time devoted to the business of the Nation, John had given up his share of the family mercantile business on the agency grounds to his brother, Lewis. And later, when he'd felt the need to move closer to New Echota, he had also turned over his thriving ferry and nearby trading post at Ross's Landing to the Methodist minister Scales, who had married his niece.

But the two-story house he'd built at Head of Coosa for his family was as spacious as the other one, with its twenty glass windows, tall, red-brick chimneys and fireplaces, and the large ten-foot-high porch, where he and Quatie could sit and enjoy the majesty of the mountains in the distance and note the change of seasons.

Smokehouses, corncribs, servants' quarters, a wagon house, a separate kitchen, and even a building where circuit riders could preach the gospel were all a part of the thriving plantation.

Coming closer, John strained to see some portion of the house against the night sky. He was rewarded with a small, steady light shining from a front window. Not ever knowing the exact time her husband would be arriving home from a meeting or journey, Quatie had always kept a light in the window for him. He smiled when he saw it.

"We're finally here, old boy," John said, patting the faithful animal that had brought him through rain and cold all the way from Washington.

As he led his horse to a stop before the house, a servant came toward him. John did not recognize the black man. Had Quatie hired him while he'd been away?

"Take my horse and put him in the barn," John said. "He's had a long journey and needs to be attended to."

The man hestitated, looking at John and then back to the house, as if undecided what to do.

"Who is it, Efrem?" a man's voice finally called from the shadows of the porch.

"A stranger, suh. Says for me to put his horse in the barn."

Puzzled at the exchange, John said, "I'm John Ross, owner of this property."

"Not anymore, Ross. Didn't you get the letter before you

left Washington?"

"What letter?"

"The one Colonel Bishop was supposed to have sent—letting you know I was taking legal possession of the property."

"No. I received no such letter."

"Too bad. But there it is. I'm afraid you've come back for nothing."

"But my family," John said. "My wife and children. Are they not here?"

"No. They're gone. Your wife was sick for a while, so the missus and I let her stay in the farrowing house until she felt better. Then she and the children left."

"How long ago? And where?"

"Well, let me see." The new owner thought for a moment and then said, "Several weeks ago. But I have no idea where she went."

"Did she take the horse and family carriage?"

"Now, you know, Mr. Ross, I got everything on the property, including the animals," the man responded, sounding a little miffed at such a question.

"Then she and the children set out on foot."

"Yes. But it was not like she had far to go. She must be somewhere nearby. You'll find her soon enough. But since it's so late, I'll allow you to board your horse for the night. And you can even sleep in the barn, too."

"I'm much obliged," John replied, his heart heavy at the tragic turn of events.

That night John wrapped the blanket about him. But he got little sleep. His homecoming had turned into a nightmare. His wife and children had been turned out of their house, and he had not even been present to protect them.

It was a high price to pay, being the leader of a nation. But he would have to remember—others were hurting that night just as much as he and his family. And it was for the good of the entire Nation that he must redouble his efforts to seek legal redress from the U.S. Congress.

By morning, when the rooster in the barnyard announced the arrival of the sun, John Ross arose from his bed of straw, paid the servant for the care of his horse, and set out to find his family.

Six-year-old Silas filled his water jug from the nearby spring and took it to his mother, who rested under the pine boughs he'd placed over the two young saplings tied together.

"Here, Mother. I've brought some water for you to drink."

"Thank you, Silas."

"Are you feeling better?"

Quatie smiled at him. "Yes, much better, my son. Soon I'll be able to begin our journey again."

He was a beautiful little boy, with an engaging smile, so like his father. And he had the same sense of responsibility.

"I'll take George Washington, and we'll go to check on the rabbit trap. If we're lucky, we'll have meat for our meal."

He took his younger brother by the hand and led him quietly into the wooded area where he had set up the trap earlier.

Seeing the animal in the snare, little George said, "I want to play with the rabbit."

"No, brother. He is our food. Our mother needs to eat to make her strong." Then Silas made another suggestion. "But if you're good, I'll let you help me build the fire."

The pout turned into a smile, and the child began to search for small twigs and pine cones.

Soon the aroma of rabbit roasting on a long stick told Quatie that Silas had been successful. Now they would have nourishment to last them the day.

She was sorry, for the children's sake, that she had

slowed them down by stopping far too often to rest. The walk toward the council grounds at Red Clay, just over the Georgia line, was a long one. But that was the only place that she could think of where John would be sure to find them. Not knowing what was happening in the rest of the Nation, she was taking care to avoid the main roads. Soldiers were everywhere, and she was afraid of them.

"Mother," Silas called. "Come to the fire. Our meal is almost ready."

She sat down on the ground and watched her son take his knife and carefully divide the cooked rabbit into three portions, placing each piece on a sharpened stick. "You have learned the ways of the hunter, Silas," she said. "I'm so proud of you."

"I helped, too," little George said, wanting a share of his mother's attention.

"And I'm proud of *you*, George Washington, for helping your brother."

After the brief meal the three gathered their few possessions and set out again, heading in a northerly direction through the wilderness.

On the same afternoon John Ross reached New Echota, he went immediately to the mission school to seek out Laurel.

She was teaching in the courthouse, now vacant at all times, since the Cherokees were no longer allowed to hold court there. John sat patiently under the shade of the tree where Laurel and Night Hawk had held the conversation that had resulted in their estrangement.

As soon as the bell rang and the children, like all exuberant youngsters, rushed out to go to the ball field, John stood up and walked to the open door.

Her back was to him; for she was busy gathering up the books that had been left in a pile at the end of each bench.

"Laurel," he called, and waited for her to turn around.

He was rewarded with a smile that held both surprise and joy.

"Cousin John, how happy I am to see you. I hope you've brought good news."

"The meeting in Washington was disappointing, Laurel..."

"No. Not about the meeting. About my parents. Have you located them?"

"Are they missing, too?"

"You mean you didn't know? I thought perhaps... But no. My letter to Quatie was returned. She couldn't have known. So why are you here in new Echota?"

The two sat down on the benches, facing each other. "When I reached home last night, I found that the people who'd drawn my property in the lottery had already moved in. Quatie and the boys were gone. I was hoping that you would know where I could find them, that maybe they were with Trudie and Alex."

"For both our sakes," Laurel answered, "I hope they're all together and safe somewhere. But the only thing I know for certain is that our house was taken over, too."

Each continued to fill in the sequence of events for the other and made suggestions for finding their families. Talking with John, Laurel began to feel much better, with renewed hope that good news would come.

"I'll get word to you, Laurel, if I hear anything about your parents," John said.

"And I'll do the same with Quatie," Laurel promised.

That afternoon Elias Boudinot stood at a window of his house and watched John Ross leave New Echota. He was glad to see him go; for it would not do for the principal chief to get wind of the secret meeting the small protreaty group would be having with the emigration agents, Schermerhorn and Carroll.

In the heart of the mountains it was twilight, long past time for Quatie to stop and make camp for the night. But she would not rest until she had brought her children safely beyond the ravine, where the evening mists had begun to gather.

Holding each child by the hand, she tightened her grip and kept up the grueling pace. Their possessions had been divided, and even the little one carried his share, strapped to his back.

"I'm tired," George Washington complained.

"I know," Quatie said. "And soon it will be extremely cold. We might be lucky, though, and find a cave to sleep in."

"Like Night Hawk and Jumping Rabbit, when they were little boys?" Silas inquired.

"Yes." Quatie laughed her deep-throated laugh that the children loved. "But first we'll make sure there're no wildcats inside."

They continued around the edge of the ravine, and when it was almost too dark to see, Quatie spotted their cave, partially hidden by a small bush with its roots growing out of the upper bank.

She held back the limbs of the bush and motioned Silas to her side. "Your sight is better than mine. Do you see any yellow eyes gleaming at us?"

Peering through the opening, Silas said, "No, Mother."

"Then we've found our home for the night."

Carefully she led them only a few feet from the entrance, where she spread one blanket on the ground. With the other blanket she covered the three of them.

The boys were like little cubs, snuggling close to her for warmth. She felt very protective that night; for they trusted her totally.

Within minutes, both little boys had gone to sleep. As Quatie waited for the same drowsiness to overtake her, she thought of her husband, the life they'd shared, and the small grave she'd left behind. How different this rude shelter was from her large house, her own comfortable bedroom, with its beautiful mahogany furniture, hand-woven spreads, and upholstered chairs. But then, hearing the soft patter of raindrops begin, she was grateful to have found shelter in the cave.

At first, Quatie thought she was dreaming. But then she heard the growl for the second time. Looking out the mouth of the cave, she saw a bear rearing on its hind legs to show his displeasure that someone had usurped his den.

One swat of his powerful claw and he could do great damage to all three of them. Quatie, realizing they were trapped and at the mercy of the animal, sat up very slowly. The bear was part of her totem. And so she began the only thing she knew, to try to reach the spirit of the bear.

She sang softly, telling the bear of their kinship and apologizing to him for taking his cave. In ancient words and chants she wove a story and asked the bear's protection for her own young. When she had finished, she waited. For several minutes the bear remained, then suddenly dropped to all fours and lumbered away into the woods.

In relief, Quatie lay down again and gathered her sons to her. Knowing they would be all right for the rest of the night, she went back to sleep.

Far below the falls, John Ross traveled on the main trail. From the moment he'd left New Echota, he had found no trace of his family. But he would not be discouraged. His feeling that, somehow, they were safe was growing stronger. As the rain came down he held on to that belief.

Chapter 14

The days passed slowly in the mountains, with John still searching for Quatie. Each day was filled with hope, but by evening, as the shadows gathered and became a part of the night, the hope that had been so strong weakened and struggled against the darkness.

One late afternoon John finally reached the small, one-room log cabin that he owned over the Tennessee line. From the outside it looked deserted. Nevertheless, he dismounted, walked up the two short steps, and pushed open the door. "Quatie?"

His voice disturbed the family of field mice in the corner next to the hearth. They scampered into their cubbyholes, leaving behind the grain they had gleaned from the nearby field.

The dirt-floor cabin was more humble than his servants' quarters at Head of Coosa. Dust and cobwebs were everywhere. But the cabin had a roof and a cooking hearth, offering shelter for him and his family, once he found them.

He set about making it habitable, pushing open the door and unshuttering the windows to let air and light inside. Taking the old twig broom still resting by the hearth, he swept the rafters clear and then turned his attention to the old iron bedstead with its moldy straw-filled mattress.

For several hours he worked, until he'd done all he could without proper equipment. Then dragging the old rocking chair with a broken arm onto the porch, he sat down to watch the sunset, as he and Quatie had done in earlier years of their marriage, when he had been at home more often.

The landscape was overgrown, almost obliterating the trail his horse had taken. Although John's eyes were directed toward the horizon between land and sky, his mind soon turned to the next day's journey.

For that reason he was only slightly aware of the bird that swept across the sky, followed by a movement of color against the field in the distance.

But then, as the sun caught the glitter of mica in a rock, with its brightness forcing him to turn his head, John became interested in the diminutive, plodding figures below.

He stood up, shaded his eyes, and took a few steps nearer, until he was off the small stoop and walking down the path in the direction of the moving figures. Faster he went, his heart trying not to be too hopeful, lest it doom him to disappointment again. Then he was running and calling for all the wilderness to hear.

"Quatie! Quatie!"

The wind took up his cry and brought another voice back to him through the trees.

"John? Is that you?"

With Silas and George Washington beside her, Quatie began to run, too, past the small ridge and the stream, and up the red clay hill, until she was in her husband's arms.

"I looked for you everywhere, Quatie," John said. "I've been out of my mind with worry."

"I stayed behind the trails, John. The soldiers were all over the Nation."

"Are you my father?" George Washington asked, tugging at John's trousers to get his attention.

"Of course he is," Silas answered, although his father had been away for so long that even he had trouble remembering what he looked like.

"Yes, I'm your father, George. But we'll all have to get to know each other again." John bent to the ground, took a son on each knee, and hugged them both.

"Will you be going away again soon?" Silas asked.

"Not for a while. We'll have most of the summer together, I expect."

John stood up, took Quatie's bundle, and began to lead the way to the small, rude cabin above.

Not so many miles away from New Echota, the proud Night Hawk sat at the dining table with his wife, Running Brook. She smiled at him shyly as the servant replenished their plates.

Much had happened since that day at the council meeting when he'd sought out Laurel to tell her of his feelings. His pride had been hurt when she'd spurned him. But he'd waited for several weeks, hoping she would change her mind. Then finally realizing she would not, he had hardened his heart against her, and he had found another woman—one who seemed pleased to be his wife.

Night Hawk had not treated Running Brook especially well at the beginning of their marriage. All he'd wanted then was a woman to warm his bed and take his mind off Laurel. But a number of months later he'd realized he was beginning to care for her and to look forward to being with her.

He watched his wife daintily eating another piece of wild turkey. It was to be expected, now that she was with child, that her appetite would increase. "Do you think our son would enjoy a bowl of peaches and cream for dessert?" Night Hawk teased.

"I think our *daughter* would prefer the pie," Running

Brook answered, with a twinkle in her eye.

"Maudie, cut my wife a piece of pie," he said. "But wait a few minutes before you serve it. I have something to show her."

Running Brook wiped her fingers on the white linen napkin and looked quizzically at her husband.

He stood up and said, "Let's go into the parlor."

The sunlight, filtering through the leaded-glass window, touched the chair in which Running Brook sat, framing her in a golden glow. She was small, with her long ebony hair held back by a beaded headband, purple and white, matching her loose-fitting garment of calico. Only the slight bulge of her stomach hinted of the future.

Night Hawk walked to the Philadelphia-made mahogany desk and retrieved a small box from its hidden drawer. In a serious voice he said, "Running Brook, this is a gift that I vowed I'd give my wife someday. It would please me to see you wear it now." He handed her the box and waited for her to open it.

Her fingers were nimble, lifting the lid of the decorated wooden box. Her pleasure at the gift brought an excited murmur. "Tskĭ-lĭ′, it's the most beautiful necklace I've ever seen."

As she took the golden chain with six golden nuggets attached to it out of the box, it seemed to hold the gift of the sun.

"Those nuggets are the first ones I found at my gold mine," Night Hawk explained. "They have a special meaning for me. That's why I want to see you wear them. Wait, I'll fasten the clasp for you."

As Night Hawk knelt to fasten the necklace about Running Brook's neck, he tried to forget that he'd had the necklace made for Laurel. It was Running Brook's now, and this was his way of finally putting the past behind him.

"Thank you, my husband," Running Brook said, a small

tear traveling down her cheek. "I will wear this in all honor because you gave it to me."

"Now, for your pie," Night Hawk said, getting up off his knees.

Seeing the two make their way back to the dining room, Maudie, pretending she'd heard nothing from the other side of the carved door, quickly took her position again at the table.

Edward Farraday raced his mail coach the last few miles to New Echota. He was carrying a letter addressed to Laurel from Principal Chief John Ross. Hoping that it contained news of her parents, he was eager to deliver it.

He had another reason as well to reach the town as soon as possible. The schoolchildren had gone home for their brief summer holiday, and he would have Laurel to himself for the rest of the day.

Less than an hour later Laurel heard the familiar sound of the coach. She hurriedly removed the apron used to protect her dress and ran to the hall mirror where she checked her appearance. Seeing a loose strand of hair, she repinned it to the nape of her neck.

By the time the horse arrved, Laurel was on the porch. "I'm happy to see you, Edward," she called out.

He grinned and said, "And you'll be even happier when you see what I've brought you."

"A letter? From my parents?" she asked hopefuly.

"Well, not exactly. One from your cousin, Ross. But I'll bet he has some news."

Laurel could hardly wait for Edward to unhitch the horses and lead them to the water trough. She rushed to the well and began to draw up a bucket of water.

Edward laughed. "I never thought I'd see the day when Laurel MacDonald would be helpin' to water my horses."

She laughed. "This bucket is for you, Edward. So stop

teasing and finish with the horses so you can bring in the mail."

A few minutes later Laurel paced up and down on the upstairs porch as she waited for Edward to sort out the mail inside.

"Here it is," Edward said, walking to the open door to hand her John's letter. He stood and watched while she carefully tore it open and began to read. When he saw her look of disappointment, he said, "He didn't find your parents?"

"No." Then she brightened. "But Quatie and the boys are safe."

Edward turned and went back inside while Laurel sat down in a rocking chair and continued to read the long letter.

"...Because of the unfortunate happenings in Georgia, I am sending a wagon soon to remove the printing press to Red Clay, where it will be safe. It is our only means of communication with our people and the outside world, and it would be a tragedy for it to fall into the wrong hands."

John also told her of the decision of the council to use money from the national treasury so that Mrs. Worcester could go to visit her husband Samuel, who was still incarcerated in Milledgeville.

Laurel was glad.

"Well, I've finished," Edward announced. As soon as he spoke, the people who had been gathering in the yard walked up the steps to receive their mail and to give Edward their packages and letters to stamp.

Laurel went back to the kitchen, where she packed the picnic basket and then folded a hand-woven red cloth over the food. It was a beautiful day, and there was no need to eat inside. The mossy bank by the nearby stream would be much more pleasant, with the softness of the breeze and the chattering of the water over the rocks providing a musical accompaniment for two people rapidly falling in love.

Ten miles farther north the Georgia militia had also chosen the same stream as a stopping-off place to cook their meal of the day before resuming their march to New Echota.

Chapter 15

Elias Boudinot sat at his desk by the window and reread the last paragraph of the resolutions he was drawing up.

"Resolved, that we are firmly of the opinion that a large majority of the Cherokee people would prefer to move, *if* the true state of their condition were properly made known to them...."

He was bitter that he had been so thoroughly disregarded by the vast majority, who supported John Ross. It seemed that all he did nowadays was spend his time writing a minority view that never reached print.

He pushed into the back of his mind his betrayal of the Cherokee constitution and his acceptance of what some would call bribes. More important was Elias's vast need to show the Nation that he was smarter than the principal chief. For by going along with the government agents on a course he considered inevitable, Elias had kept his own property intact, with the military helping to guard it, while John's property had been seized. Yet, Elias could not quiet his doubts completely,

He stood up and walked to the window, his mind going back and forth, from past to present, reliving the years that had given him such hope and then such despair.

Had it been almost twenty-five years ago that his father, Oo-Watie, had sent him to the Moravian school at Spring Place? He had been so young, but having his cousins, Nancy and John Ridge, already there had helped keep him from becoming homesick for his mother, Susanna.

How he'd worked those years, learning so much more than just the formal curriculum. And how proud he'd been at graduation when Cornelias of the Foreign Mission Board had noticed him and invited him to become a student at the mission school at Cornwall, Connecticut.

But what had made the most impression of all on his life was their visit along the way with the president of the American Bible Society, Elias Boudinot, the old man who was convinced that the Indians were the lost tribes of Israel.

By the time he'd arrived at school, he was no longer Buck Watie, but had chosen another name in the ancient tradition of the Cherokees.

"And what is your name?" the enrollment officer had asked.

"Elias Boudinot."

Remembering that time, Elias smiled.

But then his heart grew sad as he recalled the disfavor when his older cousin John Ridge had married the daughter of the school's white steward. But that was after *he* had been forced to come home because of illness, rather than following John to Andover, to prepare for the ministry.

Loving Harriet Gold, another student, as he did, Elias saw his own marriage to a white woman doomed. Especially when he received the letter from her father, forbidding her marriage to a half-breed, no matter how well-educated.

But her father had not reckoned on Harriet's stubbornness and religious belief that she had been chosen to become a wife to Elias and a missionary to the Cherokee Nation. Seeing his daughter wasting away, Mr. Gold had finally relented and allowed the marriage.

Yet Elias's joy had been tempered with sadness. For it was this second mixed marriage among students that had caused the townspeople to rise up in arms and force the closing of the Cornwall school.

Now the same wasting disease had returned, and Elias could do nothing for Harriet, except to see to her needs and make sure that their children did not disturb her.

Ten years previously, when he had married Harriet, his hopes had been so high that they would fit into the white man's world. But the prejudices against them were now stronger than ever. In the ancient Cherokee tradition, his own line was dead, as well. The continuation was through the mother. So when he died, his children could not claim their Indian heritage.

Perhaps that was the reason so few Cherokees listened to him when he told them they should give up their land and move—that, and the ingrained belief that west was the direction of death.

Along the meandering stream Laurel and Edward finished their meal. As Laurel began to put the utensils back into the basket, Edward reached out and took her hand.

"Laurel," he said, clearing his throat.

"Yes, Edward?"

Her hand trembled; for she'd never felt this way before.

"I don't want you to misunderstand—"

She shook her head, assuring him that she would not.

"—what I'm going to say."

He cleared his throat again, and Laurel smiled. Dear Edward. He was finding it so difficult to express his feelings.

"I love you, Laurel."

How long ago she'd heard those same words from Will Podewell. But this time, rather than being annoyed, she was pleased. "I think I love you too, Edward."

"But we have a problem, don't we?"

Her smile turned into a frown. "All young people in love have problems. It's the nature of things."

"But ours are a bit more complicated. You see—" He looked at her limpid topaz eyes, with their hurt expression, and he suddenly laughed. "But why worry about something that may never happen?"

He drew her to him, and when she didn't resist, he began to explore her face tentatively—with small, sensuous kisses, as light as butterflies. And when she still did not object, he became bolder, finding her lips and taking from them the sweet nectar of love. "Oh, God, Laurel," he whispered against her mouth, "I want you so."

Laurel felt shameless, hidden in the glen, her conduct so alien from that prescribed by their culture. But she had never felt this way before—the fever of wanting someone so much. Then her senses slowly began to call to her, reminding her that she was allowing far too much liberty, despite her own desires.

She finally pushed him away. "No, Edward. We must stop."

He groaned and stood up, walking from her to stare down at the water rippling over the rocks. For a few minutes he said nothing. By the time he finally turned to Laurel, he saw her searching the mossy bank. "What are you looking for?" he asked.

"I've lost a hairpin, Edward. I have to find it, because I can't return to the mission looking so disheveled."

The sound of a musket going off in the distance and a sudden shout stopped the search. "Listen, Edward. What do you think is happening?"

"I don't know. But it sounds like trouble."

Laurel and Edward began running toward the town, and in the end no one noticed the condition of Laurel's hair. The Georgia militia had arrived, and the soldiers were marching straight toward the newspaper office.

"No," Elias said, trying to stop the destruction. "You weren't supposed to destroy the press—merely take it into safe keeping for me to use."

But the soldiers could not be contained. Within a short time the syllabary that Sequoyah had created, the only type ever made from it that had taken months to shape and forge, the press, the paper, and the remaining books were all destroyed.

The era of the printed word for the Cherokee had ended.

From that time on John Ross had to send runners into the Nation to alert the people of what was happening and to gather the council for the Cherokee meeting.

* * *

During this time John Howard Payne, the American actor and playwright, had reached Georgia on his promotion tour of the United States to enlist subscribers for his new literary magazine. Everywhere he went, he heard his famous song, "Home, Sweet Home," which he'd incorporated into the libretto for the opera *The Maid of Milan.*

Because of the *Cherokee Phoenix,* Payne was aware of an existing manuscript that described the great oral traditions of the Cherokees. Interested in acquiring a copy translated into English for his magazine, he set out for New Echota.

The journey through the wilderness was long and tiring. But he did not mind. His eagerness to obtain something so valuable kept him going, and on a late afternoon in October, he arrived at his destination.

He was a tall, bearded, theatrical-looking man, with a voice that resonated like thunder off the mountain.

Stopping his horses and carriage at the first tavern within the Indian town, he walked inside and introduced himself.

The few customers at the tables merely stared at him without responding. He spoke again, with still no response. And then it finally occurred to him. He needed a translator.

But before he could indicate his wishes in sign language, a loud rap at a small window of the tavern drew the proprietor's attention. Payne watched as the small window slid open to reveal a disheveled man standing on the outside.

Happy to see someone else, Payne called out, "Tell me, my good man, do you speak English?"

"Little," the man responded.

"Then will you please come inside? I need some information."

"Drinking Bear not allowed in tavern," he said.

"Then I'll come outside."

But the exchange was fruitless. The man did not understand what Payne was looking for.

About that time Laurel and her schoolchildren rounded the corner on their way back to the mission. They had been on a walk to gather herbs, but it was also their day's lesson in English.

"No, Kama´mă," Laurel called out. "You must stay with the rest of us."

"Pardon me, ma'am, for being so bold," Payne called out. "May I speak with you for a moment?"

Redbird giggled and Deer Stalker merely stared curiously at the tall man with so much hair on his face.

"Yes?"

"Allow me to introduce myself. I'm John Howard Payne..."

"Not *the* Mr. Payne, who wrote 'Home, Sweet Home.' "

Howard smiled. "The same." He was delighted that his fame had preceded him, even to the wilderness.

"I've ridden many miles in search of a manuscipt on the oral tradition of the Cherokees. Could you tell me with whom

I might talk about it?"

"I'm Laurel MacDonald, teacher at the mission school down the way." She gazed at the tired, thirsty horses and then back to the writer. "Once you attend to your horses, I'll be happy to talk with you. The children and I would also be happy to share our refreshments with you."

"Why thank you, Miss MacDonald. That's quite kind." He smiled. "I accept."

"Then just follow this street to the end, where you'll see the two-story mission house."

Laurel gave the signal for the children to begin walking again. John Howard Payne stood and watched, then hurriedly went back to water his horses.

For Payne, the experience of having afternoon tea with Indian children in a mission school prompted him to repay the kindness. He stood on the porch and recited several long poems that kept his young audience spellbound.

Black Moccasin watched his every gesture, noted his voice that changed from loud to soft, slow to fast, swaying him from sadness to happiness and back again, even better than the orators that he had heard arguing their cases before the supreme court and the councils of the Nation. And he filed away the experience in his mind so that he could recall it one day when *he* was a chief.

All too soon Black Moccasin heard Laurel's voice. "Students, you must thank Mr. Payne and then see to your homework."

The man bowed at the applause and waited for the students to leave. Black Moccasin lingered as long as he could, but in the end he was forced to follow the others.

With her helper Wind Flower hovering in the background, Laurel invited Payne inside to the fire. The evenings in the mountains were beginning to turn cold again, with winter hovering on the peaks, waiting to slip unannounced down the trails to the valleys.

"I have been thinking, Mr. Payne," Laurel began, "of your search. I recall that my father once spoke of our former chief, Charles Hicks, who, I believe, had the traditions recorded in several manuscripts."

"Then I might get them from your father?" Howard asked, the eagerness in his voice undisguised.

"No, Mr. Payne. My father—" She struggled to keep her voice even. "My father never saw them. But I believe my cousin John might have them in his possession."

"And where could I find this Cousin John of yours?"

"He's the principal chief of thr nation—John Ross. Since his property in Georgia was taken from him, he now lives at Red Hill, a very humble abode near the council grounds at Red Clay, Tennessee. If you leave here by tomorrow morning, you'll be able to find him before the annual council meeting begins."

Taking a piece of paper, Laurel drew a map for him to follow.

"I'm eternally grateful to you, Miss MacDonald," he said, standing to leave.

"And I'm grateful to you, Mr. Payne. This afternoon was a wonderful experience that my students will never forget."

Early the next morning, as Elias worked on his resolutions, he stopped to stare out the window. The tall white man, with damask vest and morning coat, walked out of the tavern where he had rented a room for the night.

Soon a trail of dust obscured the path the carriage followed out of town.

Chapter 16

Howard Payne stopped his carriage and looked down at the map Laurel had drawn. Then he looked again at the humble, rude cabin in the distance. Surely this couldn't be where the most powerful man in the Cherokee Nation lived. Howard had heard of the vast wealth of their chiefs, their fine houses, and ferries that brought in over a thousand dollars a year in tolls.

But then, as he watched, he saw a large band of Indians stop before the gate of the rude cabin. They stood there, quiet and waiting, until a man, smaller than they, came out of the cabin and took his place in the yard.

Howard continued watching, seeing the Indians loosen their blankets that were flung over their backs and hang them on the fence, along with their tin cups. In silence they walked inside the fenced yard and formed two diagonal lines. One after the other they drew near John Ross and affirmed their loyalty and devotion in a handshake, until all had done so. Then, still without a word, they took up their blankets and tin cups and resumed their journey down the road to the council grounds.

A lump formed in Howard's throat. Never before had he seen such majesty, such dignity, in such a humble setting.

But in the end, the essence of the drama, like the finest Shakespeare, had transcended the setting. It was the magnificent action that had reduced him to tears.

Fifteen minutes later Howard sat before the fire in the small cabin and faced John. "I have the advantage over you, Mr. Ross," he said. "You don't know me, but I feel as if I already know you. You see, I waited until your other visitors left before coming to the gate myself. I saw what happened."

John smiled cordially at his tall, impressive visitor. "I'm well aware of *your* credentials," he replied. "You see, I was in the audience in Philadelphia last year when you gave one of your fine readings."

Quatie moved quietly, replenishing the refreshments. Then she took her two small sons outside to gather pine cones for the fire.

"What does that man want, Mother?" Silas asked.

"Yes. Why is he here?" little George said.

"He's interested in the stories of our people," Quatie answered.

"Is Father going to tell them to him? If he is, I want to go back inside and listen."

"Yes, I want to hear the stories, too," George affirmed.

"Your father has them on the *talking leaves,*" Quatie said. "It will not be necessary for him to tell the man. He can read them for himself."

By the time Quatie and the boys returned to the cabin, Howard was saying good-bye. "I'll guard these with my life, Mr. Ross," he exclaimed. "As soon as I make a copy, I'll bring them back to you."

"Since you're staying nearby, Mr. Payne, perhaps you'd like to attend the council meeting. That way you'd be able to meet some of the older members who can give you much firsthand information that isn't contained in the Hicks papers."

"Why, I would be honored."

The council meeting began the next day, with the principal chief's annual message. He brought the delegates up to date on his work in Washington, and the favorable resolutions in the Senate that he knew President Jackson would not consider binding.

The council also dealt with the propositions of an unfair removal treaty offered by the Reverend Schermerhorn, known by the Cherokees as the Devil's Horn, since he had swapped his spiritual title for the more advantageous one of Federal Commissioner. They denied his petition for a hearing before the council, much to Schermerhorn's anger.

But perhaps one of the most important items on Ross's agenda was to try to heal the split between the Ridge faction and the rest of the leaders in the Nation. "Let us be united so that the pages of history will never dishonor the name of the Cherokee Nation."

Twenty men were thus appointed to meet and work out their differences. And a delegation, with John Ross as head, was elected to return to Washington in December.

* * *

By November, Howard Payne felt as if he knew the Cherokees intimately. John had welcomed him as a guest to remain in the Ross cabin as long as he needed to finish copying the manuscripts. He was nearly finished, but was in no hurry; for he enjoyed the company of the cultured and brilliant Ross.

It was almost midnight on a Saturday evening, and still John and Howard sat before the fire and talked. Outside, the rain came down in torrents, sometimes mixed with the sound of sleet.

"I believe winter has come to the mountains," Howard

said, drawing closer to the fire.

"Yes. I felt it this morning," John agreed, "when I took Silas and George to search for acorns. The squirrels were unusually busy, gathering them, as well."

"That reminds me of one of the stories I finished copying, about the otter and the rabbit—' Howard stopped. "Listen, John, do you hear something outside?"

From the cautious look on John's face, he knew the man was already aware of the furtive sounds.

The two became quiet, continuing to listen. But suddenly the door to the cabin was broken in, and before John and Howard could rise from their seats, members of the Georgia Guard streamed inside, one after the other, the twenty-five soldiers taking up every inch of space in the small cabin.

"You're both under arrest," Sergeant Young barked at the two men.

John did not raise his voice. He merely looked at the young man and calmly said, "You're over the state line, Sergeant, by about twenty-five miles. You have no power to arrest *anyone* in another state."

"But we'll all be back in Georgia before morning," the solder answered.

Realizing the soldier was planning to kidnap him and drag him over the state line, John inquired, "What charge are you bringing against me?"

Sergeant Young smiled. He had been well rehearsed by Bishop. "Impeding the census of the Cherokees."

John Ross made no protest as Young began to search for his public papers, confiscating everything he could find.

But when Howard saw the sergeant walk over to his laboriously copied manuscripts and pull them roughly from their leather folders, he stood up.

"Now, just a minute, Sergeant. I'm a citizen of the United States and those are my personal papers you're—"

"Hold your damned tongue," the soldier ordered, striking

Howard so hard across his face that his nose began to bleed. "You're either a French spy or an abolitionist, and we have orders to deal with you, too."

John, seeing his friend so roughly treated, said, "You're mistaken about Mr. Payne. He's—"

"Shut up. We know who he is."

Quatie, behind the blanket that shielded the bed, remained quiet, a protective arm around each sleeping child. She could not see beyond the blanket, but from the snatches of conversation, she knew that, somehow, soldiers had come for her husband. Ever since they had been reconciled, she had waited for this day to happen.

Within a few moments the only sound was the howling wind rushing through the open door, seeming to vent its anger against the embers on the hearth. Then the noise of the wagon wheels and horses leaving the yard combined with the rain, until only the rain was left.

As the open wagon, holding John and Howard, rolled along the trail toward Spring Place, the driver, dressed in a poncho to ward off the freezing rain, began to sing "Home, Sweet Home." John Howard Payne, its author, looked at his friend John Ross. Neither commented, but both were aware of the irony.

Quatie finally rose from the bed to brace the broken door from the wind and cold. John had not spoken a single word to her, had not even said good-bye. It was as if she and the children had not existed. But in her heart Quatie knew the reason. It was her husband's way of protecting her and the children from the soldiers, who had not thought to look behind the blanket.

She knelt before the dying embers on the hearth and began her mournful song, willing her grief to be taken upward by the smoke to the Great Spirit above. By morning she was still kneeling by the hearth.

Beyond the ridge, past the former MacDonald property, Rebecca and her father, Julius, rode along the north boundary. Thistle, the pony, was still stubborn, but the young woman had finally made him see who was the boss.

The day before, when Julius was hunting, he'd seen smoke rising over the hill. And from that he guessed they might have neighbors he didn't know about.

He thought about it all evening. Just over the ridge there might be some young man, sitting on his new property, all alone, and hankering for a woman like his daughter, Rebecky.

"Why do you want me to dress up, Pa? We're just goin' ridin', ain't we?"

"I seen some smoke comin' out of a chimney, Rebeccky," he'd told her. "If they're new settlers, then it would be the neighborly thing for us to go over and say howdy."

Julius glanced at his daughter as they rode. She'd gained weight these past several years, and he'd had to buy her a lot of material for her to make new clothes, once she'd outgrown the ones that had been in the house. But he could afford it.

"What are ya lookin' at, Pa?"

"At *you*, Rebecky. You're a fine-lookin' woman, all except the freckles. I was thinkin' I might buy you one of those jars of cream I seen over at the store at the Carter settlement the next time I go."

Rebecca started pouting. "I know what you're doin', Pa. Tryin' to get rid of me so ya can marry that Lulu."

"That's not true. I'm only thinkin' of your future. But don't think it ain't crossed my mind to marry again once *you're* settled."

They continued on their journey, crossing the stream and then proceeding toward the small spiral of smoke that had come into view.

"See, I told you we had neighbors, Rebecky."

At the small house in the secluded triangle of land owned by Two Feathers, Daisy and her two small children, Billy and little Ina´li, named by Two Feathers in honor of his friend, walked in the snow toward the house. The two boys carried the basket of eggs Daisy had just gathered from the nests in the barn.

She was happy as Two Feathers' wife; for he had treated her with such kindness. She remembered nothing of her earlier life, except a feeling sometimes that she'd run from something terrible. But when she had the nightmares, Two Feathers always comforted her and made everything right again.

"Look, Mama," Billy said. "I see someone coming."

Daisy, gazing in the direction her son pointed, saw the two strangers riding toward them. As they approached, she began to tremble; for she was seized with a terrible fear that they were coming to take her away. Quickly, without speaking, she gathered up her sons, ran into the house, and latched the door.

"Pa, did you see her?"

"Yes, Rebecky. A white woman dressed like a squaw." He'd also noticed the two little boys, one so fair, and the other so dark. His jaw was firmly set. "Come, let's go back home. We ain't got neighbors, after all."

By the time Two Feathers returned with the deer slung across his shoulder, Billy ran to meet him. "Papa, Papa. Some people came today and scared Mama half to death."

"What did they do, Billy?"

"They rode into the yard and stared at the house for a long time. Mama latched the door so they couldn't get in. Then they rode away."

Two Feathers calmly strung the deer to the rafters and

walked to the outside trough, where he broke the ice to wash his hands and face. Billy followed him, waiting for him to speak.

"What did they look like?" Two Feathers asked, his voice still unemotional.

"I think one was a woman, but she was ugly. The man had a beard."

Two Feathers nodded in relief that they were not surveyors coming to measure his land. "They probably meant no harm. Maybe they're the ones who live over the ridge on the MacDonald property."

"Then go inside and tell Mama," Billy said. "She's still hiding in the bedroom."

"And where is Ina′li?"

"Asleep in his bed."

Two Feathers took Billy by the hand and walked back to the house. Once inside, he took off his coat and said, "Stay by the hearth, Billy, and finish working on your moccasins. I'll go to see about your mother."

Obediently, Billy went to his little workbench by the fire while Two Feathers walked into the bedroom, called to Daisy, and closed the door.

She was still hovering under the covers. When she saw her husband, she reached out to him.

"It's all right, Agitsi′," he said, sitting down on the side of the bed and putting his arms around her.

"But I was so afraid," she said. "And you weren't here."

He smiled at her total trust in him. For a number of months she had remained mute. He had not even been sure that she *could* speak until that night when Ina′li had been born, with the help of Tansee

His only concern back then had been in taking care of the woman and her two children. It had not occurred to him to make her his wife. But then, several months after Ina′li had been born, she had begun to have violent nightmares.

And he guessed what had happened to her, and why she had run away.

He had seen the same behavior in horses that had been treated cruelly early in life by their masters. They were good for nothing, unless someone had the patience to erase the cruel treatment from memory. How much more valuable was a woman, especially one who had the kiss of the sun upon her hair and eyes the color of the mountain bluebird's wings.

"I want you to comfort me, Two Feathers," Daisy said, drawing her husband to lie beside her on the bed.

He kissed her gently, soothingly, taking his time, never by his actions alarming her. Casually he removed his shirt and his trousers. Then his hands gently slid along her thigh, not rushing her, but giving her time for her desire to build until her need begged to be satisfied.

"I want you," she whispered. "Now."

Only after she had spoken did Two Feathers assume his position. Mindful of Agitsi´'s need, he did not allow himself his own pleasure until she had cried out in joy.

Daisy lay quietly, satiated, with her arms wrapped around him. She knew that she was giving him vast pleasure, too. And when she felt his body finally shudder and heard him moan in a language she could not understand, she felt complete as a woman, and unafraid again.

* * *

The old Moravian mission station at Spring Place had always been sacred to the brothers and the Indians. Moravian and Indian alike had been buried in "God's Acre," the graves tended lovingly by those who followed in the footsteps of the original missionaries.

But Colonel Bishop had confiscated the mission, turning out the brothers and making it into Camp Benton, headquarters for a particularly vicious group of men whom he had enlisted as the Georgia Guard, a special unit apart from the regular militia.

The chapel was now a courthouse, where questionable justice was administered, according to Bishop's whims. And the missionaries' house had been converted into a notorious grogshop and brothel.

This was the place where John Ross and his friend Payne were being held captive.

While John waited for an answer to his letter to the re-elected Governor Gilmer in Milledgeville, he and Payne were kept chained in a dark and damp log cabin that served as a jail. Overhead, the corpse of a Cherokee, who had been executed several weeks prior, hung from the rafters.

John and Howard had been visited by both Bishop and John Ridge, leader of the opposition, who, despite his stand, was appalled that the principal chief of the Cherokee Nation had been arrested on the flimsiest excuses and dragged back to Georgia. The action would only serve to cement Ross's power in the Nation.

At the state capital Gilmer stared down at the letter. "Nothing can be settled," Ross had written, "until a delegation with sufficient powers reaches Washington in December. I assure you that, if I'm released, no exertion shall be wanting on my part to favor the adjustment of the problems before us."

"That's damn blackmail," Gilmer said to his secretary.

"Does that mean you'll release him?"

"I have no other choice," Gilmer answered. "Write out the orders for Bishop to let him go. And I'll sign it."

On November 16, nine days after he'd been arrested, John was freed. But Payne had to wait four more days, until John could arrange his release, as well.

Payne knew who to blame for his situation. In his college

days he'd been a classmate of Schermerhorn, who was the source of the Cherokees' present troubles. And he knew that the man feared him and his pen.

By the time John Howard Payne was released from his chains, he was a staunch friend of the Cherokees. And he used his pen to alert the nation to the tragic and senseless events that were unfolding.

Chapter 17

At the Carter settlement, Tilda Mae and her daughter, Lulu, sat in Ellie's warm kitchen and drank a second cup of tea, with the freshly made scones just out of the oven.

"It's been such a long time, Ellie," Tilda Mae said. "You'da thought Daisy would have gotten in touch with you by now."

"You know Daisy never learned to write, Tilda Mae."

"Then Horace should have sent word to you where they were goin', after Bishop took over the Vann property."

"They went out west. And if the two are happy together, then that's all that matters."

Seeing Ellie's strained face, Tilda Mae decided she'd better change the subject.

"Julius Parker sent word to Lulu that he'll be visitin' again soon."

Loosening the tight grip on her teacup, Ellie said, "My, that sounds like you just might be a Christmas bride, Lulu."

"Not unless he's already married off that ugly daughter of his," Lulu responded with a pout. "The last time he was here courtin', he said he wasn't planning on marrying again until he had Rebecca settled in a house of her own."

Ellie stared at Daisy's friend. "Then you just aren't playin' your cards right."

"What do you mean, Miss Ellie?"

"Why, you have to convince Julius how much company you and Rebecca would be for each other, since you're the same age and all. Tell him how you've always missed havin' a sister, bein' an only child."

"But I don't want her around, lordin' it over me, once I marry Julius."

"With a new wife as young and pretty as you, he won't want her around for long, either. Once he begins to see you in his house, with Rebecca still there, then hit him with the other barrel."

"What do you mean by that, Ellie?" Tilda Mae asked, extremely interested.

"Lulu could mention how helpful she would be, as his wife, in entertainin' families with eligible sons. He'd have to be mighty dense not to understand what she was drivin' at."

"Miss Ellie, you're a genius," Lulu said, smiling at the woman. "Yes, I can see how it might work out."

"But you'll have to practice so it won't sound *planned,*" Ellie cautioned. "Let him kiss you first. And when his juices get to stirrin', that's the time to strike."

Tilda Mae hurriedly set down her empty cup. "Come on, Lulu. Time's awastin'."

"Yes, Mama."

"Jake's got in some white rabbit's fur that would be beautiful trimmin' for a winter weddin' suit," Ellie called from the doorway as the two disappeared down the wooden walk.

"Pa, I'm scared to stay by myself," said Rebecca. "Let me go with you."

Julius shook his head. "No, girl. You got Elvira here to keep you company while I'm gone."

"But she don't like me, Pa."

"Then treat her better, Rebecky. Besides, it's powerful cold outside, and it looks like more snow's comin'."

"If it's that dangerous, then *you're* better off stayin' at home, too, instead of gallivantin' all the way over to the settlement."

"Mind your manners. You're talkin' to your pa."

His voice was severe, something she wasn't used to. He'd always been so good to her, before he'd started going over to see that Lulu. Rebecca hated her already.

She stood at a window and watched the black man, Kepp, Elvira's husband, bring the carriage around to the front. And then her pa was gone, with only the tracks in the snow left behind.

"Elvira," she called. "Where are you?"

"Upstairs, mistress," the plaintive voice answered.

"Well, stop what you're doin' and come here. I need you."

The new snow was soft and melting in spots on the road. But by late afternoon it began to freeze again, making the way slippery.

Rebecca was right. He had no business traveling so far in weather like this. But Lulu had been on his mind ever since he'd seen the squaw woman.

It didn't make sense for him to own the finest house around and miles of property, when across the ridge, that other man, whether he was red or white, had the comfort of a pretty woman and *he* didn't.

But he'd made a promise to Rebecca's mama, that he wouldn't bring another woman into the house until after the girl was married. How much longer would *that* take, when she never met anybody?

Lulu wasn't going to wait forever. Julius knew that. But he couldn't go against his promise to a dying woman. Maybe he'd better buy *two* jars of cream for Rebecca while he was at the settlement store.

The days were growing much shorter, and several miles before he reached the settlement, the sun went down. The wind howled through the trees, and a deer bolted across his path, causing the horses to shy. They slipped and slid before finally regaining their footing on the icy road.

Julius's loaded musket, lying on the seat beside him, was his only protection. Traveling in the dark, with the meager glow of the moon on the snow, a half-frozen Julius began to long for his own warm bed. A man his age oughtn't be out in such foul weather with wild animals all around him. But then he thought of Lulu, waiting for him.

She sat in the parlor, tapping her foot in impatience. The food had been warming on the hearth for over an hour, and still Julius had not appeared. "Papa, why don't you take the lantern and look one more time down the road?" Lulu asked Obadiah. "If you don't see him, then we just won't wait for supper any longer."

"Yes, Obadiah," Tilda Mae said. "But be sure to put on your overcoat. I wouldn't want you to catch pneumonia."

Obadiah looked at his wife and then his daughter. "You better get the man to pop the question tonight, Lulu. Else you'll be a widow before you're a bride."

"Now, Obadiah, that doesn't make sense," Tilda Mae chided.

"You know what I mean. The man can't make many more long trips in weather like this and expect to live a long, ripe life."

"Just go and get the lantern. Lulu doesn't need your advice."

Coming out of the dark woods, Julius stopped the carriage long enough to relieve himself. Then he gave the signal for the horses to continue. As soon as he rounded the curve in the road, he saw a lantern light flickering at the end of the lane. "Yo-ho!" he shouted, his voice carrying through the crisp air all the way to the house.

"Sounds like Mr. Parker," Tilda Mae said, listening from the window. "Quick, Lulu. Pour a mug of hot grog and be ready to give it to the man when he steps inside the door."

Down the lane Obadiah saw the carriage come into view and then slow. "Greetings, Julius," he said. "We'd about given you out."

"For truth, Obadiah, I wondered if I was goin' to make it, the weather's so bad."

Obadiah climbed onto the side of the carriage and held out the lantern so that Julius could see his way to the barn. A few minutes later the two men walked back to the house.

"Look who's here, Lulu," Obadiah said, opening the door.

His daughter smiled the pretty smile she'd been practicing before the mirror. "Julius, how nice to see you. I was really worried about you." She immediately handed him the hot grog and began drawing him to the warm fire.

"It was a long, cold trip. But I finally managed to get here, Lulu," Julius replied, following her to the hearth.

"Mr. Parker," Tilda Mae said, nodding at him as she put a plate of steaming hot corn bread on the table.

"Tilda Mae," he answered, acknowledging her briefly before returning his eyes to the lucious Lulu.

What he saw made all his hours on the road worthwhile.

"I'll just put your valise in the bedroom," Obadiah said, walking past.

"Much obliged," Julius replied.

The dinner went well, but Lulu was disappointed that things did not go according to plan afterward. She had no time alone with Julius. After a brief visit with Obadiah by the hearth, while she and Tilda Mae cleaned up the kitchen, their visitor stood up, excused himself for the night, and retired to the bedroom.

"Well, the man isn't that young," Obadiah whispered, seeing the disappointment in his daughter's eyes. "He's had a long, tiring trip. But you got all day tomorrow to work on 'im," he added.

That night Tilda Mae shared her mattress with Lulu, since Julius had been put in the other bedroom. The displaced Obadiah had to be content with his pallet of quilts on the floor, in the corner of his own bedroom.

Several hours after her mother had gone to sleep and Lulu could hear her father's snoring, she got out of bed and went into the keeping room, where she put on another log and sat on the hearth with her quilt draped around her.

She began to think of all the plans she'd made, with the circuit-rider preacher invited to dinner the next night, along with Ellie and Jake, her parents' best friends. The blue wedding suit, trimmed with white rabbit's fur, was hanging in her mother's room. It wouldn't do for Julius to see it, since he was sleeping in her bedroom. Of course, if her plans didn't work out, no one would be the wiser. Julius would think they were just being extra hospitable, having other people to dinner to meet such a wealthy man.

Julius slept heavily, and then awoke as he often did after several hours of sound sleep. He opened his eyes and looked around him, finally realizing where he was.

He smiled to himself. He was in Lulu's own bed, sleeping on the same pillow where her pretty little head usually lay. He began to think about her and imagined her right beside him. But no, that wouldn't do.

He got up, wrapped his blanket around his long underwear, and tiptoed into the keeping room to light his pipe by the embers of the fire.

"Lulu," he said, seeing her sitting by the hearth. "I'm

sorry to disturb you. I was just goin' to light my pipe."

As he started to walk away she said, "It's all right, Julius. Come back to the fire. You aren't disturbing me."

"I woke up."

"So did I," she responded.

He stared at Lulu, with her long, dark hair streaming down her back. In the glow of the fire, she looked like an angel. Feeling self-conscious, he tightened the blanket around himself and sat down on the hearth beside her. But all desire to smoke had left him. A stronger desire had overcome him.

She smiled at him, her dimples showing her pleasure. "We didn't really get a chance to talk tonight," she said. "Did Rebecca mind that you came to see me again so soon?"

"She was a little pouty when I left," he admitted.

"I know how she feels," Lulu said, her voice filled with sympathy.

Surprised, Julius said, "What do you mean?"

"Oh, how lonely she must get, being an only child. You see, I always wanted a sister to share secrets with. Thinking about Rebecca sometimes, I thought about how much fun it would be, the two of us together, since we're so close to the same age—"

Julius frowned. "But I never thought of you as a sister to Rebecky. I thought maybe one day, you and I could, you know—"

"Oh, I would look on Rebecca as a companion, Julius. We could never be sisters," Lulu leaned her head a little closer to the fire, her hair brushing against Julius's cheek.

"Lulu?"

She turned her head. "Yes, Julius?"

"You think it's all right, bein' together like this?"

"Mama and Papa are in the next room. It's not like we're in the house by ourselves."

Her lips, half-parted, were irresistible. Julius leaned over to kiss her, and Lulu did not protest. "Oh, my sweet, beautiful girl. How I ache for you. But I made a promise—"

"Hush, darling. Just hold me close." Lulu put her arms around Julius. And with the quilt slipping off her shoulders, only the delicate white muslin gown separated them.

Julius was aware of her soft breasts, and aware of what her closeness was doing to him. "If only I hadn't made that promise."

"But it was the honorable thing to do, promising that you would take care of Rebecca's future. Wasn't that what it was all about?"

"Well, I reckon so."

"But your wife didn't know how hard it would be for you, a widower, without someone to help you entertain and bring eligible young men to the house for your daughter to meet."

"That's true."

She laid her head against the curve of his neck and stared into the fire, giving him time to think about what she'd just said.

"I guess it's the spirit of the promise after all," Julius finally said, eagerness to his voice. "With a woman in the house to help me, it would be much easier."

Lulu moved away from him, the tip of her breast barely grazing his hand.

"Lulu, will you marry me?" Julius asked suddenly.

She hesitated. "I'm not sure. As much as I care for you, I can't see myself waiting another year or two until you —"

"No. I mean right away. As soon as we can get a preacher."

Lulu laughed. "If I didn't know better, I'd think you had it all planned ahead of time, knowing Preacher Jenkins will be coming to dinner tomorrow night."

"Then it's fate. If you say yes, we'll get him to marry us and I can take you back home as my new bride."

"But what about Rebecca?"

"Leave her to me. I can see this is the best thing for her. Say yes, Lulu," he pleaded.

"I may be sorry, getting married in such haste. But yes, Julius, I'll marry you."

In the bedroom, Obadiah stopped snoring. "Tilda Mae, do you hear voices in the other room?"

"Shut up, Obadiah, and go back to sleep."

Chapter 18

"Mama, are you awake?" Lulu asked, slipping back into bed.

"Yes, but don't talk too loud. Your papa's just gone to sleep again."

"Julius asked me to marry him. Tomorrow night, when Preacher Jenkins comes to supper."

Tilda Mae smiled in the dark. So her daughter had been successful. "Imagine that. My Lulu married to one of the richest men in the county."

"And he's so generous. He said not to worry about a trousseau. That he'd buy me lots of pretty things once I was his wife."

"I must remember to do somethin' nice for Ellie," Tilda Mae said. "That's a woman with a good head on her shoulders. Now go to sleep, sweetheart. We'll have to get up awful early to do everything that needs doin'."

"Yes, Mama." Lulu turned on her side and stared toward the shuttered window. A few silver moonbeams crept through the crevices and entered the room. For a time she watched their shadow dance and listened to the howling accompaniment of the cold wind. Then she closed her eyes and crossed her fingers so that nothing would happen to spoil her wedding day.

By early morning Julius was out of the house and on his way to the settlement store. He had a lot of things to get—including a ring for Lulu. Not that it had to be anything fine. He just needed something he could use for the ceremony. Later he would have his dead wife's gold ring cut down for her.

"Mr. Dodge, I'm Julius Parker. I stopped off once before—"

"I remember you, Mr. Parker," Jake said, nodding at the man coming toward the counter. "In fact, Tilda Mae and Obadiah told us you were comin'. They invited my wife and me to supper tonight, to get to know you ."

Ellie, in the storage room directly behind, came out to get a good look at the man. "Good mornin', Mr. Parker. I'm Ellie, Jake's wife."

Julius smiled and nodded. "I come to do a good bit of shoppin'," he confided. "You see, me and Lulu Hanson will be gettin' married tonight."

"Well, I do declare," Ellie said. "You couldn'ta found a sweeter, prettier girl than Lulu."

"You're right about that. But I certainly did take the girl by surprise, proposin' the way I did. I been a widower for a long time. But once I made up my mind to marry, I decided there was no need to wait, what with the preacher comin' for dinner. You can't imagine what I stirred up over there."

Ellie had an idea, but she kept her mouth shut.

"Lulu and her mama are all in a swivet this mornin', so I decided it was best if I left the house for a while."

"And you've come to the right place," Ellie said. "Jake, why don"t you show Mr. Parker a pair of those blue checked flannel pajamas that came in last week. I think I'll go on home now and bake a nice weddin' cake. That's the least I can do for Tilda Mae."

Julius nodded. "That's mighty kind of you, Miss Ellie."

As Ellie turned to go, she said, "By the way, do you have a weddin' ring?"

"No. That's one of the things I had on my list. Something that would do until I can—"

The eager Ellie didn't let him finish. "We got a beautiful gold band taken in trade by a prospector that traveled this way. Might be just the thing for you."

Jake frowned, but Ellie paid no attention to her husband.

"Well, I was thinkin' of something just for tonight. You see, I got a perfectly good weddin' band at home."

"It belonged to your first wife?"

"Yes."

"Oh, but that's bad luck, Mr. Parker. Better for you to start fresh. Not that it couldn't be used by some other member of the family."

"Well, now, I hadn't thought of that. I got a daughter, Rebecky."

"Then she's the one who should wear her mama's ring. Sentimental, the way it is. Tell you what—I'll just go over to the house and bring back the ring I was tellin' you about. It's mighty pretty."

Ellie left the store, and when she'd reached the boardinghouse, she carefully removed a brick from the chimney hearth and pulled out the small sack of things that had belonged to Horace. Dumping its contents on the kitchen table, she retrieved Bess's gold wedding band, a circlet engraved with forget-me-nots.

Poor Daisy. She'd never had a chance, with Horace wearin' the ring around his neck the whole time they were married. He hadn't loved her at all. And as far as Ellie was concerned, he got what he deserved.

She'd long ago given up hope of ever seeing Daisy again.

But each night she prayed that her daughter was still alive and all right. Sighing, Ellie returned the other small items to their hiding place and then polished the circlet with her apron. It would be good to get rid of the ring and make a little money, too.

By the time she returned to the store, Julius had bought quite a share of Jake's stock. But when Ellie laid the gold band on a piece of black velvet and stood back for Julius to get a clear view, she knew from his eyes that she'd just made the most profitable sale.

Wrapping it in a scrap of cloth with a blue ribbon around it, Ellie said, "You did right, Mr. Parker, to buy it. I know Lulu will love it."

"I never seen one so pretty," Julius commented. "I just hope it'll fit."

"I expect it will. Now, be sure to tell Tilda Mae that I'm bringin' the weddin' cake tonight," Ellie reminded the man as he left on foot in the direction of the livery stable.

While Jake carried Julius's purchases to the door and watched for the carriage, he said, "Ellie, I hope you're not makin' a mistake with that ring."

"We should be gettin' rid of *all* of Horace's things, Jake. Havin' them in the house just keeps the past alive."

The carriage and the two beautiful bays came to a stop before the store, and Jake rushed out with the packages while Ellie took care of opening and closing the door. There was something awfully familiar about the fine horses and the crest on the carriage. She knew she'd seen them somewhere before.

After the carriage had left, Ellie put on her cloak. "I'll be leavin' now, Jake."

On the slippery path back to the house, Ellie still thought about Julius Parker's carriage. Suddenly, she remembered where she'd seen it. It was there, right before her eyes all the time. Horace and Bess had arrived in the same carriage, and later it had been claimed by Two Feathers.

Then Julius Parker must have been the one who'd drawn Alex's property in the lottery. That was why the man was so rich. He was living off Alex's years of hard work.

Ellie tightened her jaw. If she'd known that, she never would have encouraged Lulu. But what was done was done. She'd keep her mouth shut. It wouldn't do Lulu any good to know.

Shortly before dark, Ellie and Jake set out for their friends' house. "Now try not to get the wheels in any holes, Jake," Ellie cautioned. "I'd hate for anything to happen to the weddin' cake."

"I'll do my best, Ellie."

They rode along in silence, until Ellie had something else to say. "I been thinkin', if it's all right with you, I might ask Tilda Mae and Obadiah to come back and spend the night with us. That would give Lulu and Mr. Parker a chance to be alone on their weddin' night."

"What about the preacher?"

"Him, too. We got the empty bedrooms."

Jake nodded as he usually did and continued the steady pace.

By the time they arrived, the small log house was filled with aromas—fresh pine boughs and holly berries decorating the mantel and the trestle table, and the tantalizing smell of wild turkey and venison, sweet potatoes, dried britches beans, and loaves of bread. Outside, hidden under a wooden bucket with a large rock on top to keep the animals from getting to it, was the large bowl of snow pudding, made with spices, sugar, and milk stirred into the snow and whipped into a frozen cream.

Tilda Mae's tired face brightened when she saw her friend. "Oh, Ellie, I'm so glad to see you and Jake. I'm so nervous about everything. The preacher thinks we should have the ceremony first, then the supper. What do *you* think, Ellie?"

"Why, that sounds like a good idea. That way Lulu won't run the danger of spillin' gravy on her beautiful new suit before the ceremony. Now, calm down, Tilda Mae. Don't worry about a thing. I'll help you." She turned to Jake. "Just set the cake down on the other end of the table."

"I wish we had some music, like at Daisy's weddin'," Tilda Mae said.

"I don't see why we can't. Preacher Jenkins could lead us in singin' a song from the Scottish Psalter. I'll speak to him about it."

Several minutes later, as Ellie and Preacher Jenkins raised their voices in "Glory be to God on High," Lulu in her blue suit trimmed with white rabbit's fur walked toward the preacher and Julius.

The nervous groom, dressed in his dark suit and new shirt purchased from Jake, had been worried all afternoon—first about what his daughter Rebecca would say when she found out she had a new mama no older than herself, and second about the bath he'd taken. December was not the best time to take one, and he wondered if he might not come down with pneumonia. But then, seeing Lulu, he forgot all his worries.

With six people in the room, Preacher Jenkins took the opportunity to preach one of his new sermons before he began the vows. Tilda Mae kept glancing back toward the hearth and heard little until the actual ceremony began.

"The matrimonial estate is made in heaven," the preacher began.

At his words Lulu felt Julius squeeze her hand.

"If there be any to object to this marriage between Julius and Louise, let him come forward or forever hold his peace—"

For some reason Lulu held her breath. But then she gradually relaxed when no voice thundered from the door and the preacher continued. Julius slipped the ring onto her finger. And although she had no intention of obeying anybody, but doing as she pleased, Lulu repeated the words when prompted to love, cherish, and obey.

Then the ceremony was over, and she was a married woman, waiting for her husband to kiss her.

"Congratulations!" Preacher Jenkins was first, followed by Jake and Ellie. Tilda Mae and Obadiah beamed.

"Well, come on," Ellie said. "Let's get the weddin' supper on the table."

The entire evening went well and Ellie was glad to see that her iced pound cake was such a success. But knowing that Lulu and Julius were eager for them all to go, Ellie said," We'll see you in the mornin', Lulu. You two be sure to stop over at the boardin'house to say your good-byes."

"We will, Miss Ellie. And it's awful kind of you to invite Mama and Papa for the night."

"That reminds me of the Old Testament story of—"

Ellie cut off the preacher's long-winded remarks. "Save that for us old folks, Preacher, over a nice cup of hot tea once we get back to the boardin'house. I want you to have enough time to tell it the way it should be told."

Within moments, only Lulu and Julius were left in the house.

"You're not afraid of bein' alone with me, are you, Lulu?" he asked.

She smiled a shy smile. "A little. But I know you'll be"—she hesitated, searching for the right word—"*kind* to me, since I don't know anything about being a married woman."

"And that's the way it should be."

An hour later the lamp in the bedroom was burning low, and Lulu waited for Julius to appear. It hadn't taken her long to remove her blue wedding suit and put on the gown she had stored with the sachet bag of dried flowers. She had brushed her lustrous long hair the required number of strokes, stared at the beautiful gold ring on her finger, and practiced her look of innocence. Now she was merely impatient for her husband to come to bed.

Finally she heard his steps and saw the door opening. He was dressed in his blue-checked pajamas. "Lulu."

"Yes, Julius?"

He picked up the lamp and held it briefly so he could look at her. Then he cupped his hand, blew out the lamp, and climbed into bed. He was eager and awkward with her at first, and Lulu did nothing to help him.

Much later, as he snored beside her, she watched the moonbeams through the crevices of the shutters and smiled. He was pretty good for an old man. Of course, not as good as Ned. But Julius had other things that Ned didn't have—a big house and a large acreage.

Chapter 19

At New Echota, the December winds swirled around the mission house where Laurel sat at Worcester's writing desk.

"Dear Cousin John," she began, and then put the quill back into its holder while she stared at the white paper. How could she write him such discouraging news—that he and the entire Cherokee Nation had been betrayed while he was in Washington? There were no words that she could use to make it more acceptable. And so she took up the pen again and continued.

"My heart is heavy as I write this letter. Behind your back, Commissioner John Schermerhorn called an illegal meeting of the Cherokee Nation to negotiate the same treaty for removal that was rejected at the October council meeting. The other commissioner, Governor Carroll, is ill and not here. But Major Ridge, Elias Boudinot, and your brother Andrew are, along with Currey, the emigration agent. And we are all surrounded by the Georgia militia.

"A few days ago, while Currey read the terms of the treaty, the roof of the courthouse caught fire. Some said it showed heaven's wrath at the unlawful meeting. But the

Ridge factor pushed the treaty through, with the voting taking place this morning.

"The good news is that most Cherokees stayed away, with only eighty-four of our sixteen thousand present. So it is not a legal document in any sense. I understand that Schermerhorn, on his own, did not have the authority of the United States to sign it, and certainly the few Cherokees present did not have the authority of the Nation. But I know that this action can drive a great wedge in our cause, and you will have one more irksome problem to deal with.

"I overheard the naming of a committee to take the fraudulent document to Washington. They may even arrive before you get this letter. So I am rushing to finish it while Edward Farraday is waiting to take it with him."

Laurel began to shiver with the cold. Drawing her shawl closer to her, she stood up and walked to the fire, where she held out her hands to warm them. When they were not quite so stiff, she walked back to the desk and took up her quill.

"I have heard nothing from my parents. But the news each day from other sources is quite unsettling. I've stopped speaking to Elias, unless absolutely necessary. I'm sure you've already received the news that his brother, Stand Watie, has joined the militia, so he is well protected in his treachery. You will more than likely see Elias, since he is one of the men selected to take the treaty to Washington.

"I pray that your negotiations will be successful, and that you will be home again soon so that you might heal this breach that has occurred in your absence."

"Laurel," a voice called from the doorway. "Have you finished your letter? I need to leave now."

She looked up and saw Edward, who had come down the outside stairs with the mailbags. "Yes. I have only to sign my name and seal it."

A few minutes later, with a lingering kiss, Laurel said

good-bye and stood on the snow-covered porch to watch Edward depart. Then she hurried back inside to the fire.

Gazing at the flames that hissed and crackled, she became pensive. All around her she felt a shroud of sorrow, like the gathering of waters rushing down the mountain ravines to the unsuspecting valleys below.

But she still maintained hope that each day she might hear from Alex and Trudie. A letter, or perhaps a visit from Tansee in the dead of night. For so long she had listened to the night sounds, the brushing of branch against branch, the sudden creak of the porch steps. And more than once, she had risen from her bed and rushed to open the door, to be greeted by nothing more substantial than the wind.

With Edward gone, and the students not due back to the school for another two days, Laurel felt completely alone. But then she walked to the mantel, where she picked up Edward's gift to her—the miniature snow scene, with a deer and green fir trees. She shook the small glass globe and saw the snow begin to swirl magically into a fantasy of white. Watching it, Laurel became lost in her own fantasy that everything would be set right again in her world.

In the parlor at the Parker house Lulu sat near the hearth and took up her sewing while she waited for Julius to return from the barn. She paid no attention to the silent Rebecca, who sat at the window and glared at her with accusing eyes. But she would never forget the tantrum the girl had thrown two weeks previously, on that cold winter evening when she and Julius had returned home as man and wife.

"Rebecky, this is your new mama, Louise. We got married yesterday."

"No, Pa. She don't belong here. Send her back where she came from. You made a promise to Mama."

"My promise, Rebecky, was to see you in a house of

your own. And I need Lulu to help me. So say your welcome and then go and git Elvira to help with the boxes."

"I ain't never goin' to say welcome to 'er, Pa." She glared defiantly at both of them.

Lulu, sensing his anger, said, "Julius, the poor girl is just taken by surprise. It's all right. Really it is. We'll have plenty of time to get acquainted." She gazed into his eyes in a loving manner. "I'm a little tired from the long trip. So if you'll show me to our room, I think I might rest awhile."

"You'll come back dowstairs for supper, won't you?"

Lulu hesitated. "Maybe Elvira could bring me a little something on a tray. That will give you and Rebecca time together." She touched his hand. "But don't linger too long, darling. I'll be awfully lonely without you."

"Elvira," Julius shouted.

She appeared at the head of the stairs.

"This is your new mistress, Mrs. Parker. Show her to the main bedroom and do whatever she asks you."

"Yes, master."

Now, as Lulu sat at the fire, she smiled, thinking of that first night. Within one hour she had become the mistress of the house, with Elvira as her devoted servant.

Rebecca, still glaring at the satisfied Lulu, broke her silence. "I heard you and Pa again last night," she accused. "Groanin' and pantin' like animals in the barnyard."

Lulu set down her sewing. "Rebecca, you've got to learn that what goes on between a man and his wife is sacred. But listening, with your ear against the door, isn't nice. And *speaking* about it even worse. But if it upsets you so much, maybe you'd better move farther down the hall."

"I won't move. You might think you took my mama's place for good. But it'll only be a short time before you're gone."

"If I didn't know better, I'd think you were threatening me."

"Take it for whatever it's worth."

Julius's footsteps kept her from retorting. "So how is the cow?" she asked, smiling in Julius's direction.

"Got a new little steer," he said, grinning. "Already standin' on his legs and sucklin' before I even left the barn."

That night the sounds began again. And Rebecca, listening as usual, heard her father's voice. "You're the best wife a man ever had, Lulu. If I didn't know you was a virgin on our weddin' night, I'd think you'd had lots of practice in givin' a man pleasure."

"It's all *your* doing, Julius," Lulu whispered. "Showing me how."

She heard the pride in his voice as he responded. "I *do* have a lot of stayin' power for a man what's been a widower for all these years."

"I think, darling, you've been storing up all your love to give to *me*."

"I'd like to give you somethin' else, too, Lulu. Watchin' that little steer bein' born this afternoon, I began to think how nice it would be for the two of us to have a baby together."

An eavesdropping Rebecca, outside the door, fled back to her room. She hadn't even thought of that. She had to get rid of Lulu before her father could make a baby.

A satisfied Lulu, hearing Rebecca go, said, "That would be the most wonderful present in the world. Only..." She hesitated.

"What is it, precious?"

"We have something else to do first. Find a husband for Rebecca."

"I'd forgotten about that. I guess you're right." He began to nuzzle her again until Lulu stopped him.

"No, Julius. We'll have to stop this, so I can put my mind to Rebecca."

"You mean, just for tonight?"

"No. As much as I love you, I think I'd better move into the other bedroom so my entire energy will be on our project."

Julius groaned. "No, Lulu. I just got used to you bein' in the bed beside me."

"And I'll be again, darling. I promise. After Rebecca is married, we'll make love every night—for hours at a time, if you want to. And then we'll begin our *own* family."

What could he say to that? His sweet Lulu, willing to give up her place beside him to put her mind on his daughter. Surely he could control himself for that long. Especially with the vision of what would happen later.

In Washington, John Ross stared down at Laurel's letter. She was not the only one to have alerted him to the "Christmas trick" by the Reverend Schermerhorn, who had been unsuccessful for six months in getting anyone to sign up for voluntary removal.

But the damage had been done. Despite the canvas of the Nation, undertaken by the National Committee and National Council, with the document of fourteen thousand signatures protesting the unauthorized treaty arriving in Washington by February, Secretary of War Cass paid no attention to Ross's protest that the treaty had been made "without Cherokee authority, false upon its face, and against the known wishes of the Nation." He had what he wanted—a signed treaty. And it made no difference who had signed it.

Cass also ignored Major William Davis, the man appointed as an enrolling agent for emigration. "This isn't right, Cass. Schermerhorn's actions have been nothing but a series of blunders from first to last."

Despite Henry Clay's eloquent speech in the Senate against the treaty, the vote was taken along party lines to ratify the treaty. And General Wood was dispatched to the Cherokee Nation to prevent possible hostilities in reaction against the treaty.

For two months Julius Parker had been unhappy. A war had erupted in his house between his daughter and his new wife. And he was the loser.

Lulu had worked so hard, inviting the surrounding families to dinner, to parties where they'd introduced Rebecca to the eligible young men in the community. But Rebecca had been sullen, and no one had bothered to look at her. He couldn't blame them, with Lulu to look at instead, with her smooth, fair skin and her beautiful dark hair.

"Pa, Lulu's been mean to me again," Rebecca cried as soon as he'd arrived home from Milledgeville. "She's had me locked in my room for the past week, starvin' me to death."

"Lulu, you haven't been treatin' my girl bad, have you?"

He remembered how hurt Lulu had looked, with those soft brown eyes. "Julius, just look at your daughter. Isn't she pretty now? Elvira and I worked on her complexion and kept her away from the table, where she couldn't take second helpings of everything. You can see she's slimmed down enough to get into her new dresses. That's all I wanted to do—with the party coming up next week." A tear slid down her cheek and her voice quavered. "But I guess nobody appreciates how hard I've tried...to be Rebecca's friend."

"Oh, forgive me, Lulu. I didn't mean to accuse you." He glared at his daughter. "I don't see why you have to be bellyachin' the minute I get home, puttin' thoughts against Lulu in my head. You ought to be ashamed, girl."

"Yes, Pa." Rebecca saw that she had lost. It wouldn't do any good to speak against the woman who'd taken her pa from her. She'd just put her first plan into action, to get rid of Lulu for good.

She'd start being nicer and then she'd persuade Lulu to

go riding with her over the ridge, to that place where the snow still hid the large crater....

* * *

For weeks now Quatie had waited for John to return from the west, where the western Cherokee legislation had met and passed a resolution against the fradulent treaty. They had also appointed a delegation to accompany Ross to Washington to discuss the treaty and the annuities owed them.

John's brother Lewis, with no reason except that he was against the treaty, had already been arrested and confined. And there were rumors that anywhere along the route he was taking, John might be arrested also.

Hearing a sound, Quatie said, "Silas, go and look down the valley. See if your father is coming."

"I want to go, too," a small voice said.

"No, George. You must stay in bed. Your cough is still bad," Quatie said, soothing his brow with her hand.

Silas put on his coat and went to the edge of the ridge, his eyes following a pattern of color in the snow. Taking his hands, he cupped them to his mouth and made the special sound his father had taught him. Within moments he heard the same sound returned to him from the valley. His father was coming home.

In excitement, he began to run back to the house. "Mother, Father is coming," he shouted. "With a lot of men."

"In uniform?" she questioned, caution clouding her eyes.

"No. With friends."

"Then go to the shed and bring more wood, Silas. We need to have hot food and drink ready when they arrive."

She stood at the door and welcomed them all, but her smile was reserved for her husband. "I'm glad to see that you're safe."

"And I'm glad to be home, Quatie."

"I've been sick," George said, deliberately coughing for his father.

As soon as the delegation had eaten, they moved on toward Red Clay and their eastern relatives, leaving John alone with his family. But then, two days later, a runner brought a letter, and Quatie, resigned to what it might say, watched her husband open it.

"It's from Lewis," he commented. He read it in silence.

"John," his brother began. "There is nothing more certain than that you will be arrested if you remain another day at home. So I advise you to put out from home tomorrow morning, crossing the Hiwassee at Patton's ferry...."

He continued reading, realizing that if he wanted to get up to Washington, he and the western delegation would have to start as soon as the sun was up.

"Quatie—"

"I know." Her voice was sad. "You will be leaving again."

Chapter 20

In the same week that John left for Washington, a seemingly repentant Rebecca changed her tactics in dealing with Lulu.

As they both sat before the fire in the parlor and waited for Julius, Rebecca cleared her throat. "I guess I've been pretty mean to you," she said.

A suspicious Lulu merely looked at Rebecca without commenting.

"Well, don't just sit there. *Say* somethin'."

Lulu took another stitch in her sampler. "Yes, you have," she agreed.

"But you haven't been nice to me, either."

"Good behavior begets good behavior," Lulu said, repeating one of Tilda Mae's axioms.

An exasperated Rebecca glared at her. "Can't you see I'm tryin' to bury the hatchet?"

"Why?"

Lulu was not making it any easier for her. "Well, we both love Pa, but I notice he's been mighty miserable lately." She hesitated and then added, "I think he'd feel a lot better if we could start bein' friends."

Lulu set down her sampler and put her entire attention on her stepdaughter. Had Rebecca really had a change of heart? Or was she only playing a game?

Lulu had not enjoyed the forced separation from her husband. She was hot-blooded, as Ned had found out long before Julius appeared at the settlement. These past weeks of spending the nights alone had been every bit as hard on her as on Julius.

If Rebecca stopped being so irritating, then Lulu could go back to being a wife again. That didn't mean that she would be satisfied for the girl to remain in the house for long. But while she continued to try to get her married off, the waiting would be much easier to bear.

Finally she said, "For your papa's sake, I'm willing to call a truce, if you are."

"Oh, thank you, Lulu."

"There's one thing, though, that you'll have to promise."

"What is that?"

"You won't spy on Julius and me anymore at night."

Rebecca frowned. It wasn't in her plan for them to share the same bedroom again. But then a smile erased the frown. Lulu would be dead soon, so a few days wouldn't matter much. "I promise."

"Then come and give your stepmama a hug," Lulu said, willing to forgive her.

Rebecca laughed as she walked to Lulu, who was a lot smaller than she. "I couldn't ever think of you as my mama. We're the same age."

"I know," Lulu said, giggling.

Julius, walking into the parlor, said, "Well, what's this? Are my eyes deceivin' me? Sounds like the two of ya are actually gettin' along."

Rebecca turned to face her father. "We are, Pa. It just took a little gittin' used to—havin' *two* women in the house."

"Now we can become a *real* family, Julius," Lulu said.

He looked at his wife with questioning eyes. He wasn't

sure he understood her. But when he saw her nodding and smiling at him, his heart leaped to his throat. His nights alone were finally over.

That evening Lulu moved back into Julius's bedroom, and Rebecca, trying not to think about what was happening between them, carefully made her plans, to take effect as soon as Julius went off to his meeting.

Rebecca lay in bed and prayed for another snowstorm. A few flakes had already fallen that afternoon from the buttermilk sky, and as she listened to the howling wind outside she knew her prayer might be answered.

When morning came, Rebecca hopped out of bed and went to the window. She smiled. As far as she could see, the land was white, with all the trees covered in ice. Now it wouldn't be long before Lulu got her comeuppance.

For two days the bad weather kept up. But on the day her father was to leave, the sun came out, dazzling the landscape with its brilliance.

Julius was a man of property now, important to the community, and he had been asked to serve on the committee to establish a bank in the county. He wasn't sure that he wanted to turn over the care of his own money to a bank. Burying the strongbox in a good hiding place seemed safe enough for him. But he would go and listen to what the banking men from Calhoun had to say.

So by midmorning of that day Julius saddled up Cloud Maker and prepared to leave for William Brogdon's house five miles west.

He waved to Lulu and Rebecca, both standing at the parlor window, and started down the lane, where great drifts of snow lay against the fence.

Rebecca waited until her father was out of sight. "Are you as tired as I am, Lulu, bein' cooped up in the house all this week?"

"Yes. It would have been fun to go with Julius today. Mrs. Brogdon should've had a tea party and invited the wives."

"Well, I think this afternoon I'll take my pony out for a ride."

"Not by yourself, Rebecca. It's too dangerous."

"Why don't you come along, too? We could saddle up Sundance for you."

Lulu hesitated. "But I haven't ridden in a while."

"Then you should get in some practice. Pa likes a woman to ride with him. In fact, that's what we used to do together, before you came. We rode all over the property. Did you know we saw a squaw woman once over the far ridge?"

"An Indian?"

"No. A white woman. But she was dressed like a squaw. Had two little boys with 'er. One had blondish-red hair, and the other was dark, like a little Indian."

Rebecca could tell that she had gotten Lulu interested. "We could ride over in that direction, if you'd like. Maybe we'd see 'er again."

"That would certainly be more interesting than starting another sampler," Lulu admitted.

"Then let's do it."

"All right," Lulu agreed. "But we can't stay out too long in all this cold."

"No. Just long enough to—to see the woman."

Later that afternoon, Kepp, the black man, saddled up Sundance for Lulu and Thistle for Rebecca. "Be careful, Miz Parker," the man cautioned as he brought the two animals to the front of the house. "This horse is mighty high-spirited."

"Oh, dear, I'm not sure whether I'll be able to handle him."

Rebecca quickly said, "Then here, Lulu. You ride the pony and *I'll* ride Sundance."

Looking at the smaller animal, Lulu said, "That's awfully nice of you, Rebecca."

As the two left the yard Kepp stood and watched. The pony, Thistle, was twice as mean as Sundance, mainly because of the treatment he got. Kepp didn't understand why Rebecca had suddenly decided to swap with her stepmama.

"I forgot to tell you. Sometimes Thistle bites."

Lulu, having difficulty with the pony, barely heard Rebecca. The glitter of the sun on the snow brought tears to her eyes, and she couldn't seem to get the pony to go in the right direction. But after awhile, with Lulu patting him and crooning in his ear, the pony settled down a bit.

Disappointed that Lulu had not been given a vicious nip, Rebecca picked up the pace, leaving her behind. The scattered snow from Sundance's hooves was lifted by the wind, and the stray icy flakes slapped at Lulu's face with a sharp sting.

Riding along, she began to think that maybe this wasn't a good idea. But then Rebecca stopped and waited for her. As they rode side by side she began to relax and enjoy the scenery, the beauty of the hills and the frozen streams. Julius owned all this land, and she was his wife.

Later Rebecca pointed toward the small spiral of smoke that curled above the trees in the distance and vanished into the blue sky. "That's where the squaw woman lives," she said.

Lulu nodded and then turned her head to see if she could see her own house. She searched for the smoke rising from the chimney, but the two had ridden too far over the hills and ridges. Only a vast sweep of white, with a few evergreen trees interspersed in the landscape, was visible behind her. She was completely disoriented. "Are you sure you can find your way home again, Rebecca?"

"Of course. Didn't I tell you? Pa and me rode over every

inch of the property."

"But not in this much snow, I vow."

"Yes, we did. Last winter, after a storm, when one of Pa's calves was missin'."

"Did you find it?" Lulu asked.

"Yes. But it was too late. The poor thing had already froze to death."

Rebecca, seeing the effect her words had on Lulu, laughed. "What's the matter? You afraid I'll ride off and leave you to freeze to death like the little calf?"

"No, Rebecca. You wouldn't do such a horrible thing."

"You're right. Pa would grieve somethin' awful if anything happened to you."

"But I think we've been out long enough. We should start back home."

"We're almost there," Rebecca protested. "See, it's just over the next hill."

"Oh, all right. I guess a few more minutes won't matter. But I'm getting awfully cold." Lulu brightened. "Maybe we could stop and ask the woman for something hot to drink before we start back."

That was not in Rebecca's plans. But she nodded anyway.

They continued riding in the direction of the other house, getting closer all the time to the crater, bordered on one side by a stand of trees. But the small circle of boulders surrounding the crater was completely invisible because of the snow.

Rebecca knew it was dangerous for her, going so close to the edge with Lulu. On purpose, she allowed the pony to get slightly ahead of her. And Lulu, so eager to reach a warm fire, picked up the pace, urging Thistle forward. But sensing something wrong, Thistle began to balk. "What's the matter with your pony, Rebecca?" an exasperated Lulu asked, as the girl rode up behind her.

"Just stubborn, I guess." Rebecca reached out with her whip and struck the pony.

Thistle whinnied in protest and took off through the snow in an effort to get away from the sharp sting. His right front leg struck one of the hidden boulders directly in front. He went down, throwing Lulu from his back.

As she plunged headlong into the crater Lulu screamed, "Rebecca, help me!"

But Rebecca merely watched the end of Lulu's blue scarf that slowly unwound and traced the route she was taking. Only the fringe remained visible to the eye. But by evening the snow would have covered it, too.

For a moment, a satisfied Rebecca sat on the protesting Sundance and listened to the muffled cries of the woman below and the bellow of pain coming from Thistle. Noticing that the pony was unable to stand, she wheeled around and slowly began to trace her path back to the house.

* * *

Almost an hour later Two Feathers and Billy were returning home from their hunting. Billy had caught his own wild turkey and he proudly carried it across his back in the same manner as the older man was carrying his.

"Papa, do you hear something?" Billy asked.

"Yes, son."

They stopped to listen. The sound of the pony in pain was unmistakeable.

"We must go to see," Two Feathers said. "Someone's in trouble."

The crater was in no-man's-land as far as the original Cherokee boundaries were concerned. The old law that governed the Nation stated that each man could take as much land as he wished to use, but a quarter mile must be left between that land and the next man's property.

But the crater was also looked upon as a place where

the spirits communed. The rocks were sacred, and the crater was sacred. It was best to avoid it rather than risk offending the spirits who dwelled there.

But as Two Feathers followed the sound he realized where it was leading him. He approached the area cautiously.

"Look, Papa. The pony's been hurt."

Two Feathers recognized Thistle, the pony that had once belonged to Laurel. The animal's eyes were filled with pain. And examining him further, the Cherokee saw that his foreleg was shattered. The pony would have to be destroyed.

He began to chant, soothing the animal and apologizing for what he had to do. Lifting his musket, Two Feathers was quick. But a great sadness welled up inside him.

With Billy some distance back, he stood, peering down into the crater. That's when he saw the tip of the blue scarf. By it, he knew that the sacred crater had claimed Thistle's rider.

Chapter 21

"Oh, Papa, I blame myself," Rebecca cried. "I should've told Lulu she had no business ridin' off on her own like that after I decided to come home. But it was so cold and I was gittin' chilblains again. She said she could find her way by herself."

Rebecca's face was tearstained as she faced her tired father. "When she didn't come back by suppertime, Kepp went with me to see if I could find her. But then it got dark, and we barely made it home again ourselves."

"Did the pony come back?"

"No, Pa."

"Then there's still hope. I got to find her, Rebecky. My poor Lulu's lost out there, not knowin' which direction to take. Go get Elvira to light the lanterns. I'm goin' after 'er."

"No, Pa. You'll only freeze to death, too."

Julius, looking mortally wounded, whirled around. "Don't ever say that, girl. My Lulu won't freeze to death. She's smarter'n that. Maybe she found shelter. Maybe she went to that there cabin we seen last year."

"Yes, Pa."

Holding the flickering lanterns, Julius and the black man

started out. At regular intervals Julius called his wife's name. The wind continued to howl and the snow continued to fall, but no answer came.

"It's a wide territory, Kepp," Julius said, aware of the mission that his daughter felt was futile.

"Yes, suh." Kepp hesitated.

"Well, what is it, Kepp?" Julius asked.

"Sundance and Thistle's been stall mates for a long time. Maybe if you kinda allowed Sundance her head, she might lead you to the pony."

"You think so, Kepp?"

"Wouldn't hurt to try."

Julius relaxed the reins, letting the horse take her own course. She immediately changed direction.

"Lulu?" Julius shouted to the right.

"Miz Parker," Kepp called.

The two took turns calling her name as they traveled through the snow, with only the lanterns to show where they were going.

The lights from the Parker house dwindled in the distance and soon disappeared. As the men kept traveling Kepp took note of certain trees that would point their way back home.

Steadily over the hills and ridges Sundance went, as if she knew exactly where she was going. And Cloud Maker was content to follow.

An hour later Sundance stopped at the edge of the crater and gave an agitated whinny. When Julius got down, Kepp said, "You better watch out, Mr. Julius. There's a deep hole right in front of you. Can't see it, but it's there."

Carefully, Julius took a few steps forward, holding the lantern before him. A small patch of red stained the snow, and Julius, holding the lantern closer, reached down and scooped up some of it in his hand. As the snow melted he groaned. Sticky, congealed blood was left in his palm.

Kepp, closer to the crater, swung his lantern over the edge of the boulders, to peer downward. "Look over here," he said.

Julius moved beside Kepp and held his own lantern high. A much wider swath of stained snow was caught in the shadow of the moon. At the sight he began to cry. Now he knew what had happened to Lulu.

"The pony must have stumbled and taken her right over with him," Kepp said. "And with the snow so deep, we won't be able to get 'em out 'fore summer."

"I can't believe it. I've lost my sweet Lulu."

"I'm powerful sorry, Mr. Julius." Kepp stood beside his master, waiting for him to give the signal to leave.

Finally Julius rubbed his nose on his sleeve, turned, and walked to his horse. "Let's go home, Kepp. We don't need to go any farther."

That night, with her face suitably solemn, Rebecca tried to comfort her father as best she could. But deep in her heart she was glad. Lulu would never be a threat to her again.

Julius, however, refused to be comforted. Losing Lulu was his punishment for going against the wishes of a dying woman.

At the cabin over the hill Lulu was still shaking from the cold. Wrapped in two warm quilts, she sat by the fire and drank the mug of hot coffee. Half-frozen to death, she'd been completely disoriented when the Indian and the little boy had rescued her and brought her to the cabin. But then, seeing Daisy bending over her, she knew she had completely lost her mind.

"Daisy? Are you Daisy?"

The blonde-haired woman shook her head. "My name is Agitsi´. Who are you?"

"I'm Lulu. But I *know* you're Daisy. Don't you recognize

me? We were best friends at the settlement. I stood up with you when you married Horace."

The woman looked distressed. "No. I don't know you. And my husband is Two Feathers. He'll tell you."

Seeing her agitation, Lulu quickly said, "I'm sorry. It must be the cold that's addled my brain. For a moment I thought you were someone else." She smiled and said, "Thank you, Agitsi′, for your kindness."

Now, as she sat by the fire, next to her wet clothes that had been spread to dry, she continued to look at the woman she knew to be Daisy. Only Daisy didn't seem to remember who she was. Lulu glanced toward the other end of the hearth, where Billy and the other child, Ina′li, were working at the little bench. Of course, it was hard to tell what Billy would look like after five years, but the coloring and even the name were the same, linking the older child to Horace's son.

But why was Daisy here with the Indian? And where was Horace?

Slowly, as she sipped her coffee, Lulu began to think of a conversation with Ned one night, not long after Daisy and Horace had left the settlement.

"I swear, Lulu, I saw a man hidden under that bearskin Jake was cleanin'."

"What a wild imagination you've got, Ned," she'd teased.

"Wasn't my imagination to see Miss Ellie and Jake actin' so strange. And they sure shooed me away fast enough, not lettin' me go close to the bear."

"I thought that was old Runy's doing, Ned."

"Well, the dog *did* snarl and bare his teeth at me. But Jake could've called him off, if he'd a mind to. Later that night I heard him diggin'. I bet if a man wanted me to look, we'd find something buried behind the barn."

"And if you really want to, you can go ahead and start spreading lies about my friends. But I warn you, Ned. If you do that, then I think we'll just have to stop seeing each other."

"No, Lulu. You're the best thing that's ever happened to me. I guess it *was* just my imagination," he'd added quickly.

But had it been his imagination, after all?

What if Ned had been right, and Jake had buried Horace?

Lulu tightened her hand around the mug. Too many questions bombarded her brain. She looked again at Daisy. She seemed happy enough. But Miss Ellie wouldn't be happy if she knew where Daisy was living.

All at once Lulu felt a great need to protect Daisy. Perhaps it was better for her to say nothing, rather than risk opening up some Pandora's box. The past was the past.

Soon after the sun came up, Two Feathers rode with Lulu as far as the ridge nearest the Parker house,

"I will go no farther," Two Feathers said.

"But what about your horse?"

"He'll find his way home on his own."

"I can't thank you enough, Two Feathers. If you hadn't wrapped your rope around the tree and crawled down the crater for me, I'd be dead."

"The spirits were good to you," Two Feathers answered, "making a pocket of air for you to breathe."

"Yes. And not letting me fall all the way down to the borrom of the crater. Well, good-bye, Two Feathers. Good-bye, Billy."

* * *

At New Echota, where the sun rose slowly over the silent blanket of ice and snow and peeked into the windows of the mission house, Laurel lay beneath the warm bedcovers. She pulled the quilt up to her chin and snuggled deeper while her mind struggled to recall what had happened during the night.

She smiled in sudden remembrance. She'd been given a power dream. Thistle had called to her, and they had raced together through the valley in perfect freedom, perfect grace; woman and pony as one in body and spirit. Then Thistle had vanished into the mist, leaving Laurel to race on alone, but with an ancient rhythm and strength she'd never felt before.

What had it meant? She'd sensed such joy, and such sadness, too, in the dream. "Thistle," she whispered, climbing out of bed and tiptoeing to the window to peer out at the vast sea of white.

It had snowed even more during the night, but that did not discourage Laurel. Shivering, she put on her warm riding clothes and boots, wrapped the scarf around her face, and headed for the barn. Within minutes, she'd saddled up a horse and led him into the yard.

"You see, it snowed again, old boy," she said, patting him on the right flank. "But you don't mind, do you?"

He replied with a steamy snort through his nostrils.

Soon Laurel had passed the tavern. And with the horse stepping high as if to avoid sinking into the treacherous drifts, she finally reached the main road.

Looking around at the pristine beauty on each side, at the pines bent low by the weight of the ice on their limbs, Laurel felt a great love for this beautiful land of her ancestors. What a tragedy if John should not be successful in saving it.

She had been riding for over twenty minutes when Deer Stalker called, "Laurel! Wait for me!"

Surprised to see the boy, Laurel watched him maneuver his pony, urging him forward in a trot to catch up with her.

"I can't believe you're out of bed this early," Laurel teased.

"I saw you from the window," he answered. Then he confessed, "It's hard to talk when everyone else is around."

Laurel noticed his serious expression. "Did you want to talk with me about something special?"

He nodded. But still he hesitated.

"What is it, Deer Stalker? What's bothering you?"

Once he started, the words tumbled out rapidly. "What Elias said several days ago. He told some men outside the tavern that Chief Ross is making a grave mistake."

"Oh? Did he explain why he thinks that?"

"He said that while he's in Washington, trying to negotiate with the government, all the good land out west is being taken over by the other tribes, like the Choctaws and the Chickasaws and the Creeks. If that's true, and we lose this land, then we won't have anywhere to live."

"Oh, Deer Stalker, don't let Elias scare you. Land has been reserved for all sixty tribes in various parts of Indian Territory. And Cherokee land can't be taken over by another tribe."

Seeing the relief in Deer Stalker's face, Laurel did not feel it necessary to burden him with a new concern—that it was not the other tribes they had to worry about. Although the government had promised the new land in perpetuity, white settlers were already moving in. And when they did, it was only a matter of time before the treaties were extinguished, pushing the Indians farther and farther west, until they had been pushed across the entire continent and into the sea.

This John believed. He had seen the way other tribes with no counsel had been taken advantage of. And this was why he had been unceasing in trying to work out a legal settlement with the U.S. government.

Looking at the thin jacket Deer Stalker was wearing, Laurel said, "Let's ride back. Breakfast should be ready. Are you hungry?"

"Yes."

Suddenly Laurel asked, "What would you do today if we

all had a holiday from school?"

An eagerness crept into his voice. "Black Moccasin and I could set some rabbit snares in the woods."

"If you promise to wear a heavier coat," Laurel replied, glad to see a measure of happiness return to the boy's eyes.

* * *

At the Parker house Elvira hurried back from the barn with freshly laid eggs for breakfast. Not that Mr. Julius would feel like eating anything, being so heartbroken. But nothing ever took away Rebecca's appetite.

As she rounded the corner Elvira looked up to see a woman covered in snow riding a horse into the yard. Thinking she was seeing Lulu's ghost, she dropped one of the eggs and ran screaming into the house.

"Hush, Elvira," Rebecca scolded. "Don't you know this is a house of sorrow?"

"But I saw her."

"Saw who?"

"Miz Parker's ghost. All in white, and comin' toward me on a horse."

"That's impossible."

"Is it, Rebecca?" Lulu asked, shaking the snow from her cloak as she entered the hall.

Seeing Lulu back from her icy grave, Rebecca started screaming. She ran up the stairs and locked her bedroom door. Lulu was supposed to be dead. But she wasn't. Something had gone wrong.

Downstairs, Lulu was reassuring Elvira. "You're not seeing ghosts, Elvira. I'm real. See?" She held out her hand. "Pinch me."

Julius, hearing Lulu's voice, ran from the dining room. Seeing his wife standing there, he rushed toward her. "Oh, my sweet Lulu. I've been grievin' myself to death, thinkin' I'd lost you for good."

"No, Julius. An Indian found me. I spent the night with the people across the ridge. But I'm afraid poor Thistle is dead."

"That don't matter a bit. You're back home safe and sound. That's the important thing. But you're never to go ridin' alone again."

"Yes, Julius." Lulu smiled and turned back to Elvira. "Well, hurry on to the kitchen with those eggs. I'm starving."

Later, as she and Julius enjoyed their breakfast together, Lulu was strangely quiet about Rebecca's part in her accident. But the girl would not go unpunished. Lulu would see to that herself.

Chapter 22

John Ross and his delegation arrived in Washington in February. By March, Martin Van Buren was inaugurated as president of the United States and Secretary of War Cass was replaced by Poinsett.

This was what Ross had been waiting for, employing delaying tactics and all legal maneuvers in expectation of the eventual sweeping clean of the old regime. There was always the possibility that the new one might look more favorably on the Cherokee petitions and declare the fradulent treaty of 1835 null and void.

The months following began to look a little better. John's brother Lewis was released from Georgia confinement; for he was the treasurer of the Nation, with power to handle their financial affairs. And then a private emissary from Poinsett sought John Ross's help in another matter, with the assurance that it would be a favor to be repaid in kind.

"The secretary of war is asking your help in quieting that firebrand Osceola," Colonel Sherburne began. "We've got to bring the Seminole War in Florida to an end."

John was well aware of the situation that had caused the war. The Seminoles, protesting a removal treaty repudiated by the majority of their tribe, had chosen to fight rather than attempt legal redress like the Cherokees. But it was folly to make war on the United States. John knew it could only end in tragedy for the Seminoles.

He hesitated. "Before I agree or decline, I would need certain assurances from Poinsett and the Department of War."

"Then I will set up a meeting with Poinsett."

A short time later John was face-to-face with Joel Poinsett in his private office. "Come in, Chief Ross, and have a seat. Cigar?"

John shook his head at the proffered box. He waited in silence while the secretary of war cut off one end of his cigar, put it in his mouth, lit it, and began to draw on the smoke.

Seeing that Ross was not intimidated by him, he set his cigar in the ashtray and got down to business. "Sherburne has already outlined the favor we're asking. And I want you to know we will not forget your help. The department is eager to get this war settled."

"Before we discuss what I might do to help, I have several important questions to ask you."

"Fire away, Mr. Ross."

"Are you authorized by the president of the United States to guarantee safety and protection to the lives of Osceola and the other chiefs that might compose the Seminole delegation?"

"I am."

"And you would be prepared to offer them a liberal treaty of peace?"

"Absolutely."

"Now, as to expenses incurred by the Cherokee delegation—"

"I assure you that our government will be quite generous. Money will be no object."

"Then, with your assurances, I'll do what I can. I'm a stranger to the Seminoles, Mr. Poinsett. So I can only write a letter to them, as a brother, asking them to give up their war and enter into peace negotiations with the United States."

"Excellent, Mr. Ross." Poinsett picked up his cigar.

"I *will* accept a cigar now, Mr. Poinsett."

As the two smoked together they discussed the details and the timing. Then the two shook hands and John left the secretary of war's office.

That night he began to draft a letter to the Seminoles.

"To all Seminole Chiefs, greetings from John Ross, Principal Chief of the Cherokee Nation.

"Although we are strangers, I am writing to you as a brother, and as one who understands the anguish of division and removal.

"I know that a brave people, when driven to a state of desperation, would sooner die under the strong arm of power than die the death of a coward.

"But I will speak to you as a friend, also, and with the voice of reason advise you, as a small but brave people, to act the part of a noble race, and at once throw yourselves upon the magnanimity and justice of the American people.

"I have received a guarantee of the sincerity of the United States in making a liberal treaty of peace with you."

John continued to work on the document, and when he was satisfied with the wording, he began to think of the chiefs suitable to make the long, hazardous journey to deliver it.

Night Hawk and Jumping Rabbit immediately came to mind, and by morning John had selected the names of the other two for the official Cherokee delegation of four to the Seminoles' stronghold in the Florida swamps.

* * *

One evening, not long after that, Night Hawk sat before his hearth and smoked his clay pipe. Walini′, his small daughter, sat on the rug nearby and sang to the doll Running Brook had made for her during the past long winter. The child was so like her mother, with her beautiful dark eyes and smile.

With Running Brook attending to his needs, he had almost forgotten Laurel. Only when the mountain laurels were in bloom did he feel that strange sadness come upon him, a sickness to be thrown off like any other fever that appeared in spring. Or in times like this, when the snow was upon the ground and he had more time for contemplation.

Hearing someone come into his yard, a cautious Night Hawk spoke to Running Brook as he reached for his musket. She ran to pick up Walini′ to hide her from sight while Night Hawk walked to the door.

"Tskĭ-lĭ′," the voice called. "It's me—Jumping Rabbit."

Night Hawk immediately opened the door to his friend.

"I have news from John Ross in Washington. He needs us to take a letter to the Seminoles. It's all here," he said, holding out the package of letters.

"Come in, my friend," Night Hawk said.

"There're two other chiefs with me. Do you suppose we might spend the night and then all start for Florida in the morning?"

Hearing Jumping Rabbit's voice, Running Brook brought Walini′ from the secret cupboard and came to greet her guests.

Much later that night, Night Hawk lay in bed beside Running Brook. "I don't like the idea of leaving you here for such a long time. But since the trip is a favor to the United States government, then you and Walini′ should be safe."

"I'll miss you, my husband." Running Brook said no more.

Armed with the letters, the delegation left on horseback

the next morning. They wasted no time, but continued in a steady, measured pace. One day passed into two, then three and four. Cautiously they rode through Creek and Uchee territory, stopping only long enough to rest, to eat, and then they were on their way again.

The mountains became the foothills, and the foothills were transformed into lowlands of saw palms, yucca, and white sand. Flies and gnats worried the horses, and thirst bothered the travelers as they finally rode into the swamps where the Seminoles were hiding and carrying on their warfare.

Then, one afternoon, the delegation made contact with a Seminole scout. Convinced of their mission of peace, he brought one of his own chiefs back with him. And Night Hawk, reading the address, was welcomed as the bearer of good news.

"Our people are starving in the swamps," the chief said. "But until you arrived, we had no other hope."

Several days later two delegations—one Cherokee, the other Seminole—left the swamps and rode toward Fort Mellon, headquarters of the area commander, General Jesup.

Upon their arrival Night Hawk and Jumping Rabbit stood together and watched from a distance as the gates to the fort opened and the solemn Seminole chiefs, with their white flag of truce rippling in the afternoon breeze, entered.

They waited until they saw the commander appear in the yard to greet the peace delegation. With the Seminoles signaling back to them, the Cherokees responded. Night Hawk knew then that their mission had been accomplished.

"I'm glad the Seminoles have taken the path of peace," Jumping Rabbit said.

"Yes," Night Hawk replied. "It's to their advantage, as well as to the advantage of the United States, for the war to end. Now let's hurry home."

The four Cherokee chiefs remounted their horses and headed north.

By the next day a Seminole scout caught up with them. "You have betrayed our people," he accused. "Our chiefs believed you, but they were made prisoners. We saw them this morning being taken out of the fort in chains."

Night Hawk became furious at the news. "If that is so, we have also been betrayed. Where are the chiefs being sent?"

"I overheard one of the soldiers say St. Augustine."

Night Hawk nodded. "Where Osceola is being held prisoner."

"What are we to do, Night Hawk?" Jumping Rabbit asked, his question echoed by the other two chiefs.

"We must follow them, all the way to St. Augustine, if necessary. We have to let the chiefs know the Cherokees had no part in this unchivalrous act."

"John Ross will be quite saddened that the United States has not kept its word."

"Yes. He has always had more faith in the white man's government than some of us."

Colonel Sherburne, the private emissary of the secretary of war, who had contacted John Ross for his help earlier, was in St. Augustine when Night Hawk and the others arrived. But he would not release the Seminole chiefs. He merely suggested that the Cherokee delegation accompany him to Washington to make any settlement. Night Hawk would have done this anyway, since John Ross should be apprised personally of what had happened.

So, convincing the imprisoned chiefs that they had no knowledge of what had been planned, they left St. Augustine and arrived in Washington at the end of December.

Their principal chief was furious, as Night Hawk knew he

would be. And his disgust at this perfidy only grew when Poinsett later allowed reimbursement of only one tenth of the expenses of the Cherokee delegation. His promises of generosity were as meaningless as his assurances of safety for the Seminoles.

Still, this was the government that Ross had to deal with, in a last stand to try to save his own people and their heritage. John Howard Payne, the Quakers, and a few missionaries were the only ones he could count on as true friends.

"Van Buren will not undo what Jackson has done," he was finally told, effectively closing the door to a new treaty. His efforts at legal address were exhausted. And removal seemed certain.

* * *

Night Hawk returned home to his wife Running Brook and his daughter Walini´. When spring arrived, although the Cherokees had been told not to plant any new crops, Night Hawk paid no attention.

One day, after his midday meal with his little daughter and Running Brook, now pregnant again, he returned to the far field where he worked along the rows of young corn, removing the weeds that had sprung up with the past rain.

Watching him from a distance was a squad of Georgia militia assigned to arrest him. But the fields were too open. He would see them coming and could easily escape before they reached him. So they decided to wait and take him when he returned home.

Just as the sun was beginning to set, one of the soldiers ran back to the house. "He's comin'."

"Well, go inside and tell Rufus to keep his wife quiet so she won't tip him off."

In the parlor a distraught Running Brook stared at the soldier guarding her. She had barely had time to hide Walini´ in the cupboard before they had burst into her house. Since she spoke little English, she could not fathom everything being said by the soldiers. She only knew that they were waiting for her husband.

She strained to see out the window, but the soldier kept her from getting too close. Then, as Night Hawk appeared near the house, soldiers with pointed bayonets rushed to surround him. Watching the fracas, Running Brook cried out and began to struggle with her guard.

Night Hawk had no chance of escape. Overpowered, he was knocked to his knees, with one of the soldiers locking an iron collar around his neck and binding his hands with chains.

"Tskĭ-lĭ!" Running Brook screamed, rushing onto the porch, her captor behind her.

"Stop that woman," an order rang out. One of the soldiers raised his rifle butt to hit her.

Seeing what was happening to his wife, Night Hawk lunged, twisting and turning, using his chains as a weapon. "No!" he shouted, but he was too late. Before he could reach her, she fell under the blow. Then the soldier turned his bayonet and stabbed Running Brook in the stomach.

Before he lost consciousness at an equally viscious blow, Night Hawk heard the satisfied voice of the soldier. "Well, that's one less Indian that'll be makin' the trip west."

He did not see when the same soldier claimed the gold necklace from Running Brook's neck.

That day, throughout the part of the Nation that Georgia claimed, families were being caught—women in their kitchens and children playing in their yards, while the men were taken in the fields and locked into neck collars and chains.

Pots on the hearth grew cold, and no one was allowed to retrieve shoes or blankets or personal possessions.

The travail of the Cherokee people had begun.

Chapter 23

"Dear Laurel,

I am writing to you from the stockade where Night Hawk and I were brought yesterday. He is gravely ill from a blow to his head, and I am caring for him as best I can. But he is much troubled. He keeps calling his little daughter's name, over and over.

"I know that Running Brook was killed by the soldiers when she ran to help him. I overheard them talking. But I do not know what has happened to Walini′. I checked in the women's compound, but she is not there. Perhaps that is what Night Hawk is trying to tell me—that she is still hiding somewhere in the house, or one of the other buildings.

"Knowing your father's high regard for Night Hawk and the mutual friendship that we have all enjoyed, I beg of you, if at all possible, to send someone who is familiar with the property to look for little Walini′.

"Whoever goes will have to be extremely careful. Soldiers are everywhere. But for the moment they seem to be interested in rounding up the chiefs first, so the rest of the Nation will be without leadership.

"Your friend, Jumping Rabbit."

Laurel stood outside the courthouse and read the letter. When she looked up, the runner had vanished.

All day it had been difficult to keep her mind on the lessons. And now she knew that it was useless to continue. She went back inside and waited for Deer Stalker to finish his oration. Then she dismissed the class.

"Why are we stopping so early?" Redbird asked, walking back with Laurel to the mission house.

Careful not to alarm the young girl, she said, "Oh, it's such a pleasant afternoon that I decided you might all enjoy going on a nature walk. I was thinking that I might ask A´wani´ta to take you. And you could all have a picnic later."

At New Echota, Elias had been the only other one familiar with Night Hawk's property. But he had already left voluntarily for the west. It was up to Laurel to look for the child.

As soon as she had arranged the care of her students, Laurel, dressed in her English clothes, set off on horseback, with the sidesaddle securely in place. She had removed all Indian trappings from the bridle. If she were spotted, she wanted to make sure that no one suspected her heritage. Especially since she had strapped a musket to her saddle.

Up the ridges and into the valleys she rode, the new leaves of the hardwood trees softening the blood red of the earth, and the clumps of flowers trembling at the pounding rhythm of hoofbeats.

Another trip was etched into her mind, when she had rushed headlong to her own home to find her worst fears confirmed. Remembering her anguish, she said, "Please, for Night Hawk's sake, let me find his child safe."

She felt sad about the estrangement she had caused between them. But she'd been so young then, and her feelings for Edward so new. Yet, if he had not come into her life, Night Hawk's child could well have been her own. But then she would be dead, like Running Brook.

Laurel, aware of someone's coming from the opposite direction, left the road and hid in a small copse. A few moments later she watched as a squad of Georgia militia marched down the road. She'd barely had enough time to hide, much less obliterate the telltale hoofprints. So she kept her fingers crossed that no one would look down and notice the fresh tracks along the trail.

After the first few soldiers had kicked up the dust, followed by the others, and kept on marching, Laurel began to feel less tense. Still, she hid until they had completely disappeared. Then, when she could trace no sound to them, she rode out of the copse. This time, she was careful to leave the trail at intervals, choosing to ride at the edge of the forest, crisscrossing back and forth and at times backtracking so that her path would be difficult to follow.

Finally, on a rise overlooking Night Hawk's property, Laurel stopped her horse. She sat and stared toward the house. It appeared deserted, and no sounds of life came from the pastures or the barn. It was a strange, frozen tableau, more suitable as a wilderness setting for one of Freneau's gentle pastoral poems than as the scene of death and heartbreak the day before.

Urging her horse forward, Laurel galloped into the deserted yard. With the sun already low in the sky, she had no time to waste in caution.

Sliding from her saddle, she tied the horse's reins to the hitching post, removed her musket, and dashed up the steps. Avoiding the dried blood on the porch, she entered the two-story house.

The hall and parlor were in a shambles, their destruction a familiar calling card of the riffraff that followed behind the militia, looting and carrying off any valuables.

"Walini′," she called, speaking in Cherokee. "I'm your father's friend. He has sent me for you, Walini′. Can you hear me?"

She left her musket propped against the hearth. Going from room to room, upstairs and downstairs, Laurel listened for the smallest sound. She was rewarded only by the sudden scurrying of a squirrel across the roof, nothing more.

She opened every door, looked into chests, under beds, in the chimney nooks, and even crawled into the eaves. She kept calling until her voice was almost hoarse, and then she left the house to seek out the kitchen, looking into the ovens, the churns, and large boxes. From there she went to the corncrib, the smokehouse, and the barn, crawling into the hayloft, looking under troughs, seeking out all the secret places where she herself had played when she had visited with her father.

Walini′ was not in any of them.

Thoroughly discouraged, she walked back into the parlor and sat down in the rocking chair by the hearth to rest and to think where else she might look. On the stone mantel lay a clay pipe, similar to her father's.

At first Laurel paid little attention to the piece of calico cloth half-hidden under the overturned upholstered chair across the room. But then she stopped rocking and went to examine the cloth. Lifting the chair, she began to pull the cloth toward her. A rag doll, with one arm half-torn from it, popped into sight.

When she realized that it must be Walini′'s doll, tears began to stream down Laurel's cheeks. Taking the pathetic little doll in her arms, she went back to the rocking chair and, holding it close to her, she began to sing the lullaby that all little Cherokee girls were taught. Her mother had sung it to her when she was a little girl. And she knew that Running Brook would have sung it, too. She hoped that wherever Walini′ was, she could hear it.

"*Ha′-mama′, ha′-mama′, Udá hale′yĭ, hi′lúñnû, hi′lúñnû ...*"

When she had finished, Laurel rocked in silence.

The sound was almost imperceptible at first, a child crying softly somewhere beyond the hearth.

Laurel stopped rocking. She got down on her hands and knees, with her ear against the wall. She listened again for the sound.

"Walini′," she said. "Answer me, darling."

But the child would not answer. Only another little sob gave away her hiding place.

Frantically Laurel began to search the wall and the nook beside the hearth. There had to be a secret cupboard somewhere, and a way to open it. But where? How?

So involved with finding it, Laurel did not hear the horsemen come into the yard. But then her horse's whinny alerted her. Running to the window, she saw two men. From their actions it was apparent that they were in the army of scavengers following the soldiers. One had already begun to untie her horse's reins while the other was busy removing the saddle.

No. They would not get away with it. She had lost too much already.

Laurel ran back to the hearth, retrieved her musket, and returned to the closed window. But before she could raise the sash sufficiently, shots rang out from several directions.

"Jesus, we're surrounded," one man said.

"Yeah," the other agreed. "Let's get the hell outa here."

Unable to resist, the older man reached again for the reins of Laurel's horse. But another shot grazed his hat and discouraged him. With only the saddle as booty, the two quickly disappeared from the yard in a red cloud of dust.

Still wary, Laurel waited for the others to make their appearance in the yard. But the only sound was an owl hooting, its eerie cry answered quickly throughout the woods. From the signal Laurel knew that unseen protectors were surrounding her.

She put down the musket amd went back to the hearth,

feeling along the ridges of the mantel like a blind man; for shadows were overtaking the room. In desperation her hands traced each Cherokee rose carved into the wood. Nothing happened. But when she touched the sixth one, the squeak of moving hinges to the side of the hearth told her that she had found what she had been seeking. With her fingers wedged into the small opening, she pulled toward her until the cupboard came open, revealing a small child, sitting in the dark, with her arms wrapped around her knees and her little face stained with tears.

"Oh, Walini′, I've found you," Laurel said, and reached out for the child.

For a few moments she held her in her arms, soothing the little girl who had burst into almost uncontrollable sobs. Then she picked up the doll and handed it to Walini′ for comfort. But realizing how hungry and thirsty she must be, Laurel took her to the kitchen. There she found a wooden bucket half-filled with water. Tasting it first to make sure it was all right, she offered it to Walini′.

Greedily the child drank from the dipper, swallowing the liquid in great gulps. And when she had satisfied her thirst, Laurel, still holding her, began to search for food. She finally found part of a loaf of bread in a pan near the cooking hearth. Walini′ needed no prompting. She reached out immediately for the bread.

Later, with the child clutching the remainder of the bread in one hand and clinging to her doll with the other, Laurel set her on the horse's bare back. She climbed on behind her and, with her musket slung over one shoulder, she began the long trip back in the dark to New Echota.

Chapter 24

For several days Walini′ was Laurel's shadow, sleeping in the bed beside her, sitting in the classroom with the doll in her arms. Everywhere Laurel went Walini′ went, refusing to be separated from her rescuer even for a moment.

But gradually, with the help of Redbird and Kama′mă, the child grew surer of her surroundings and began to play on the upstairs porch with the other children. Although she could not see Laurel, she was still within calling distance of her voice.

Laurel tried to give her the love that Running Brook would have given. After several weeks the trauma that the child had been through seemed to be diminishing, at least in outward appearances. But she still cried out in the night, seeking to be comforted.

As soon as Laurel had gotten back to New Echota, she'd addressed a letter to Jumping Rabbit and given it to Edward to deliver to the fort where he and Night Hawk were being held.

"Give it personally to him, Edward," Laurel had asked. "Otherwise, he might not receive it."

When Edward returned, he said, "You were right, Laurel. I had to smuggle the letter to him through the stockade fence. He's watched almost constantly, and all writing paper has been taken from him, so he will not be able to write letters influencing others. But he asked me to tell you how grateful he is that you found little Walini′."

"And Night Hawk?" Laurel prompted. "Did he say how he is?"

"He's improving slowly. When Jumping Rabbit told him that his daughter was safe, that seemed to calm him."

"I'm glad. Thank you, Edward."

Several weeks passed, with a pall upon the land. No one knew what each day would bring. Several hundred Cherokees, persuaded earlier by the emigration officials to move west, had met with such extreme difficulties that the survivors had despaired halfway and returned home, to the consternation of the officials. Attaching herself to that group was the black woman, Tansee, lifelong servant to the MacDonald family, who was attempting to get back to the Nation.

As Edward once again drove to the capital Tansee remained hidden in the trunk lashed to the top of the mail coach. Edward knew the penalty for what he was doing, transporting a former slave, whose disappearance had been reported by Julius Parker. But because of his love for Laurel, he took the risk.

Late in the afternoon, when twilight threatened to overtake him, he rushed toward his destination. But when he'd crossed the ferry, he was stopped by members of the militia, guarding the road. "You're not transportin' anything contraband into the Nation, are you, Mr. Farraday?"

"Only three missionaries," he answered.

The soldier scowled and jerked open the coach to look inside. When he saw it was empty, he realized the joke. His scowl turned into a smile. "Then proceed on. The poor souls will have need of comfort in the next few weeks."

Tansee, listening uneasily to the exchange, was relieved when the coach began moving again, although her hiding place was cramped and each jolt of the wheels added another bruise to her large body.

She had traveled far with Alex MacDonald's message for Laurel. None of his letters had ever been answered. Of course, it had been impossible to contact his daughter at first, hiding out as he had in the caves of the North Carolina wilderness.

"Are you still doing all right, Tansee?" Edward called.

The woman's reply was muffled. "Yes. But I've changed my mind about bein' buried in a coffin."

"We shouldn't be on the road much longer," he assured her.

"Well, when we *do* get there, it's gonna take a crowbar to get me out of this trunk."

Edward continued his race down the post road, stopping at intervals to rest, but it was too dangerous for Tansee to be given the same consideration as the horses. Almost as soon as she climbed out, she was forced to return to her cramped quarters.

Well past dark, when everyone in the mission house had gone to bed, Laurel heard the familiar sound of wheels along the ruts in the lane. Quickly she got out of bed, being careful not to awaken Walini′ or the two older girls. She threw a mantle over her nightgown and rushed down the stairs.

"Edward," she whispered, opening the door to him. "I had almost given up on you."

He grinned. "Give me a kiss, Laurel. Then be prepared for a big surprise."

"What are you talking about?"

He shook his head. "First the kiss."

Standing just inside the door, away from any curious eyes, he took her in his arms and gave her a slow, lingering kiss. "I can't take this much longer, Laurel," he said, nuzzling her neck. "We'll have to get married soon."

"Yes, Edward. Just as soon as Cousin John negotiates the new treaty and it will be safe in the Nation again." She stepped back out of his arms and said, "Now, what's your surprise?"

He took Laurel by the hand and drew her to the coach. "I've brought you something that I found at Ross's Landing."

Laurel rushed to open the coach door.

"No. Not in there."

She watched him climb on top of the coach, look in all directions, and then quickly unfasten the lid of the large trunk.

Big Tansee, dressed in her large gray coat and slouch hat, slowly sat up, then painfully began to climb out.

"Tansee!" Laurel said, forgetting to whisper in her amazement at seeing the woman.

"Miss Laurel, you don't know how glad I am to see you."

With Edward's help, the black woman, stiff from her incarceration, climbed down.

"Oh Tansee, where did you come from? And where are my mother and father? Are they safe? Why didn't they ever write to me?"

"It's a long story," Tansee replied. "But before I tell it, I got to attend to this sore and hungry body."

"Of course. Come into the kitchen."

Edward, almost forgotten, said, "Laurel, I'm going on to the tavern for a bed and something to eat. You don't need me around tonight. I'll see you in the morning before I leave."

"You'll come for breakfast?"

He nodded.

Laurel's brown eyes shone with her excitement. "I won't

ever forget this, Edward," she whispered, rushing Tansee inside the house.

Far into the night, Laurel and Tansee talked at the kitchen table, stopping only long enough for Laurel to check on the sleeping children and then to return downstairs.

"It was a shock, with the soldiers waitin' to arrest Chief Alex, as soon as that Mr. Parker took over his property. We fooled them, though, escapin' over the ridge and keepin' to the wilderness. But we were just one step ahead of the soldiers all the way. We hid out in the daytime and traveled by night. Your mama stumbled on a tree stump in the dark the first week and broke her spectacles. That was the only thing she ever complained about—losing her spectacles.

"By the time we finally got over the North Carolina line, we found some other Cherokees hidin' out, too. But then bad things began to happen. One of the young women, no older than you, went out to look for berries one day. A soldier found her in the woods and tried to rape her. She was able to get his musket and shoot him. But after that a whole army of soldiers came and rounded up everybody."

"I remember," Laurel said. "But at the time I had no idea my mother and father were in the group."

"Then you know the rest of the story—how one of the Indian men took the blame and gave himself up to protect the woman. He was hanged, and the rest of the them were forced to emigrate west. There wasn't much your mama and daddy could do, except go along."

Tansee looked at Laurel. "But I don't understand why you never got their letter tellin' you—unless the letter was lost."

Tansee continued her story, relating the heartbreak of the trip to Arkansas—the cholera along the way, the children dying of measles, and everywhere the lawless scavengers following, ready to steal anything they could when no one was looking.

"The food was the worst," Tansee said, "what little there was of it. Since I was black, I didn't get a ration. And neither did the white wives or husbands. 'The government is payin' me to feed the Indians,' the sutler said. 'So the rest of you will have to do without.'

"Chief Alex and Miss Trudie shared their food with me. But what awful stuff. No coffee. No sugar or fresh vegetables. Just flour and salted pork. You'd think the federal government would be smart enough to know almost *nobody* in the Nation eats pork."

The black woman eyed the extra piece of peach pie.

"Go on, Tansee. Finish the pie," Laurel said.

She did not have to be urged. "Chief Alex wasn't sure where you might be. He was hopin' you'd married Night Hawk. But he wanted me to get the message to you—that they were both all right, even though Miss Trudie has her spells."

"What do you mean, Tansee? How serious are they?"

"Well, her lungs bother her. She coughs a lot. But she's improvin' some. I think the worryin' over you hasn't helped either one of them. Chief Alex thought maybe *you'd* be needin' me even more than they did, so that's why he paid me to make the trip back to find you."

"I'll start writing them every day," Laurel vowed. "Surely, *one* of the letters will finally get through."

Later, with Tansee bedded down on a cot in the kitchen, Laurel climbed the stairs to the room she shared with the three girls. It would not be long before daybreak, when her duties as a teacher would begin again.

She hugged her happiness to her. Her mother and father were safe. And dear Edward had been responsible for bringing the good news to her.

Laurel gently straightened Walini´'s little body from its position across the bed, climbed in beside her and, for the first time in months drifted into a peaceful sleep.

But other events were taking shape at the same time, to destroy any peace of mind Laurel might be enjoying.

Earlier that week the Reverend Samuel Worcester had received an official letter at his jail cell in Milledgeville. He was finishing his sentence at hard labor, and his hope to return to New Echota as missionary and teacher was strong. But that hope was dashed when he began to read:

"This letter is to inform you that land lot number 125 in the town of New Echota, which has served as a mission to the Cherokees, has been drawn in the Georgia lottery by Colonel William Harden. He will be taking possession of the property within the week."

The other communiqué was issued as a proclamation by General Winfield Scott, who had been ordered, after General Wood's resignation, to take command of the forced removal of the Cherokees. Federal artillery, cavalry, and infantry numbering three thousand men were already at his disposal, with the power to call up four thousand of the state militia and volunteers. And he had chosen New Echota as his headquarters.

The chiefs and headmen, the aristocracy of the Nation, had already been rounded up, disarmed, and made prisoner in the stockades. Now it remained for the rest of the Nation to join them.

"Thousands of my troops are approaching from every quarter," the general warned, "so that escape is hopeless. If you seek to hide yourselves in the mountains and forests, my troops are prepared to hunt you down."

During this time John Ross was still in Washington, meeting with government officials in a legal last-ditch effort to save his people.

* * *

Early the next morning Laurel awoke to the aroma of breakfast being cooked. She smiled, stretched, and then woke the children. Freshly scrubbed, with immaculately clean dresses on, the girls walked downstairs to join Deer Stalker and Black Moccasin at the kitchen table.

"Good morning, Tansee," Laurel said.

"Good mornin', Miss Laurel," she replied, bringing hot bread to the table. "I decided to fix your breakfast like I used to."

"It smells delicious." Laurel proceeded to introduce her wards, Redbird, Kama′-mă, and little Waliní. "I see that you've already met Black Moccasin and Deer Stalker."

"Yes. As soon as I put the bread in the oven," Tansee said, laughing.

Laurel smiled, and soon her happiness, as visible as the sweet butter on the hot bread, had spread throughout the kitchen.

Hearing the sound of the rapidly approaching mail coach, Laurel said, "That must be Edward." She got up to place an extra chair at the table.

But at the sound of Edward's harsh footsteps across the porch. the wrenching of the door, and the look on his face as he ran inside, Laurel's smile disappeared. "Edward?"

"Quick, Laurel. All of you get into the coach. The soldiers have come and are rounding up everybody."

Walini′ started crying as Laurel suddenly snatched her from the table. "Tansee, help me," the young woman begged.

Within seconds the five frightened children, with Laurel and Tansee, were hidden in the coach as Edward raced his horses in the opposite direction, past the mission house and toward the little-used trail that led to the old road west of New Echota.

Chapter 25

Over the ridge, beyond the Parker house, a squad of soldiers stealthily approached the property belonging to Two Feathers.

It was a beautiful day, with the warm breeze filled with a resinous scent of pine and cedar flapping the wet sheets on the wash line.

Like Tansee at the mission house, Daisy had also taken great pains that morning with breakfast, preparing the dishes that Two Feathers and the children enjoyed. It seemed that her cooking was a language that spoke eloquently of her love for them.

"Will you be working in the far cornfield again today?" Daisy asked.

Two Feathers nodded. "And Billy has promised to help me."

"May I go, too?" Ina′li asked.

Before Two Feathers could reply. Billy said, "No, Ina′li. I am older."

"But by next spring you'll be able to help also," Two Feathers said.

"Mama?"

Daisy looked at her younger son, who had begun to

pout. "You can help me to feed the ducks, Ina′li. And look for their hidden nests next to the water."

The birds outside in the trees stopped their singing and began to twitter excitedly. Two Feathers, sitting at the table, stiffened as if sensing danger.

"What is it?" Daisy asked, alarmed at her husband's sudden silence.

He held up his hand for all to be quiet.

Within moments the door was broken down and soldiers poured into the cabin. At the sight of the pointed guns the boys started crying and Daisy would have, too, except for the outward calmness of Two Feathers, who remained seated at the table.

"You're all under arrest," one of the soldiers barked. "I have orders to take you to the stockade. Get up. You're to leave immediately."

"Just a minute, Corporal," an officer said, standing at the open door and watching. He walked inside, and after a peremptory glance at Two Feathers, he peered more closely at the blonde-haired Daisy and the two little boys, one so fair and the other so dark.

Mistakenly assuming that Two Feathers was Ina′li's father, the officer spoke to Daisy. "You have your choice, ma'am, being a white woman. You'll have to leave this house. But if you want to, you and the older boy can stay in Georgia."

Daisy didn't understand. In a quivering voice, she said, "What do you mean? Can't we all stay?"

"No. These two will have to go west," he answered, pointing to Two Feathers and Ina′li.

"Mama," Ina′li cried, running and putting his arms around his mother's neck.

Realizing the officer's error, Two Feathers tried to intervene. "Agitsi′, tell the man about..."

"Shut up, Indian. Let the woman decide."

Daisy had never been separated from her children or Two Feathers, even for a day. "I go where my husband goes," she affirmed. "Where my little boys—"

"Then get up. You have a long way to walk today."

"Will you let us come home tonight?"

"No. This property already belongs to someone else."

Daisy looked at her younger son. "But I promised to let Ina′li feed the ducks. You'll let him feed them before we leave, won't you?"

The officer didn't know why he should be affected by such a simple request. Disguising his emotions, his voice took on a tone of exasperation. "Go ahead, but don't be long."

When the first soldier motioned for Two Feathers to get up and follow, the Indian reached toward the mantel for his clay pipe.

"No. You're to take nothing with you, except the clothes on your back."

Two Feathers obeyed him. As he left the house and walked onto the porch, Billy held tightly to the Cherokee's hand. With the hostile soldiers all around him, the boy tried hard to stop crying. But a tear escaped anyway.

Daisy and Ina′li, holding a wooden bucket of dried corn, called to the ducks, who came waddling into the yard. In every direction they ran, quacking and downing the niblets of corn being thrown on the ground. When the corn was gone, Daisy and Ina′li set the empty bucket on the steps and joined Two Feathers and Billy. Together they began to walk away from the house, where the breeze, sweet with pine and cedar, still flapped the sheets hanging on the line.

"Halt!"

Soldiers on horseback emerged from the woods and began to give chase to the mail coach. Edward paid no attention but continued down the road, until a cavalryman caught up with him, reached out to take hold of the lead horse, and slowly brought the vehicle to a stop.

Surrounded by men on horseback, a disappointed Edward said an oath under his breath.

"Didn't you hear me?" the soldier questioned with a furious voice.

"I was in a hurry."

"You must be carrying something powerful important to disregard a militia order, Mr. Farraday."

Surprised that the soldier knew his name, Edward said quickly, "I'm carrying the United States mail. I'm already late for my next stop."

Ignoring him, the soldiers used his bayonet to push back the curtains from the post coach's window. Seeing Laurel, Tansee, and the children, he turned back to Edward. "So you have some passengers, too, I see. And where might you be taking them?"

He didn't expect Edward to answer. Returning his attention to the coach, he opened the door and spoke to its occupants. "Get out."

Laurel, holding Waliní in her arms, was the first, followed by Tansee and the other children.

The soldier gazed at Laurel for a long time, admiring her beauty, her fair complexion and lustrous brown hair. "Ma'am, are you white or Cherokee?"

"Cherokee," Laurel announced with pride flashing in her dark eyes.

From the box Edward said, "She's my wife, and the children are members of her family."

"And I suppose this one," he said, poking at Tansee with his bayonet, "is the family slave."

"She's Cherokee, too," Edward affirmed, his answer partially right. Years earlier Indian slaves, captured in war, had worked in the fields alongside the black slaves. Their white masters had sometimes forced their intermarriage.

Tansee's grandmother had been one of them.

"Mr. Farraday, we know all about you. You can't fool us with your lies. Not about the black woman, and certainly not about this woman," he said, looking again in Laurel's direction. "She's not your wife. She's Laurel MacDonald, the teacher who took over Samuel Worcester's mission school."

"But she's my fiancée," Edward said. "That's as good as being my wife."

"Not quite."

The soldier gazed back at Laurel, more insolently this time. Then he said, "I should arrest you, Mr. Farraday, for obstructing our military mission. But since you're carrying the mail, I'll let you go on your way." He was not being lenient. The soldier merely wanted to get rid of him, since he was already making plans for Laurel himself.

"Laurel, I'm sorry."

"I understand, Edward," she replied. "You did all you humanly could to protect us."

"And I'll keep on, Laurel. I swear it. Don't give up hope. I'll do something yet to help you."

"Thank you, Edward."

"On your way, Mr. Farraday," the soldier ordered.

Edward picked up the reins and whistled to his horses. As they began a slow, trodding pace he looked back at the forlorn group standing in the road, with soldiers on horseback surrounding them on all sides.

Redbird reached for her brother's hand. Their parents had disappeared, and now they had only each other—and Laurel.

"I'll take care of you, Tatsu′hwă," Black Moccasin said. "Don't worry." Yet inwardly he was just as frightened as his sister.

"All right, march!" the cavalryman ordered, directing them all to retrace their steps to New Echota.

"Are they taking us back to the mission house?"

Kama′mă asked, walking beside Laurel.

"I don't think so," she replied, trying to keep her voice steady. "More than likely we'll be joining the others they're rounding up."

"But where are we going?" Deer Stalker whispered.

"Probably to the stockade."

Their conversation was cut off by one of the soldiers, galloping up beside them. "Stop your whispering."

They continued walking, without speaking, until the mission house came into view. Walini′, in Laurel's arms, cried, "I want my doll. I want my doll." And when she began to cry, Laurel turned to the soldier beside her.

"Please, do you think we might stop off and get—"

"Shut up, and keep walking."

Big Tansee leaned over and whispered, "Don't cry, Walini′. I'll make you another doll."

Black Moccasin, still holding his sister's hand, gazed at the mission porch and remembered the tall, bearded visitor who had spoken in such wonderful words. He knew that he would never forget that afternoon as long as he lived.

Soon they joined the other citizens of New Echota, who had also been taken from their homes. With the military order given to move out, the reluctant citizens formed a slow, mournful procession from their capital.

When they reached the main road, Laurel stopped and took one quick last glance behind her. She was surrounded by memories of her civilization—the supreme court, the council, the newspaper.

Voices crowded into her mind, each demanding attention—the one belonging to Going Snake, with its distinctive grunt at the end of each passage he read, drifting through the council-house windows to the meadow where she and the children had sat and listened; the suddenly cold voice of Night Hawk when she had rejected his proposal; the soft, feminine voice of her mother, telling her the old family stories, as if she might never have a chance to relate them to her daughter again.

The voices rose and joined the others belonging to her cousin John; her father, Alex; Samuel; Vervia—and Edward Farraday.

Laurel was leaving behind more than memories. The very fabric of her life had been woven into the history of her nation, her capital, her life's work.

Yet, long ago, had she not gotten a glimpse into the future? But she had dismissed the vision—of happy children at play being hunted down by soldiers. Now it was born anew. The vision had become the reality.

Chapter 26

Two days later an exhausted Laurel, with Tansee and the children, limped into the stockade, where separate pens had been built for the men and women.

Edward had told her of the concentration camps that dotted the land, but until that moment she had never believed she would ever be an occupant. In sadness she watched as Deer Stalker and Black Moccasin were led away from her.

"You must be brave," she said. "The men will help to take care of you—Chiefs Night Hawk and Jumping Rabbit are already there."

Once again she was admonished for talking. "Get on across the grounds," one of the soldiers urged. But the route to the women's pen was cut off by a large group getting in position to move out. Laurel and the others were forced to remain where they were.

She saw a tall, white-haired Indian on horseback riding to the head of the procession. She immediately recognized Going Snake, the eighty-year-old speaker of the council. He was clothed in dignity, the tragic circumstances of the occasion unable to diminish his majestic bearing. Directly behind him several of the younger chiefs on ponies took up their positions.

"Jumping Rabbit," she called out. But she was too far away for him to hear. Laurel searched for some sign of Night Hawk, but he was not with Jumping Rabbit or among the others on horseback.

At the military commander's signal, the procession began to move out. Red dust rose over the stockade as hundreds of men, women, and children walked, their eyes looking straight ahead to their leaders in front of them.

As they passed by, Laurel searched the stoic faces of the people. Many of them she recognized as friends.

The wagons came next, loaded with flour, salt, and salted pork. Then came the squads of soldiers, assigned to guard the Indians to make sure none escaped.

When only the swirl of dust was left, the soldier prodded Laurel, Tansee, and the young girls across the square to the women's pen.

The gates slammed, shutting out trees, mountains, freedom, and hope. But for the children's sake, Laurel forced herself not to show her dismay at the squalid surroundings. "Well, Tansee, let's go and see what we can make of our new lodgings."

"Humph!" Tansee said. "This place isn't fit for pigs, much less people."

"Maybe we won't be here long," Laurel said. "Maybe we'll be moving out soon, too."

The servant did not tell her that even worse difficulties lay ahead on the trail. Instead she began to help Laurel look for a nook where there might be room for them all. The crude pen was hardly more than a lean-to, open to the weather on all sides, with patches of sky visible through the shoddy roof.

Despite the number of people who'd just left, conditions were extremely crowded. With the tired children in tow, Laurel and Tansee edged past one group after another.

Nowhere did either one see an empty place large enough to lie down, much less enough space for all five of them.

By the time they reached the far corner of the pen, convulsive sobs from one of the women rose above all the other sounds. The noise had evidently caused the other women who'd arrived at the same time to seek a position as far away from the grieving woman as possible. But Laurel determined to ignore the noise, settling Walini′, Redbird, and Kama′mă in the small amount of space beside her.

"Are you by yourself?" Laurel asked, first in Cherokee. But getting no response, she spoke again in English.

The woman raised her tear-stained face to see who had spoken to her. Seeing a sympathetic Laurel, she said, "They took my husband and little boys."

"I'm sorry. I know how sad you must be."

A fretful Walini′ began crying, too, upset by the woman's tears.

Redbird whispered to Kama′mă. "Look. She has yellow hair."

"You'll have to excuse them," Laurel apologized, still trying to soothe Walini′. "They've never seen someone with your light coloring before."

Still staring at the woman, the younger girl said, "My name is Kama′mă. It means 'butterfly,' for that was the first thing my mother saw after I was born."

Redbird, not to be outdone, said, "And my name is Tatsu′hwă."

"What does that mean?" Daisy asked, suddenly interested in the pretty girls.

"Redbird. I was born at the winter moon."

Daisy looked at the smallest, in Laurel's arms.

"Walini′," Laurel said. "You would call her Polly. This is Tansee, and my name is Laurel."

"My mama named me for a flower, too," Daisy said suddenly.

"Which one?"

Daisy hesitated, as if she were thinking hard. "I don't remember. It was so long ago." She brightened. "But my husband calls me Agitsi′. That's the name I go by now."

At the mention of the Indian name Tansee suddenly stared at the woman. Could she be the same one she had been midwife to in Two Feathers' house? It was possible. But it was probably better not to mention it, especially since she had been swown to secrecy.

Unaware that Daisy was now Two Feathers' wife, Tansee, along with Laurel, befriended the forlorn woman, who seemed to them almost as helpless as the children

That night they all shared the small space together. Walini′ and Agitsi′ were the only ones to shed tears as they went to sleep. It would have been so easy for Laurel to join them. Only her hope that Edward would be able to get them out soon prevented her.

On the other side of camp, in the men's pen, Two Feathers knelt down and examined Night Hawk's injuries. The young chief had obviously received a vicious blow and a severe lashing. But Two Feathers, used to the ancient way of healing, realized that the man's heart was sicker than his body.

"What's wrong with him, Papa?" Billy asked.

"He has had a great sadness."

"Then why doesn't he cry?" Ina′li said.

"Tears are not the right medicine for a chief," Two Feathers replied.

"Do you have the right medicine?" Billy inquired.

"Perhaps."

That night several of the soldiers stood on the porch of headquarters and listened to the sounds of chanting and dancing coming from the men's pens.

"Listen to that," one of them said. "It just goes to show you they're *all* heathen under the skin."

The other agreed. "Looks like the missionaries and the schools were just a waste of time."

"And to think their chief had the gall to suggest they might become citizens."

Listening to the mounting sound that swept through the camp, the first said, "You think those peddlers slipped some whiskey to them?"

"Wouldn't put it past them. Maybe we'd better add a few more guards, just in case."

But the dance and the chant soon ended, and a quiet swept over the stockade. By morning Two Feathers was pleased that Night Hawk had vastly improved during the night.

Several days later Laurel was selected to go outside the gates of the women's pen to draw water from the pump. She had no comb and none of the other conveniences of civilized life. The hem of her skirt was dirty from the red dust, and her crumpled white blouse had been stained by Walini's tears. Yet, with no mirror to remind her, her appearance did not seem important. Her entire attention had shifted to the problem of survival.

As she walked across the square Laurel was greeted by hoots, whistles, and crude comments by the soldiers on duty. One of them began to follow uncomfortably close behind her.

Laurel knew better than to protest; for one of the other young women the day before had been stripped of her clothes and whipped in full sight of the laughing soldiers. Even the ones on duty in the towers had done nothing to stop the whipping.

"Didn't you hear what I said?" the voice behind her asked. "...what I'd like to do to you right now?"

Pretending she didn't understand him, Laurel continued to walk to the pump, where a man, already drawing water, had his back to her. While she waited her turn, the soldier who had followed her also waited.

Standing with her empty bucket, Laurel curiously regarded the raw, raised welts on the Indian's back. Then when he turned around, she recognized Night Hawk. "Tskĭ-lĭ," she said, so glad to see him.

"Laurel." Aware of the nearby soldier, he began to speak quickly in Cherokee. "When were you brought here?"

"Several days ago. Walini′ is with me."

"All right, get on back to the men's pen," the impatient soldier ordered Night Hawk.

"I will never forget your kindness," he said at the same time he received a jab with the end of the soldier's rifle.

Setting her bucket down, Laurel began to pump the water. She watched a proud but sad Night Hawk cross the square. His progress was slow and seemingly painful. But spirit had blazed in his eyes, briefly and dangerously.

With the bucket nearly full, Laurel began her trek back to the women's pen. Once again, the soldier fell in step directly behind her, and the hoots around the square started up again.

"What are you goin' to do, Butchie, when you catch up with her?"

Grinning and making an obscene sign to his friends watching him, he was not aware when Laurel stopped suddenly.

As he bumped into her she let part of the water slosh from the bucket, soaking the front of his trousers.

At his oath she quickly turned and apologized in Cherokee, then rushed to get inside the gates of the pen. She could still hear the soldiers' hoots and whistles, but they were not directed at her this time—merely at the soldier they called Butchie.

Tansee, waiting for her inside the gate, took the bucket of water. "You might be sorry for that, Laurel," she said. Then her face burst into a wide grin. "But oh, what a laugh you gave all of us."

The women made room for the two as they wound their way back to the corner of the pen.

"Is Walini′ still awake?"

"She might be asleep by now. Agitsi′ started singing to her."

Before they reached their place, Laurel heard the song. It was Two Feathers' song, the one he had made up. By tradition it could never be sung by anyone else.

So what was this woman doing, singing it? Did she not know the penalty for singing someone else's spirit song without permission?

"Agitsi′," she said, forgetting everything else. "That song belongs to Two Feathers. What are you doing singing it?"

A puzzled Daisy stopped and looked up at Laurel. "He is my husband. He taught it to me."

"Do you mean that Two Feathers is here—in this stockade?"

"Yes. I told you, Laurel. I came here with my husband and two little boys. But they were taken away from me."

"Oh, Agitsi′. I know him well."

"You do? But I never saw *you* before."

"It doesn't matter. We know each other now."

Chapter 27

For over eight years John Ross had labored, seeking an alternative to removal. But in the end, the Senate, caught up in regional politics, had finally decided, by one vote, to ratify the fraudulent Treaty of New Echota.

Despite the efforts of Henry Clay and a few others, the two-year grace period had run out. Now there remained only one route to be taken—west.

John and Quatie's daughter Jane withdrew from Salem Academy. And his sister's sons, whose school fees had been paid by their uncle, came home from New Jersey also. The older William, graduating as valedictorian, had planned to enter Princeton in the fall. But his hopes had been dashed by the forced removal.

In a meeting with the six-foot-four General Scott, John, as principal chief, and his brother Lewis, as the Nation's treasurer, discussed the financial complexities of removing over fifteen thousand people in an orderly manner.

They would have to hire physicians and conductors, buy teams and wagons, provisions, and contact government contractors for the goods that would have to be purchased overland, once their initial supplies ran out. But most important to his people's survival was food.

"I estimate it will take eighty days to travel the eight

hundred miles," General Scott said. "Figure on food for that number of days."

John nodded. "When do you plan for the entire group to move out?"

"I've already given the protreaty party permission to leave voluntarily. The rest, as soon as you can get the provisions together. But I want everyone west by October first."

"I've heard that the severe drought is causing problems with the river vessels," Lewis said.

"A few of the boats had to be abandoned because of the amount of draw," Scott conceded. "But the rains should begin soon."

"And what is your latest information on the cholera epidemic?" John asked.

"I've been told that it's no longer a problem. But you'll have doctors traveling with you."

At the next meeting with General Scott, John and Lewis presented their estimates for all expenses—totaling sixty-five dollars and eighty-eight cents per person, including sixteen cents a day for food.

"That sounds extravagant," Scott complained. "Go back and refigure."

The two did so, but in the end John realized that he had underestinated the expense, since they had forgotten to include certain items.

Soon, white contract seekers and all manner of office holders, dreaming of the enormous amount of money that could be pocketed at the expense of the Indians, began to vie for the contracts. They bombarded Scott to let them bid, with the lowest bidder receiving the contract.

"General Scott, the health and comfort of the Cherokee people are much more important than a few dollars saved," Lewis argued.

Scott sat in silence and then finally spoke. "All right, we'll let the contract stand as it is. But I'm sure the government will think the coffee, sugar, and soap unnecessary expenses."

Coming home from Washington to oversee the mass emigration and arrange for his own family's move, John stopped off at the Cherokee Agency at Calhoun, Tennessee. Hearing of his coming, thousands surrounded him, all wanting to greet him with a handshake and a word of encouragement, for the treatment of the Cherokees at the hands of the government had become a scandal and a national disgrace.

A few days later, after seeing Jane home and visiting with Quatie, Silas, and George, John returned to Calhoun for the giant task ahead.

He divided the Nation into thirteen groups of a little over a thousand men, women, and children each, and assigned each group a conductor, wagon master, physician, interpreter, and commissary agent. Contracts for food along the way were let, so that the people would not go hungry. And he remained in Calhoun, waiting to see each detachment off personally.

At the stockade where Laurel waited for some word from Edward, the time passed slowly.

The federal and state troops who guarded the young Cherokee women had been surprised that so many of them were graceful, pretty, and well educated. But they were also prisoners. And so the troops followed their own code of frontier behavior, doing as they pleased, with no one to censure them for their drunkenness, rape, and murder. In the prison camps the soldiers were the ruling law and authority.

Sickness had also devastated both men and women in their crowded conditions. In Laurel's compound a large number of women and children had already died. With apology, their clothes had been removed before burial and washed so that others might use them.

Laurel, bargaining with another young woman her size, had swapped her own skirt and blouse for a more traditional cotton calico dress and woven vest.

One evening, after she had been there for several weeks, she stood before the gate of the women's pen and waited for the guard to finish his evening rounds. Then she slipped out to get water. Night Hawk was waiting for her. Their words were brief.

As she got ready to leave he suddenly asked, "Where is your white man now, Laurel?"

His taunting words angered her. She never should have confided to him earlier that Edward was coming to get her. "I don't know. But he made a promise to me. And I believe him."

"All our paths have been sown with the white men's promises," he spat out. "But like daggers, they only serve to wound us as we walk by."

Laurel, understanding his hurt and pain, tried to make him understand her own feelings. "I know you have reason to hate them all," she said, "but Edward is different. He's kind and considerate, and I love him."

Night Hawk's face showed his contempt. But before he left, he quickly handed her two slightly shriveled peaches. "These are for you and Walini′," he said, and then vanished.

Hearing the order for the outer gates of the fort to be opened, Laurel rushed back to the women's side as a member of the cavalry rode into the prison camp.

"My, this little piece of a peach sure does taste good," Tansee said, and the others agreed with her.

Laurel had divided the two peaches so that the three women and the three children shared equally. As she fed

Waliniʹ her portion Laurel said, "Do you realize that this is the first fruit we've had since we got here?"

"We have two hundred peach trees in our orchard at home," Redbird said wistfully.

"That's nothing," Kamaʹmă answered. "Chief Vann had over a thousand in *his* orchard."

"Did you count them all, Kamaʹmă?" Daisy asked.

"No. My father told me. He used to go to the racetrack all the time. You know, the one the chief built near Spring Place."

"I wonder where all his blooded racehorses are now," Laurel commented, remembering the times Night Hawk and Jumping Rabbit had ridden them in contests.

"Probably being ruined by Bishop and his men," Tansee replied.

"Next week I hope someone gives us an *apple*," Kamaʹmă said, settling down to go to sleep.

In the middle of the night Redbird woke Laurel. "I don't feel so good," she complained. "My stomach hurts."

Soon, the other children awoke too, each with the same complaint. Laurel had tried to dismiss her own queasiness. But now she grew afraid that they were all coming down with the same devastating illness that had swept the compound.

For the rest of the night they were attended to by Tansee and Agitsiʹ, the only two who had not been affected.

The next morning a weak Laurel received a summons to appear at headquarters. Thinking it might be news from Edward, or even Edward himself, she dragged herself from the sleeping shelf, quickly washed her face, and hurried from the compound.

Standing at the door of headquarters, she said to the guard, "I'm Laurel MacDonald. I was asked to come here."

The guard nodded and opened the door. A captain sat at the desk inside. She waited for him to look up.

"Laurel MacDonald?"

"Yes."

"Lieutenant Wayne needs a woman to cook and wash for him. How would you like to leave here for the time being?"

A man stepped from the shadows and smiled at her. She recognized him immediately as the one who had stopped Edward's post coach and subsequently marshaled them back to New Echota.

The weeks of frustration, of being treated like an animal in a pen, had taken its toll on her pride. With her eyes blazing in anger, she dismissed the young man's offer and returned her attention to the captain. "Your lieutenant has made a terrible mistake," she said. "I am the daughter of a chieftain. And before our property was stolen from us, we had slaves in the fields and servants in the house. I'm afraid I don't know *how* to cook and wash. But if he wishes to learn how to read, or eat with a fork, then I might be able to teach him."

"That is quite enough," the captain said. "You have no choice in the matter. You will go with him now."

Laurel bolted for the door. Thinking she was attempting to escape, the two followed her. "Guard, stop that woman."

But the guard looked on helplessly as Laurel bent over by the side of the porch and lost the small amount of food she had eaten for breakfast. "I think the woman is ill, sir, like so many of the others," the guard said.

"Then get her out of my sight. I won't have her dying on my doorstep." The captain turned to the lieutenant. "You're better off getting someone else, Wayne. Unless you want to come down with whatever she has."

Later Laurel lay on the sleeping shelf in the women's pen. Sick in body and spirit, she realized that if Edward did not come soon, it might be too late.

* * *

The days passed and Laurel began to feel better. Only Redbird remained ill. But then she began to grow stronger, too. Tansee finished the new doll for Walini′, and Agitsi′ fashioned a dress for it from the remnants of cloth and ribbons she'd begun to collect.

"Sing, Laurel," Walini′ urged. "Baby bear song."

While Walini′cradled the cornhusk doll in her arms, Laurel sang, *"Ha′-mama′, ha-mama′, Udâ hale′yĭ hi′-lúñnû, hi′luñnû ..."*

Soon other women and children joined in, the memories of happier days feeding their hearts and souls.

The first detachment left the Nation, then another. But with news of the epidemics of cholera along the entire water route and equally devastating disasters waiting at every point along the overland route, Scott decided that he would have to call off the emigration until later in the year.

So the people remained in their prisons during the summer months and on into the fall.

By this time John Ridge and the other members of the protreaty party, including Elias Boudinot and his brother Stand Watie, had arrived in the west, with their wagons, servants, spinning wheels, bedding and dishes, horses and farm implements—all their personal property that the government had allowed them to keep, with cash reimbursement for what they had left behind.

But they had also brought with them the knowledge that they had betrayed their nation, and might suffer the penalty of treason at any time.

The danger was in two directions— from the western Cherokees who had settled in the west years before, and from the majority of the Nation who would be arriving later. This thought was never far from their minds as they cleared their land, built new homes, and planted new crops.

On an unseasonably cold day in October the captain at the stockade received his order. The news spread rapidly throughout the pens. They were finally leaving for the west.

"Laurel, I can't find my blue ribbon," Agitsi′ cried, getting down on her hands and knees to look for the small scrap.

"Here it is," Redbird said.

They hurriedly strapped their meager possessions to their backs and began to move out of the women's pen.

"Ka′mamă, hold Tansee's hand," Laurel said. "We don't want to get separated."

"I hope my husband and little boys haven't forgotten me," Agitsi′said.

As the six took their places Laurel saw Night Hawk, mounted on his pony at the front of the procession. Riding beside him was Two Feathers, honored as a medicine man by the Cherokees.

The captain had not been pleased to give Night Hawk his place at the head of the procession. But he knew that without a chieftain to lead them the people would not follow.

"I see my husband, but I don't see my little boys," Agitsi′said, frantically looking in all directions.

"They will be with Deer Stalker and Black Moccasin," Laurel assured her. "We'll be able to find them tonight when we make camp."

Tears filled Laurel's eyes. So long ago, on the day they had arrived at the stockade, she had seen Going Snake and Jumping Rabbit at the head of that procession, with all of the people looking in their direction.

Now the scene was replayed. But this time she and Walini′, Tansee, Redbird, Kama′mă, and Agitsi′ were in the crowd, with the four boys somewhere. Laurel knew better than to rely on the soldiers. For the next three months their very existence would depend upon Indian leadership.

They moved out. In the center were the wagons. On all sides they were surrounded by guards. As they marched to the ferry at Hiwassee the flames behind them demolished the squalid pens where they had been imprisoned for the past five months.

Chapter 28

Edward Farraday raced his coach unmercifully, with the crack of a whip urging the tired horses onward.

He was not usually this insensitive to winded animals, but the smoldering ruins of the former stockade where Laurel had been kept indicated that time had run out. If he did not catch up with her before she crossed the ferry, it would be too late.

He had spent all summer in correspondence with the Georgia authorities, his impatience tempered by the realization that he must do nothing rash to jeopardize his special request concerning Laurel. Just as he had begun to make headway with the governor's office, the man's personal secretary had resigned, forcing Edward to start over with the one who had taken his place.

Now, with the long-awaited correspondence folded in his coat pocket, he followed along the road where Laurel and the other prisoners had traveled only three or four hours previously, judging from the tracks still visible in the dust.

Overhead, a covey of quail flew in formation, their feathers suddenly ruffled by the roguish wind that swept over the hills and then touched down to tease the low places before regaining momentum and seeking other sport, other mischief.

As Edward passed by an ancient stand of hardwood trees, a shower of leaves tumbled down, making a carpet of gold and red on the forest floor. Visible above the bereft, tall branches were the newly built squirrel nests, sturdy and strong for the hard winter ahead.

By the time he reached the hidden spring and the small, trickling creek that ran beside it, Edward realized that for the sake of the horses he must stop. Unwillingly he brought the coach to a halt and unhitched the animals. While they immediately made for the familiar creek to slake their thirst, Edward headed for the spring with its four crawdads, placed there to keep the water pure, lazing at the bottom of the crystal pool.

The steady trot of an animal coming from the opposite direction caused Edward to get off his knees, put his hand on his revolver, and turn around. But then, seeing a bearded old man on a mule, Edward relaxed. The fellow looked harmless enough.

"Howdy do," the stranger finally said, nodding toward Edward.

"Howdy," Edward replied, speaking in the same manner. "Have you come far?"

"Right far, I reckon," the man answered non-committally, getting down from his mule and leading him to the stream.

"You didn't pass by the Indians, did you?" Edward asked.

The old man stared at him for a moment. "Might have." He returned his attention to his mule. When he'd made sure the animal was taken care of, he spat out his wad of tobacco and unfastened a tin cup from the rope around his waist.

Edward knew better than to ask another question while the man approached the spring.

After he'd taken a long, deep swallow of water, the stranger looked over at Edward. "You aimin' to catch up with 'em?"

"The Indians, you mean?"

"Yep."

Edward nodded. "But from the tracks it looks like they've gotten a good head start."

"No business of mine, but if you set off now, you could probably catch up with 'em 'fore nightfall."

Edward suddenly grinned. "Then I'll rehitch my horses and set on out."

For over an hour he traveled north, following the heavy marks of wagon wheels and the lighter prints of both moccasined and bare feet. Each time he saw the print of a slender foot, he wondered if it might have been made by Laurel.

Too late Edward realized that he should have brought shoes and clothes and a coat with him. Perhaps even something for Laurel to eat. But he'd had no time, once he saw the charred remains of the stockade.

Another hour and a half forced him to stop to rest the horses again. The brisk wind had calmed.

Only a stray purple martin glided past the billowy clouds, gathering like sheep toward their evening fold. And in the ensuing quiet Edward heard the almost imperceptible sound of the wagon migration.

He suddenly took up the reins again, cracked them and shouted, "Gee-haw!" The surprised horses responded immediately, taking off down the road in a burst of speed.

The enormous swirl of dust in the distance made visibility impossible. But the sounds, growing louder, indicated that Edward was directly behind the procession. Then the mass creaking of wheels stopped, and the dust gradually lifted, rising to join the blanket of fog beginning to settle over the mountainous terrain.

A few minutes later Edward saw the small campfires sputtering into flame in every direction across the land. The wagon train had evidently stopped for the night, but several hundred people were milling about.

Into this throng Edward raced. Up and down the road he went, shouting, "Laurel! Laurel MacDonald! Where are you?"

From the makeshift corral where the ponies were being cared for, Night Hawk heard the voice, and then he saw the mail coach speeding past. So Edward Farraday had come for Laurel, after all—just as she'd said he would.

Night Hawk's disappointment was mixed with a grudging acknowledgment. The long trip west would be hazardous for them all. In his heart he knew that it was safer for Laurel to remain behind. But let Edward find her for himself. Night Hawk was much too busy to help.

While Edward continued his search for Laurel, Agitsi′ was also searching around each campfire for her family.

Her frustration grew with each passing minute until, suddenly, a child's familiar voice called out, "Mama! Mama!"

As she turned and saw her children running toward her, Agitsi′s face lit up. She began running to meet them, her arms outstretched. "Billy! Ina′li! Oh, how glad I am to see you." She hugged each one to her and kissed them over and over. "My precious little boys. I've been looking for you all day."

"Did you see Papa riding at the head of the procession?" Ina′li asked.

"Yes. But I haven't seen him since we stopped."

"He's looking for you," Billy said. "He told us to stay by this fire. That he would be back when he found you."

"But he won't be able to find me. Because I'm here with *you.*"

Seeing the distress in his mother's eyes, Billy said, "Then stay with Ina′li, and I'll go for Papa."

"You won't get lost?"

"No, Mama. I'll be able to find my way back."

Reassured, Agitsi′ turned her attention to Ina′li. Hugging him again and smoothing the dark hair from his eyes, she said, "Your hair has grown so long."

"Papa plaited it. But it came loose while we walked."

Under Two Feathers' tutelage Billy and Ina′li had grown considerably in the past five months. They had learned so many things—the old stories and the dances. They could even speak haltingly in Cherokee. Even though they'd been hungry and thirsty, and missed their mother terribly, they'd enjoyed being with the men and other boys, especially Deer Stalker and Black Moccasin.

Listening to Ina′li tell her of these things, Agitsi′ settled down by the fire and was content while she waited for Billy and Two Feathers to return.

All over the camp families searched for their loved ones. But the guards, determined that no one would escape in the approaching darkness, soon curtailed their movements.

Edward's actions also claimed the attention of one of the armed guards. But as he cast a wary glance at the approaching vehicle, he recognized the official insignia of the postal service. So he lowered his musket and allowed the coach to pass.

Farther down the road Laurel and Tansee were busy preparing the first cooked meal of the day. A short distance away, Kama′mă and Redbird were playing a game with Walini′. The sun had already sunk behind the line of trees, leaving only a sparse rim of light.

Over the hissing noise , as droplets of fat fell into the cooking fire, Laurel heard her name.

"Laurel! Laurel! Where are you?"

"Listen, Tansee. It sounds like Edward." In her excitement Laurel dropped the sharp stick that served as a cooking fork.

Tansee strained to hear as the voice called out again. "I believe it is, Laurel."

"Oh, Tansee, this is what I've prayed for all these months. He's come for me at last."

"Don't get your hopes up, child," Tansee cautioned, "'til you know for sure."

But Laurel was past all caution. Unmindful of the guards' earlier admonition to remain near the cooking fire, she ran in the direction of the voice. "Edward, I'm here!" she shouted, while curious groups of people silently watched the unfolding drama.

Laurel waved to catch Edward's attention and flag him down. While she ran to meet the coach, memories of another day—when her mother and father had disappeared—enveloped her. He had found her on that day, too. Dear Edward. How could she ever have doubted his love?

Yet, as she watched him jump down from the box and rush toward her, a sudden shyness overcame her, forcing her to stop. She was shabby and dirty. Her long auburn hair was no longer lustrous, but dull with the dirt and dust of the road.

Aware of her appearance, she quickly brushed her fingers through her tangled hair and straightened the collar of her faded dress.

For a moment Edward stood silently drinking in the sight of her. When he'd found his voice again, he cried, "Laurel! What have they done to you?"

"Don't look at me like that, Edward." Her smile was tremulous as she struggled with her own emotions.

"No, of course not," he replied, taking himself to task for showing his dismay at her appearance. He reached out for her hand. "I've ridden all day to find you. And I was afraid I wouldn't reach you in time."

"But you're here, Edward. That's all that matters."

Edward cleared his throat. "I worked so hard all summer, trying to get you free. I bombarded the governor's office with my petitions. And I waited and waited for the authorities to come to a decision."

"And they did?"

"Yes. I received the official letter yesterday. It's in my pocket."

Laurel's happiness at the news was marred as she thought of the children who had depended on her for so long. Then there were Agitsi′ and Tansee, Two Feathers and Night Hawk, and all the others. Remembering the past months together, she said, "It will be difficult to say good-bye."

"I know," Edward answered sympathetically. "But I felt you deserved that much from me, at least."

"What are you talking about, Edward?"

He pulled the letter from his pocket and handed it to her.

In the last vestige of light through the trees Laurel was barely able to make out the words. "The governor regrets that he is unable to grant your request concerning one Laurel MacDonald, Cherokee. The matter of all Indians is now out of his hands, so there can be no further petition to this office."

Struggling to maintain her composure, Laurel silently returned the letter to Edward.

In a pained voice he cried, "I wish it could have been different, Laurel." He took her into his arms and began to kiss her, his frustration magnified by the softness of her body, by the long months of forced separation.

Emotionally drained, Laurel remained unresponsive. Finally she turned her head away. "Thank you for coming,

Edward," she whispered. "But now I need to get back to the cooking fire."

Edward released her. With one final, anguished look, as if storing up a picture to last a lifetime, he turned his back and walked toward the waiting horses.

Past curious eyes watching him from the fires along the road, Edward retraced his route. He would head northeast now, and stop for the night at Kyle's trading post.

At the corral Night Hawk saw the coach pass again. A sense of desolation overcame him. Laurel was gone. For a long time he remained at the corral. Then he left to seek out his little daughter, Walini'. From that night on, the child would be his responsibility entirely.

Chapter 29

"He's gone, Tansee."

The black woman looked at Laurel, her heart going out to the forlorn figure standing in front of her.

"His request was turned down. Edward only came to tell me good-bye."

Tansee went back to stirring the fatback and dumplings. Staring down at the bubbling mixture, she quietly said, "He must love you an awful lot to come this far."

"Yes." As Laurel was lost in the past the noise of the children playing brought her thoughts back to the present. She brushed a tear from her cheek and shook her head, as if doing so, she could erase her misery. "I'll get the wooden bowls," she said, seeing that the food was done.

She held each bowl while Tansee filled it, placing them all in an orderly row upon the ground. "Redbird, Kama′mă, bring Walini′ to the fire. We're ready to eat."

They needed no prompting. Hungrily they knelt down and looked to Laurel to thank the Great Spirit for the meal. Before she'd finished the short prayer, Walini′ had already stuck her finger in the bowl to taste the food.

Once their initial hunger had been assuaged, Redbird asked, "Why are you so quiet, Laurel?"

Laurel forced herself to smile, "Because it's been such a long, hard day."

"And she's tired, like the rest of us," Tansee defended. "Just look at Walini´. She can barely stay awake long enough to finish eating."

"Do you think Agitsi´ found her little boys?" Kama´mă asked.

"I expect so. And we'll find Deer Stalker and Black Moccasin, too. Tomorrow, when the sun comes up," Laurel assured her. "Now, if you're all finished, we'll rinse our bowls and then go to sleep."

A few minutes later Laurel spread her blanket over the drowsy children and anchored each corner with a rock to keep the wind from removing it. Soon Tansee hugged her old gray coat around her and went to sleep also. But Laurel sat by the banked fire and gazed into its dull embers for a long time.

There she finally made peace with her past. Her path, her future, now lay with her people. But perhaps, in her heart, she had always known that.

On the other side of the camp, where another fire was banked for the night, Agitsi´ snuggled against her husband, Two Feathers. "All those months I was so afraid we'd never be together again," she said, tears running down her cheeks.

"We have a long journey to take, Agitsi´," he warned. "But I'll be beside you. I will always take care of you and my adopted sons."

Perhaps more than any of the others that night who slept around the fires, Two Feathers was aware of what was to come; for he had been given a vision. He gently wiped away Agitsi´'s tears. For him, they were a symbol of the hardship that lay ahead on "the road that cried."

* * *

When Night Hawk had tired of remaining by the ponies, he slipped through camp, looking for Deer Stalker and Black Moccasin. Finding them by another cooking fire, he quietly led them to the campsite where Walini′ and the others would be sleeping.

By the faint glow of the fire he sought out the shape of his little daughter, whom he hadn't seen since the day the soldiers came to his house. He watched the steady breathing of the sleeping child. Tenderness for Walini′ was mixed with gratitude for Laurel. If it had not been for Laurel's rescue, Walini′ would have died in the house.

His eyes took in Redbird and Kama′mă on either side of Walini′. He saw Tansee, too, her large body curled up beside them. But farther into the shadows, where Deer Stalker and Black Moccasin had chosen to lie down, still another form was silhouetted in the meager light.

No, it couldn't be. And yet... Night Hawk's throat betrayed his emotions. It was Laurel. She had not gone with Edward after all.

What had happened? Had she deliberately chosen to stay with the children? Or had there been no choice? As he tenderly spread his own blanket over Laurel and the two boys, he knew he would never mention seeing Edward.He had taunted Laurel enough.

Night Hawk walked back to the campfire, where he put on more twigs. He reheated the small portion of food left in the pail. And when he'd finished eating, he, too, lay down to sleep.

"Good morning, Laurel."

Her body protested at being awakened so early. She opened one eye. But the sun, filtering through the trees, blinded her, and she put her hand across her face to blot out the glare and the man standing over her.

"You'll have to get up. I need your help."

Laurel pushed herself up on one elbow. But as she did so she collided with the person sleeping beside her. The boy merely turned on his side without waking.

Quickly Laurel sat up. She stared from Night Hawk back to Deer Stalker. And then she saw Black Moccasin.

"I couldn't find them last night. Did you bring them here?"

"Yes."

"And you've seen your daughter?"

"Asleep."

"Then it's time for you to see her awake." Laurel took the child in her arms. "Walini′," she said gently, "your father is here. Open your eyes. He's been waiting such a long time to see you."

The little girl stretched her arms and her head drooped against Laurel's shoulder.

"Walini′," Laurel called again, rubbing the child on her face with the soft tips of her fingers. "You have someone here who wants to see you."

Slowly the little girl came awake. Night Hawk, stooping beside Laurel, smiled and held out his arms. "Walini′?"

The child stared at him as if he were a stranger.

"I don't believe she recognizes me," Night Hawk said, attempting to conceal the disappointment he felt.

"That's to be expected, Tskĭ-lĭ′."

"Is it?"

"Yes. She's been away from you for such a long time. She'll have to get used to you again."

The noise also woke Tansee. Seeing Night Hawk, she nodded to him as she left the campsite.

"You said you needed my help," Laurel prompted.

"Yes. As soon as you can, I'd like for you to go around this section of the camp and talk with the people. A good many are sick and weak. Find out how many and take their names."

"And then what?"

"Report to me at that tall sassafras tree across the road," he said, pointing in the direction of the tallest tree. "When we know how many, we'll select the sickest to ride in the wagons to the ferry."

Knowing that Night Hawk had little authority until they actually reached the embarkation site, she said, "Will the soldiers allow it?"

"If we take the supplies out and carry them on our backs."

Night Hawk walked away as Tansee returned. Soon Laurel saw him on the pony, making a path through the hundreds of people, still closely guarded by the soldiers.

A few minutes later Laurel gave each boy a loving hug. "Black Moccasin, Deer Stalker, wake up. Tansee has our breakfast ready."

Redbird smiled shyly at her brother while the more ebullient Kama′mă stared from one boy to the other and said, "Where did you two come from?"

"New Echota," Deer Stalker replied, causing the little girls to giggle.

Laurel smiled and Tansee laughed. Walini′ laughed, too. It was good to be together again.

As soon as the meager breakfast was over and Laurel was ready for the day, she began the task of walking through her section of camp. Some of the people spoke only Cherokee, while others spoke English as well as she. But everywhere she went, she was appalled at the number of unhealthy people—from the very old ones to small babies, lying listlessly in their mothers' arms.

She had no pen, no paper to record their names. So it was a lesson in remembrance, with only a sharp rock to mark the number on the pieces of soft tree bark that she carried in her hands. But as Laurel progressed she realized she could never remember all their names and resorted to using berry dye to identify the sick, like the mark of Cain upon their foreheads. The women who were eminently expecting babies received a special mark of their own; for they would still be able to walk until the time of delivery came upon them.

But one old woman refused to be marked. "No. I will not have the mark of death on my head," she said. "For the raven mocker will see it and take me before my time."

Understanding the ancient beliefs, Laurel replied, "But this sign is a good one. It will help to save you from the raven mocker."

Only then did the woman submit to the mark on her forehead.

By the time the people were ready to move out, the wagons had been filled with the most severely ill. But many of the others were forced to walk, their packs strapped upon their backs.

For Laurel, seeing Two Feathers coming toward her with his family, the reunion was a joyous one. "I see that you have been busy in the last few years, Two Feathers," she teased.

His eyes showed his love for Laurel. Relinquishing his wife and adopted sons to her care, Two Feathers left them and joined Night Hawk at the head of the procession.

At the Parker house Lulu also prepared to leave. But she was merely going back to the Carter settlement to visit her parents—and to take care of a little matter that would concern Rebecca.

"I hate to see you go," Julius said, holding on to her gloved hand while she waited for Kepp to bring around the carriage.

"I'll be back before you miss me," she said, raising her face for his good-bye kiss.

When the carriage arrived, he helped her into it, closed

the door with the MacDonald crest still emblazoned on it, and then stood in the circular drive to watch until the vehicle disappeared.

"There goes a fine-lookin' woman, Rebecky."

"Yes, Pa."

Rebecca had waited month after month, knowing that Lulu would get even with her in her own good time. She'd seen it in her eyes, even though Lulu had never said a word. Because of it Rebecca had even lost her appetite, and now she was only a shadow of her former self. Her pa had been pleased to see her less fat, but she knew that it was nothing but worry that had done it.

With Lulu gone for several days, though, she could relax. Tonight she wouldn't even have to push the piece of furniture against her bedroom door, as she'd done every night since Lulu had come home from the grave.

Inside the carriage Lulu also relaxed. God, it was good to get away for a few days by herself. It had been so boring with Julius lately. He wasn't nearly the lover he'd been at first, and sometimes he couldn't do it at all.

One night, lying in bed, unsatisfied, she began to think of Ned. And that's when she'd come up with a plan that would make everybody happy, except Rebecca. Or Julius, if he found out. But she'd see to it that he never did.

"Julius, I've been thinking," she had said.

"About what, love?"

She ignored the embarrassment in his voice. "About the property that Indian left over the ridge."

He breathed a sigh of relief at the turn in the conversation.

"Well, it's already been drawn in the lottery. Only, the owner ain't claimed it yet."

"That's exactly what I was thinking. He might be willing to sell it to you."

"But I already got more'n enough land to manage, Lulu."

"No, not for *us.* Actually I was thinking what a nice wedding present it would be for Rebecca and her husband."

"Well, that ain't likely, the way she's goin'."

"But there's a nice boy over at the Carter settlement. Honest and hardworking. Single, too. I'll bet if I just happened to mention the land and house that you'd given Rebecca, he'd be mighty interested in her."

"You think so? What's his name?"

"Ned Bates."

"How could they get together?"

"We could invite him to come back here on a visit with Mama and Papa. Then let nature take its course."

"That's a good idea, Lulu. I'll have to check into that first thing tomorrow at the land office."

"And we could have another party. Mama and Papa would love to meet some of our rich neighbors."

Now, while the carriage continued on its way, Lulu thought of that earlier discussion with Julius. It had produced what she wanted. He had bought the property. She would just have to persuade Ned that marrying Rebecca was what he wanted, too.

Lulu wrapped the fur rug around herself and began to think of her secret trysts in the past with Ned. The well-sprung carriage swayed gently from side to side, and the polished wheels turned steadily as Cloud Maker and Sundance raced toward the Carter settlement.

Chapter 30

At the landing John Ross watched the wagons rolling into position. He saw the thousand faces, solemn with the knowledge that they were leaving their beloved homeland forever. His heart ached for the people as each savored one last glance of sacred cedar, red clay earth, and ancient waters that had pulsed with life as long as any could remember.

John had waited to oversee the departure and say good-bye to each detachment. This was the last—except for his own family and the two hundred of those too ill and feeble to make the trip with the rest.

He had done his best, negotiating with Washington for the necessities to help prevent unneeded hardship. But already the birds were flying south, and winter was fast approaching. It was not a good time for the weakened and demoralized people to be traveling.

The whips of the drivers, the sound of oxen and horses were temporarily hushed as, in a body, the people looked toward their principal chief, who stood on a makeshift platform.

Holding his arms upward in supplication, John began a prayer for their safe journey. His voice lifted on the wind and touched the hearts of everyone who heard. When he had finished, the military bugle sounded. Then, as soldiers urged the convoy forward, the whips of the drivers and the sound of wagon wheels began again.

Night Hawk and Two Feathers, commissioned by John as the Cherokee leaders of the detachment, rode again at the head of the procession. Laurel, whom he had designated as the official interpreter, walked with Tansee, Black Moccasin, Deer Stalker, and the two older girls at the side of one of the wagons directly behind. They had given up their places to others weaker than they, while Agitsi′ took her turn watching over the children.

Laurel's role of leadership was in keeping with earlier Cherokee tradition, where women warriors had fought beside the men, and a few women had served as principal chiefs of the Nation.

With the landing still visible behind them, the children kept waving good-bye. "One day I hope to return," Black Moccasin said wistfully to Laurel, "to find the grave of my mother and father."

With the brilliance of the late October sun overhead, the wagons, holding the children, the sick and elderly, the cooking pots and blankets, rattled on while the dust gathered like a red plague around them. When they turned north, away from the river, a loud clap of thunder sounded from the cloudless blue sky. It turned into a steady rumble, providing a voice to the small spiral of dark smoke that became visible, touched the ground, and disappeared again into the still-cloudless sky. Then the thunder ceased.

Two Feathers and all those behind bowed their heads. For a moment the Great Spirit had spoken, showing his displeasure at the way his people had been treated.

More than twelve hundred walked directly ahead of them, following the same route to McMinnville and on to

Nashville, in their treacherous journey through the Cumberland Mountains.

Beyond the mountains lay the great rivers, with the Ohio and Mississippi formidable enemies. But few could think that far ahead. Sufficient to them were the anguish, the hardship of the next weeks.

The wagons continued to roll, jolting the riders. Some people continued to walk, herded like sheep by the soldiers on horseback. As one old woman, too weak to continue, fell to her knees, a soldier left his place in line and rode toward her.

Instead of dismounting to help her, he said, "Get up. I know what you're doing—pretending you're sick so you can try to escape."

His voice rose in a loud warning to those around her. "Not one of you will be allowed to go back home. You'll either keep going, or you'll be buried by the side of the road. Make up your minds which it'll be."

The old woman did not understand. Laurel, walking back, glared at the soldier as she spoke softly in Cherokee. "Come, my mother. You can ride in the wagon up front."

Deer Stalker took her pack. But as Laurel was attempting to help the woman up, Tansee appeared at her side. "Here, she's nothin' but skin and bones. I can carry her as easy as a sack of corn meal."

Big Tansee reached down and lifted the woman in her arms. She followed Laurel back to the wagon, where Agitsi′ moved the small children to make room for her.

Late in the day they were finally allowed to stop, to cook their food and make camp for the night.

Tansee received their food supply distributed by the commissary agent. Their group now numbered fourteen, including the old woman and a little girl who seemed to be alone, except for a pet duck that she had held all the way from the landing.

"Look, Laurel," Tansee said. "We have corn meal and beef—not that awful weevilly flour and rancid salt pork we've been eatin' for the past five months."

Agitsi´ also examined the supplies. And she sounded even more excited than Tansee. "We've got coffee and sugar, too. I'll go to the spring for water so we can boil some right away."

"Take Billy and Deer Stalker to help you," Laurel suggested.

"I'd like to go, too," Black Moccasin said.

"But you're captain of the firewood," Laurel reminded him. "And Ina´li can be your helper."

"What do you want *us* to do, Laurel?" Redbird asked, speaking for herself and Kama´mă.

"Watch after Walini´ and..." She hesitated. "What do they call you?" she asked, turning to the small child with the duck.

The child merely shrugged.

"Well, we'll have to call you *something.*"

"What about Carrying Duck?" Kama´mă suggested.

"That's appropriate," Laurel answered, smiling.

That evening, with Night Hawk and Two Feathers joining them, Laurel tried hard to pretend that they were merely taking a short trip, perhaps to visit relatives. But inwardly she knew better. Eight had already died since that morning. They had been allowed to stop only long enough to bury them. Then they were herded on.

Night Hawk, sitting by the fire and savoring his coffee, as all were doing, glanced from time to time at Walini´, seated on Laurel's lap. But he made no further attempt to make friends with his daughter.

That night, as they slept around the campfires, each had his own blanket, proof of their principal chief's concern for their comfort. But he could not govern the winds that swept from the mountains, bringing an icy chill and the threat of an early winter.

The next several days brought a scarcity of firewood, for as they traveled, only stumps of trees where forests had been greeted them. A sudden rain, so common in the higher elevations, turned the road into a sticky morass, with the teams of oxen slipping and sliding in their efforts to pull their loads ever upward into the mountains.

On a late afternoon, cold and gray, with the threat of more rain, one of the soldiers began to scout the area for trees. Seeing a fine stand that had not been touched by the thousands going ahead of them, he rode back to get the wagon that carried the axes and, with the other soldiers guarding them, he enlisted some of the strongest-looking men to go into the grove.

The small group stood before the trees, axes in their hands. But they refused to cut down a single tree.

The officer became angry. "What's the matter with you, you lazy good-for-nothings? Do you think *we're* going to do your work for you? Start cutting down the trees immediately."

Still, they refused.

In exasperarion he turned to one of his fellow soldiers. "Go and get the interpreter. I can't seem to get through to these savages."

Moments later, Laurel appeared. "What is it, Lieutenant?"

"These men have refused my orders. Tell them I will not tolerate their laziness."

Laurel spoke with one of the men, nodded, and then looked up at the officer. "They apologize to you for causing trouble. But you see, the cedar is sacred to us, and they will not harm a single one. But Little Eagle says if you find other trees, they will be happy to cut them down."

"There's not time for that. It'll be dark soon."

"Then we will do without supper and a warm fire tonight," Laurel said. "They will not cut down these trees, no matter what you say."

Still angry, the lieutenant rode off, leaving the problem to the corporal in charge of the ax wagon.

After another quick consultation with Little Eagle, Laurel turned to the corporal. "Little Eagle says that a quarter mile back he remembers seeing some trees that would be suitable. Why don't you get a larger brigade to help, and several other wagons to bring the wood back to camp?"

"That sounds like a good idea," the corporal replied, relieved that Laurel had come up with an alternative. In a confiding voice he said, "You know, my grandpa won't cut down a cedar, either. We got one standin' in the middle of a cornfield. Won't anything grow around it, but Grandpa don't seem to mind."

That night the fires in the camp were meager, with many sharing the same cooking fire. But the experience that day helped shape their priorities. When Night Hawk and Two Feathers heard Laurel telling of the problem, they realized what they must do. Seeking out Little Eagle and the corporal in charge of the wagon with the axes, they put their plan into motion.

By the next day the assigned Cherokees became aware of each tree along the way that might be suitable for firewood. The lieutenant was not happy about these men traveling out of convoy, going ahead to cut down trees. But then, by evening, he realized that none had escaped, as he'd feared. He grudgingly conceded that their job was a necessary part of the people's survival.

But once again the lieutenant was faced with the Cherokees' stubbornness. They would not travel on the Sabbath. It was a day of worship and honor to their Maker. And so, as he stood helplessly by on that first Sabbath and looked toward the menacing sky, he saw them gathering into small groups—Moravian, Baptist, Methodist. One of the men had smuggled a Cherokee Bible with him—one of the thousands that had been printed by the Cherokee printing press at New Echota.

Lieutenant Wright listened to the reading for a while, but understanding none of the words, he walked back to his own campsite and removed a bottle of whiskey from his saddlebag. With the sound of hymn singing in the background, he proceeded to get drunk.

The bad weather continued. The deaths continued. Each day they lost time stopping to bury their dead. And the physician traveling with the group became extremely busy, administering his medicine to the ill, in the hope that the few grains of opium would help.

But the old woman in the wagon with the small children seemed much worse by each hour. More drastic measures were needed. When they stopped, he took out his lance and cup to bleed her.

Two Feathers suddenly appeared at the fire where the woman lay. "The old mother does not need your white man's medicine," he said.

The physician protested. "But she will die without it."

"She will also die if you drain her essence from her."

"Bleeding is an accepted medical procedure," the doctor said, his voice haughty at being challenged. "Please move aside so I may continue my treatment."

But the old woman summoned enough strength to protest. "I do not want to be bled," she said, looking up at the physician.

The physician glared at Two Feathers, then put his lance and cup back into his medical bag. He would never get used to the superstitions of these poor Indians. "When we get to Nashville, I will make an official complaint at the Indian Agency against you."

Two Feathers ignored the physician. He settled on his haunches and began to speak to the old woman while the physician left in a huff.

What was he to do if the people refused his services? He had been paid a goodly sum to travel with them as their physician. Sighing at their backward ways, he finally decided he would have to resort to other means of treatment.

Less than a mile away, Howard Trask, owner of the ferry at the Sequatchie River, sat and counted his money. He was already rich. He had made a smart move with the first detachment of Indians that had approached the ferry—charging twice the amount he usually did for them to cross. Their leaders had been bewildered at the sudden price change, but in the end it had done them no good to protest.

"If you can find a better way to get across, then take it."

But of course he'd known there was no other way within miles. And they'd had to pay his price, even though they grumbled about it.

For days the wagons and people had kept coming. And he'd kept charging the same exorbitant fee. "I hear there're thousands on the way, Margaret," he'd crowed to his wife. "Do you realize how much money we'll have after they've all crossed over?"

Margaret hesitated. "Do you think it's right, charging the Indians so much more than anybody else, Howard?"

"Of course it is. I heard it's the government that's payin' for it, anyway."

But the standard fees were the ones John Ross had figured in the per capita expense of the removal. The government was willing to advance him only that amount of money, which would be subtracted later from the annuities owed the Cherokee Nation.

Hearing the approach of the final detachment, Howard quickly hid his money box and hurried to the ferry.

Chapter 31

"Seventy-three cents for each wagon, and twelve and a half cents for each horse, pony, and ox." Howard stood before his ferry and calmly demanded the money before any would be allowed to cross.

"That's extortion, Mr. Trask," the wagon master complained.

"Take it or leave it. All the others that went by paid the same fee."

Lieutenant Wright, slightly inebriated, did not feel up to arguing. He merely wanted to keep the detachment moving. "Pay it, Mr. Walker," he ordered. "So we can make a few more miles before dark."

The crossing was a mammoth undertaking, with stubborn oxen refusing to move onto the flimsy rafts. Horses reared and threatened to trample the children and old ones on foot. The scene was one of potential disaster. Night Hawk and Two Feathers did their best, marshaling the people into smaller groups away from the ferry while the drivers brought the wagons into position and waited their turns to cross.

One hour passed, then another, with the sounds of whips and recalcitrant animals echoing along the river, where a few white settlers had gathered on a hill to watch this mass migration to the west.

"Walini′," Agitsi′ called, all at once missing the small child. "Where are you?"

"She was here a minute ago," Kama′mă said. "With Carrying Duck."

"But Carrying Duck is gone, too," Agitsi′ said, suddenly fearful. She had taken her eyes from them for only a moment.

"Maybe they went down to the river," Redbird suggested.

Agitsi′ frantically began looking for the two little girls, calling to them as she walked.

After searching through the groups and walking for quite a while, with Redbird and Kama′mă following, she headed in the direction of the riverbank. "There's Walini′," she said. "Now if we can find Carrying Duck, too..." She began to walk rapidly toward the child in the distance, intent on scolding her for disappearing.

For the past half hour Laurel had been farther down the road with an old woman who was dying. The noise of a runaway wagon invaded the somber scene, causing Laurel to look up.

What she saw caused her to cry out. With the runaway wagon bearing down on her, a smiling Walini′ began to cross the road.

The child was too far away for Laurel or anyone else to reach her in time. "Tskĭ-lĭ!" Laurel screamed.

Night Hawk, hearing Laurel's voice, looked back from his position at the ferry. He saw Laurel frantically pointing toward the road. Looking in the direction she was pointing, Night Hawk's blood ran cold.

Urging his pony into a gallop, he raced down the road in a direct collision course with the oncoming wagon. Between them was his own little daughter, unaware of the danger.

It happened so fast, the wagon bearing down, Night Hawk racing toward it. Laurel's vision became blocked by the wagon and the dust. She began to run along the side of the road, toward Walini′, not knowing what she would see, not knowing whether Night Hawk had reached the child in time to save her.

The runaway wagon continued, still out of control. With people scattering in all directions, the horses swerved, missed the ferry, and plunged down the bank. As the dust began to clear Laurel saw the limp child lying in Night Hawk's arms. Heartbroken, she sat down at the side of the road and began to cry.

"She's all right, Laurel."

She lifted her tearstained face and saw the little girl astride the pony in front of Night Hawk. Relieved and angry at the same time, Laurel said, "Oh, Walini′, why did you go off by yourself? You were supposed to stay with the others."

"We took Duck to swim," she answered.

Night Hawk looked at his daughter in a stern manner. "You must obey your father from now on," he said. "You are not to go off by yourself or with Carrying Duck ever again. Do you understand, Walini′?"

"Yes, Papa."

Laurel and Night Hawk looked at each other. This was the first time she had given any indication that she knew who Night Hawk was.

Agitsi′, with Carrying Duck firmly in tow, arrived. "I'm sorry, Laurel," she said. "I turned my back for only one moment..."

"It's all right," Laurel answered, seeing the woman's distress. "The children are both safe. We'll just have to watch them a little more carefully from now on."

Later, with everyone on the other side of the ferry, the detachment pulled out. The "doggery," a small boat that traveled up and down the river to sell sweet cakes, whiskey, and more notorious services, also pulled out from its anchorage and continued upriver.

The people had been told not to drink the river water; for cholera was still widespread. But as they traveled mile after mile, hunting for a healthier source, the casks lashed to the sides of the wagons ran dry. Many of the thirstier ones were sorry that they had listened and not availed themselves of the river water.

"What does it matter?" one said to his friend. "We will die anyway."

And it seemed true. For by the time they stopped, ten of those who had crossed the ferry awaited burial.

That night, as they lay by the campfire, Night Hawk and Two Feathers heard the noise and the drunken revelry in another section of camp. Although tired from the day's journey, both got up.

Laurel, also awakening, said, "What is it?"

"They must have gotten whiskey from somewhere," Night Hawk said. "Try to go back to sleep, if you can."

Agitsi´ also awoke. Sitting up, she rubbed her eyes. "Two Feathers?"

"I'll be back later," he assured her, leaving the campfire with Night Hawk.

As the noise grew louder Laurel turned to Agitsi´. "The men are drunk," she said. "Cousin John and the council specifically asked that no one sell them any spirits. But it looks as if no more attention has been paid to that request than some of the others."

Much later the noise finally abated. Night Hawk and Two Feathers returned to the fire. But on the next morning it took much longer to break camp and start on the trail again. The soldiers had gotten as drunk as the Indians.

By noon it began to rain, a cold drizzle that promised to turn into sleet. Many of the people, who had been taken from their homes with only the summer clothes on their backs, were not prepared for the cold. Some were barefoot, while others wore only the summer moccasins that now became wet with mud and rain.

A few of the people on horseback, still with the berry-dye marks upon their foreheads, lagged behind. When one of the old men, too weak even to ride, seemed likely to fall off, Laurel put him in a wagon and took over the pony. Astride in front was Redbird, who had asked to ride for a short way.

"Look, Laurel," she said. "There's snow on the mountain peaks."

"Yes, I see." Laurel drew the army blanket closer, trying to protect them both from the rain and the cold. But she still shivered from the wind that gusted and made an eerie, howling sound as it swept over them and penetrated the thin blanket.

"When we get to Nashville in several days, Lewis will be waiting for us, with warm clothes and more blankets."

"But I'm not cold, Laurel," Redbird assured her.

"That's strange. I'm freezing." Laurel frowned. "Here, let me feel your forehead." She took her hand and raised it to Redbird's head. She expected her forehead to be chilled. Instead, it was extremely hot.

In alarm, she said, "Turn around, Redbird. Look at me."

The girl did so. Pink splotches marred her complexion, giving her the appearance of a small, spotted trout. "Darling, I think you have measles."

"I do?"

"We'll get the physician to take a look as soon as we stop."

"Am I going to die, like the other children at the stockade?" Redbird asked, with little emotion in her voice.

"Of course not. You'll be sick for the next week or so," she conceded, "But I'll take good care of you."

The Cherokees had no medicine for the white man's diseases that now plagued them—measles, whooping cough, dysentery, and consumption. They had been healthy people, living in relative isolation in a healthy land of fresh breezes, good water, and adequate food. They had prided themselves on cleanliness of body and mind, as a gentle agrarian people.

Only when they had been crowded into the pens, allowed no change of clothing, no soap, and none of the food they'd been used to, had they fallen ill.

Laurel put her arm around Redbird and urged the pony forward. Directly before them lay a tall mountain ridge, with a narrow trail winding upward and disappearing into the clouds.

The supply wagons and the ones carrying the sick had to be double-teamed to get them up the steep incline. With the freezing rain coming down in a heavy downpour, the chore was almost overwhelming.

Along the trail, at regular intervals, fires had been made so that the people walking could warm themselves for a brief time and then travel on. Wild animals, with predatory eyes the color of yellow quartz, watched from their hidden places in the rocks and waited for a misstep, an accident that would give them their next meal. It did not matter if it were an injured animal or a child losing his footing to disappear down the mountainside.

Finally, they passed over the ridge, but by the time the detachment stopped and Laurel was able to locate the physician, Redbird had become wan and listless.

"She will have to be kept warm and dry tonight," the physician said, knowing that it was easier to recommend the treatment than to carry it out.

Night Hawk and Two Feathers were too busy to help. Laurel turned to Black Moccasin. "Do you think you and Deer

Stalker might be able to find a shelter somewhere in the rocks?"

"We will look, Laurel," Black Moccasin said.

"Don't go far. And remember to be careful. I would not want anything to happen to either one of you."

Billy and Ina′li helped Agitsi′ with the cooking fire, and Kama′mă helped her prepare the food. The old woman was still a care. But Walini′ and Carrying Duck, properly reprimanded, stayed nearby. Laurel was not sure how long their penitence would last.

A half hour later, the two older boys were back. "We found a place in the rocks," Deer Stalker said, the excitement showing in his dark eyes. "It's not very large, but I think it will do."

"It's very steep to get to," Black Moccasin added.

Laurel followed them back to see. Examining it, she realized that the shelter was only large enough for the children and the old woman. The rest of them would have to sleep in front of the ledge.

With the boys' help, Laurel brought Redbird to the shelter. "As soon as everyone has finished eating, lead them all here."

"But what about you? Aren't you and Redbird going to eat?"

"I'm not hungry," Redbird said in a weak voice. "Only thirsty."

"Ask Agitsi′ to bring our share when she comes later." Laurel lifted Redbird's head and gave her a drink of water from the wooden flask that Night Hawk had carved when he was in the stockade.

When Night Hawk and Two Feathers had made their rounds of the camp, making sure the horses, ponies, and oxen were secure and fed, they carefully wound their way back to the rock ledge.

Seeing that Laurel had given up her blanket to cover the

children, Night Hawk moved over, gathered Laurel close to him, and for the first time they went to sleep together.

She was aware of his strong, lean body curved around her own. And she remembered his words eons before, when they had sat under the tree at New Echota and she had rebuffed his avowal of love, because of Edward.

"You will not be able to wait much longer, Laurel. Your response tells me that you are already a woman, with womanly feelings."

Feeling this strange, new pull to him, Laurel suddenly realized that Edward no longer mattered. She had given him up that day at Ross's Landing, when she had started on the long journey with her people.

In Night Hawk's arms she went to sleep. And for the first time in months she slept for most of the night.

By the next morning, when she opened her eyes, snow covered the army blanket wrapped around them. As far as Laurel could see, the mountains and the valleys were white. The seasons had paid no attention to the calendar. It was now winter, and they were hundreds of miles from their destination.

Slowly removing herself from Night Hawk's arms, Laurel crawled under the ledge to check on Redbird.

Chapter 32

As soon as he'd seen the last detachment off, John Ross returned to Red Hill to make preparations for his own family to leave for the west. Included in this group were his twenty-one-year-old son, Allen, and his sisters' families.

They would be traveling the same overland route as those ahead of them. But the pace would be much slower; for John was also taking with him the last remnant of the Nation—two hundred of the ill and feeble, unable to make the journey without help.

It was appropriate for the principal chief to be the last to leave his ancient homeland. All his adult life he had worked for the good of the Cherokee Nation. But when he'd fought by Jackson's side in the Creek War, he'd had no inkling that it would be the same man who would ultimately drive his people from their homes.

John stared down at the stacks of papers, manuscripts, correspondence with presidents, and treaties that waited to be packed. Beside him was the official history of the Cherokee Nation—all that was left of a vast empire of rivers and valleys, gold mines and orchards, schools and missions, mercantile centers, courts, and council houses. The history of freedom and progress of a sovereign nation lay on the floor before him, in a rude log house that had, itself, become a symbol of loss.

"Quatie, have you seen the Hicks manuscripts?" he inquired.

"They're beside the trunk, John," Quatie said, pointing near the door. "Jane and Allen sorted them last night."

Taking a leather thong, John bound them together and placed the bundle in the trunk. Carefully, he marked each consignment, until all the papers from the floor were gone. Then he closed the lid and locked the trunk.

"Father, are we almost ready to leave?" Silas asked.

"Yes. Only a few minutes more, and then we'll be on our way."

"We want to say good-bye to Chota," George said, speaking of their little calf.

"I'll go with them to the barn," Allen offered.

"And I'll go, too," Jane said.

John nodded. "And Allen?"

"Yes, Father?"

"You can bring the wagon when you come back."

Once the children were gone, he turned to Quatie, who sat in a rocking chair by the hearth. "I wish we could take your spinning wheel, but there isn't room."

"It's all right, John. I'll manage without it." She rose from the chair and walked toward him.

He put his arms around her and kissed her. "You've been a wonderful wife to me, Quatie—never complaining all these years. But I know how difficult it is for you to leave everything behind."

"I have *you*, and I have the children. That's all that matters."

Holding on to her hands, John stepped back and looked into Quatie's gentle brown eyes. "But I pledge to you, if God wills it, I'll build you another house, even finer than the one we lost. We'll start over together—like Abraham and Sarah in a new land."

She smiled, but her heart was sad. She was tired—almost too tired to begin the journey. But her husband needed her—as never before.

Soon the door opened, causing the fire on the hearth to protest against the invading wind, as Silas and George ran inside. "Father! Father! There're all these people standing around, on the other side of the road," Silas said. "Are they waiting to tell you good-bye?"

John smiled ruefully. "No, Silas. All our friends have gone."

"Then, who *are* they?" George asked.

John repeated Quatie's words. "It doesn't matter, sons. Now get your coats on and climb into the wagon."

A few feet away from the barn, Jude and his two nephews, Skeeter and Roy, who had remained in the Nation to pillage and steal at every turn, began to lead the livestock out of the enclosed area. They had come early that morning, keeping everyone else from the animals, until the wagon had pulled to the front of the house.

With the law continually after them, they knew that it was safer to take the livestock and sell it, then move on. They couldn't afford to join the people who were now milling about and arguing who would take possession of the house once the Ross family was gone.

"I got here first," one man said. "So the house is mine."

"Not if I get in it first," another challenged.

"Then we'll just fight for it."

"You'll have to fight more than Grady for it," a third man said, pushing through the crowd to face the other two. He was a large man with broad shoulders and muscular arms. Already his fists were clenched for action.

Grady, a much smaller man, took one look at the man

who was well known for winning at fist fights. "Maybe we can draw straws for it," he suggested.

"No, I say we fight for it."

The crowd, so involved with watching the ensuing fight, barely took note when the wagon pulled out of the yard.

As they traveled slowly down the road George turned his head. "Look, Mother. That man is taking Chota away."

"Yes, George. I see."

Jane, feeling sorry for her little brother, said, "Let's play a game. Can you name the first city we'll reach?"

"McMinnville." After he'd answered, he looked back again, his mind still on his pet calf.

"But I don't see why we have to go at all," Silas said. "I'd rather stay."

"All right, Silas," Jane said, trying to continue the game, despite the boys' lack of enthusiasm. "Can you spell Arkansas?"

"Sure, that's easy."

Gradually Silas and George became interested in the game. And before they'd gone far, the two also began to think of questions.

"Now I have one for Allen," Silas said. "Why is Rabbit called the trickster?"

"Because he's a tricky fellow," his older brother said quickly, leaning over and tickling Silas, who began to laugh.

John and Quatie, riding in front, with their children, the trunk, and a few personal possessions in the back, looked at each other. Their children seemed much more resilient than they. Although sad to leave their home, they had not yet realized the full extent of their loss. But John and Quatie knew that the grandeur of former days had vanished forever in the howling of the wind.

High on a snow-covered ridge a few miles from Nashville, Laurel and the others were getting ready to break camp.

The wagons were in position, and everyone was hurrying to put out the fires, round up the children, and secure the cooking pots, together with the food that had been cooked that morning to last them the rest of the day.

Redbird was still ill, but so far she was the only child in the small group to come down with measles. But Laurel, knowing how fast the sickness could spread, continued to examine the children each morning for the telltale spots.

The sick old man, who had taken a place in the wagon serveral days before, had not survived, and so Redbird was going to ride in his stead. As Laurel helped her toward the vehicle, Carrying Duck appeared and pulled at the hem of Laurel's dress.

"Have you seen Duck?"

Laurel shook her head. "Not since early this morning."

"I can't find her anywhere," the child said, the tears beginning to spill down her cheeks.

Night Hawk, riding by to check on the line, stopped when he heard the child crying. "What's wrong?"

"Carrying Duck can't find her pet," Laurel replied.

He looked at the child. "Would you like to ride with me? You can look for Duck while I finish checking on the wagons.

"Yes."

Night Hawk leaned down and hoisted the child onto the pony. "I'll bring her back before we start out."

"Papa, I want to ride, too," Walini´called from the wagon.

"Next time, Walini´."

Falling Star, one of the young women from a nearby wagon, stood and watched Night Hawk ride off. After several minutes she walked over to Laurel and said, "Your husband is very handsome."

"Oh, Tskĭ-lĭ isn't my husband."

"He isn't?" The young woman's voice took on a new eagerness.

"No. He's Walini's father."

Laurel thought little of the brief interchange; for she became busy checking the campsite to make sure everything had been packed.

Soon Night Hawk reappeared with a bawling Carrying Duck.

"What's the matter?" Laurel asked. "Didn't you find Duck?"

Night Hawk's face was somber. "We did, but it was too late. We saw the feathers by the cooking fire."

Carrying Duck, still crying, reached out her arms for Laurel. "The soldier ate her."

"Oh, Carrying Duck, I'm so sorry."

She held the child, who refused to be consoled.

The signal was given to move out. Laurel turned Carrying Duck over to Tansee and mounted her pony, to ride alongside the wagon.

On the next day they finally arrived in Nashville, where Lewis, true to his word, met them with fresh supplies—food, bear and wool blankets, and shoes for those whose feet were bleeding from the cold.

After a day spent reshoeing the horses, repairing the wagon wheels, and washing clothes, they crossed the Cumberland River and continued in a northwesterly direction toward Hopkinsville, Kentucky. Once again they were charged exorbitant prices, which they had to pay. The news had spread that there was money to be made.

Several days later, with the weather no better, they came upon a fresh grave at the side of the road. Poles with streamers surrounded the grave, and a large rock had been marked with a name, indicating that the one who had passed on to the other side had been greatly loved.

The procession stopped and Two Feathers dismounted. In sadness, he saw that it was the grave of White Path, the beloved chief who had been in charge of one of the other detachments. His people had marked his grave so that others coming later would see and remember him.

Two Feathers' voice rose in a prayer for his spirit. And when the wagons began to roll again, the people were silent as wave after wave passed by, reverently noting the final resting place of one of their beloved chieftains.

That evening Night Hawl was absent from the cooking fire. Laurel kept looking for him, even after Agitsi´ and Tansee had divided the food for the children and the adults.

"I suppose you'll have to save Night Hawk's portion," Laurel said. "Something must have delayed him."

"Oh, he won't be eating with us tonight," Agitsi´ said.

"No. He's been invited by another family to share their meal," Tansee added. "He didn't tell you?"

"No."

Laurel did not know why she should feel so abandoned. It wasn't as if Night Hawk were not free to do as he pleased. She began to think of her earlier conversation with the pretty young woman at the wagon. "Your husband is very handsome." So now she had an idea where Night Hawk may have gone. In an effort not to show that she cared, Laurel paid much closer attention to the children.

As they wrapped their blankets around themselves and settled down to go to sleep, they asked Laurel to tell them a story.

"What would you like to hear?"

"The one about Rabbit and Tar Wolf," Black Moccasin said.

Lying down beside them, Laurel began: "Once upon a time, when all the streams and rivers had dried up, the thirsty animals got together to decide what to do.

"'We should dig a well,' said Owl. And the other animals agreed, all except Rabbit. He was a lazy fellow and said,

'The dew on the grass is enough for me.' So he sat back and watched the others do the work.

"But when the water in the well kept getting lower and Rabbit kept getting sleeker, Fox said, 'That tricky rabbit must be stealing our water at night.'

"'But how can we stop him?' one of the other animals asked. 'We can't stay up all night.'"

Laurel glanced toward Walini′ and Carrying Duck. They were already asleep. But she continued the story for the others.

"'We will make a tar wolf to scare away the thief.'

"That night when Rabbit came to steal water, he looked at Tar Wolf, who guarded the well. 'Get away, or I'll kick you.' By the time the animals arrived the next morning, they found Rabbit, stuck fast to Tar Wolf. Now they had proof that he'd been stealing their water. But when they cut him loose to punish him, Rabbit ran away into the nearby thicket."

"You left out some of the story," Kama′mă complained.

"I know. But it's late. We all need to go to sleep."

By the time Night Hawk returned to their camp, he found that Laurel was not in her usual place. She had gone to sleep with the children gathered around her. So he wrapped his blanket about him and quietly lay down, alone.

That night Laurel dreamed that she was at home with her mother and father. The fire on the hearth blazed with warmth. The aroma of roasted venison and pumpkin pie wafted through the house, all the way to the parlor.

With the sun bursting over the mountains in brilliant, jagged rays, Laurel awoke, smiling. But as she looked around her the dream had vanished. She was cold. And her stomach rumbled with hunger.

Chapter 33

At the Parker house Lulu took one last admiring glance at her dining table, already set for the dinner party that night. She had done it herself, for she didn't trust Elvira to handle the delicate porcelain china and the sterling silver flatware that had come with the house. She hadn't been sure about the forks, but she'd found a book in the library that had showed her where to put them.

The fine white linen tablecloth, embroidered at each corner with green and yellow leaves and berries, had a dozen napkins to match. She had allowed Elvira to wash and iron them, but only while she watched to make sure the woman didn't scorch them.

Julius had thought she was making too much of the party, but Lulu knew better. Ned and her mama and papa were not the only guests. The rich banker, Mr. Brogdon, was coming, too, all the way from Calhoun with his wife, Derusha, and their good friends, Mr. and Mrs. Clyde Overby. She was sorry she didn't know the wife's name. But she would learn it soon enough so that by the end of the evening, or maybe by the next day when they left, she would have become good friends with both women.

Upstairs, the extra bedrooms were ready, with wood already laid for the fires, and the fine blankets and quilts covering the soft feather bedding.

Rebecca had protested giving up her room to the Brogdons. But Lulu had expected that. "You'll be in the attic for only one night, Rebecca."

"Well, I don't see why it can't be somebody else, like your mama and papa."

"The room's too small for two people. But at least Ned will be up there in the other room. You might thank me for that later, even though Julius doesn't think much of the idea."

"With Elvira sleepin' on the floor beside me, I don't think much of it, either."

"Well, try not to pout when Ned gets here. I wouldn't want you to make a liar out of me."

Remembering the earlier conversation, Lulu took the turkey feather duster and went into the front parlor. She wanted to make sure no ashes had fallen onto the hearth, spreading dust on the fine waxed finish of the mahogany furniture. At the doorway she stood for a moment, admiring the beautiful evergreen tree with the candles set in holders on the limbs. She'd never had a Christmas tree before. But she'd found a painting in one of the drawers of the desk. Evidently the former owners of the house had taken the custom from the Moravians at Spring Place. Although a Methodist, Lulu thought it was a fine idea—especially since nobody she knew had ever put one up before.

As Lulu inspected the tea table nearest the hearth she heard a carriage rolling into the yard. She ran to the window and looked out. Seeing Ned driving the little phaeton belonging to her mama and papa, she quickly hid the duster, called to Elvira, and then walked to the front door to greet them.

"I'm so glad you got here before dark," she called out. "Kepp, help Ned with the boxes, please."

Tilda Mae was so busy taking in the house and surroundings—the circular drive edged with mountain laurel, and the large, two-story house with its tall brick chimneys and sparkling leaded windows—that she stumbled on one of the steps. Obadiah steadied her and held her arm until she reached the door.

Lulu leaned over and kissed her mother. "I know you're both frozen to death. Come on in to the fire."

As they walked down the hallway she nodded in the direction of the black woman. "This is Elvira. She'll show Ned and Kepp where to take the luggage."

Tilda Mae, still speechless, followed Lulu into the parlor.

A moment later, when she heard the front door open again, Lulu turned. Seeing Ned, she said, "As soon as the things have been put in the rooms, come on downstairs. I'll try to find Rebecca for you."

He smiled a knowing smile. "All right, Lulu."

When Ned, Elvira, and Kepp had disappeared up the stairs and Lulu was alone with her mother and father, she said, "Well, what do you think of the house?"

Tilda Mae smiled. "It's beautiful. You sure did marry well, Lulu." She walked over to the large array of books on each side of the fireplace while Obadiah stood and examined the Christmas tree.

Taking a leather-bound volume from the shelf,Tilda Mae opened it and stared at the page. "It's too bad Julius can't read." She closed it and put it carefully back on the shelf.

"What do you call this, Lulu?" Obadiah asked.

"Why that's my Christmas tree, Papa. And after dinner tonight, I'm going to light all the candles."

"Ain't you afraid you might burn the house down?"

"The candles won't be lit that long, Papa. And we'll all be here to watch."

Realizing they'd come a long way, Lulu said, "I expect you'd like to go to your room and rest awhile. Elvira," she called to the woman, who had just come into the hall again, "will you show Mama and Papa upstairs?"

"Yes, ma'am."

They passed Ned on the staircase. Seeing Lulu alone, he joined her before the parlor hearth. Speaking in a low voice, he said, "Well, when do I get to see the girl?"

Lulu pretended to pout. "I thought you might want to spend some time with me first."

Ned laughed as he moved closer. "Why do you think I'm here in the first place?"

Lulu giggled as he reached out to draw her nearer, but hearing approaching steps, they both moved apart.

"Julius, come in and meet Ned Bates. He's just arrived with Mama and Papa."

"Mr. Parker, " Ned said, with an easy smile on his handsome face. "Lulu's been tellin' me you got a pretty daughter. I'm eager to meet her."

"Well, now, she ain't what I'd call pretty. More like she's passable. I tell you this so you won't be too disappointed."

"Now, Julius," Lulu teased. "Ned knows better than that."

Ned stood still while Julius eyed him, as if he might be buying a plow mule instead of a potential son-in-law. "Are you a hard worker?" he asked.

"Oh, yes, sir. I have to be."

"You drink or wench a lot?"

"Julius!" Lulu sounded embarrassed.

Ned didn't seem to mind the question. "I sometimes drink a little too much on Saturday night. But I work too hard to do the other. That doesn't mean I wouldn't like to. But I'm at the age where I'd most like a wife and family."

"Good! I don't want one of them teetotalin' Baptists for a son-in-law. Sounds like you and me might be able to do a little business."

"Now, Julius," Lulu said. "Ned hasn't even seen Rebecca."

"That's right, Mr. Parker. I won't be marryin' the wrong woman, even if she has *ten* farms."

Julius nodded. "You'll do all right, son."

Before Lulu had a chance to look for Rebecca, who, she knew, was off pouting somewhere, another carriage pulled up to the door. It was a fine vehicle, almost as beautiful as the one in the Parker barn. "There're the Brogdons now. Let's go out to meet them, Julius." Lulu put on her cloak and walked onto the porch.

With the other people arriving, Ned decided he'd rather go up to his room in the attic. He wasn't much for staying around and trying to talk with strangers. He'd have to be with them that night, and that was enough.

Besides, he hoped to run into Rebecca. He hadn't been quite truthful with her father. He'd already decided to marry her, regardless of what she looked like. He'd do anything to be close to Lulu again. The farm had only been an added incentive. But now he was anxious to see what kind of face he'd be waking up to every morning.

Downstairs, Lulu drew her other guests into the parlor. And this time she had Elvira bring the hot tea. As she served it Lulu said, "We'll have supper soon. But I thought maybe you'd like to get the chill off you with something hot."

"How kind of you, Mrs. Parker."

Lulu smiled and said, "Call me Louise. I feel as if we're already friends, with our husbands knowing each other."

"Then you must call me Derusha."

Lulu smiled. "More sugar, Mrs. Overby?"

"Yes, please."

The woman had not taken the hint. So Lulu continued to

call her Mrs. Overby.

She didn't seem nearly so friendly as Derusha. But that type never was –thin in the shank, with thin lips to match. Lulu wouldn't be surprised if she didn't stuff a few extra handkerchiefs in the bosom of her dress.

By the time Tilda Mae and Obadiah came downstairs again, they had changed their clothes, with Tilda Mae wearing her best winter dress with a brown shawl. Seeing guests in the parlor, the two hesitated in the hallway.

"Oh, Mama, come and join us for tea. And Papa, you might want to go into Julius's office. I think they have something a little stronger in there."

Obadiah, delighted at the thought of a little corn whiskey, walked down the hall, following the sound of the men's voices.

Tilda Mae was quiet, listening to her daughter making conversation with the two elegant-looking women. She was storing up every sentence, every detail to tell Ellie when they got home again.

"*Our* house is made of stone," Letha Overby commented, "with four brick chimneys. It keeps the heat in the winter, but it's nice and cool on the hottest days."

"Did you and your husband build the house?" Tilda Mae ventured.

A slight frown of annoyance crossed Letha's face. "No, it was already on the property."

"Obadiah thought about standin' for the lottery, too, but then we decided we liked where we were."

Lulu quickly interrupted. "More tea?"

"No, thank you, Louise," Derusha said. "And where is that, Mrs. Hanson?" she asked, returning to the conversation.

"Over near the Carter settlement. You may've heard of Jake and Ellie Dodge. They run a boardinghouse and a general store there. They're my best friends."

"No. I don't believe I know them. But my husband probably does."

Once the women had gone upstairs, Lulu cautioned her mother. "Mama, it might be best if you don't mention the lottery again. Or the Indians."

"I'm sorry, Lulu. I guess I'm not used to such elegant company. Ellie and I can say anything we want to each other, and no one takes offense."

"And that's the way it should be," Lulu agreed. "But I don't know these people very well, so I have to be careful what I say around them."

"I understand, Lulu."

Upstairs, Ned could hear someone moving around in the other bedroom. And then the tall pendulum clock began to strike the hour, signaling that it was time for supper.

Knowing that Rebecca was bound to come out of her room soon, Ned waited in the narrow third-story landing. He watched while her door opened and she began to walk along the narrow hall.

She was exactly as her father had described her—passable. No more, no less. Resigned to his fate, Ned turned and smiled. "You must be Rebecca," he said.

"Are you Lulu's friend?"

"Well, I'm Ned Bates," he admitted. "But I hope to be *your* friend."

Rebecca smiled at his answer. He sounded as if he didn't care much for Lulu.

He held out his arm for her. "You'd better be careful, walking down these steep stairs."

"Yes. I'm not used to them. My room is really on the second floor."

"I know. But your papa told me how nice you'd been, giving up your room for the Brogdons."

By the time they reached the dining room, Rebecca was completely smitten.

The dinner proceeded well and even Letha Overby was impressed. She narrowed her eyes to take another look at this Louise, dressed in her blue suit, with the rabbit fur trim. Usually she didn't care for pretty women, but she could see that this one was smart, too.

Although Ned seemed to notice only Rebecca, the other men at the table clearly enjoyed looking at Lulu. But she was appropriately sedate, to the other women's relief.

Far from considering the subject of the Indians taboo, the men frankly discussed the removal.

"Van Buren gave his president's message to the Senate on December fourth," Overby said. "I read a copy of his speech. He said all the Indians have reached the territory without hardship, and they're now spending the winter in their new homes."

Lulu took special note. Not realizing that Van Buren was in error and that not a single detachment had arrived, she was convinced it was now safe to write Ellie and Jake about Daisy.

The next day Tilda Mae, Obadiah, and Ned settled down for a longer stay. But after breakfast the Brogdons and the Overbys left to go home.

Still impressed with the Christmas tree that had been lit after dinner the previous evening, Derusha and Letha discussed putting one up also.

"It's a waste of a good tree," Clyde said.

"But it's so pretty and festive," Derusha argued.

William Brogdon smiled at his friend. "I guess this means that we'll both have trees in our parlors this Christmas, Clyde."

He laughed. "I hope Julius's wife doesn't keep this up. If she does, she's going to cost us a lot of money."

"I like her," Derusha said.

Letha was still debating.

"Well, Julius certainly dotes on her," Brogdon offered.

"Who wouldn't?" Seeing the look in his wife's eyes, Clyde hastily added, "She's almost as pretty as Letha and Derusha."

Chapter 34

"Dear Mrs. Dodge, I am writing to you as a friend to tell you that Daisy is alive and well."

The letter had arrived by post coach only a few minutes before, and as Ellie began reading it her hands trembled. For over four years she had kept praying that her daughter would get someone to write a letter to her and Jake, letting them know where she was. And now her prayer had been answered.

"No one else is privy to what I'm going to tell you. Your daughter is out west, in Indian Territory, with her husband. She has made a new life for herself and her two little boys.

"She goes by the name of Agitsi′, and her husband is a Cherokee. He is kind to her and the boys. If you ever decide to get in touch with her, ask for Two Feathers.

"I also know where Horace is, but your secret is safe with me."

Ellie almost dropped the letter. Someone knew what they had done. Frantically she turned the unsigned letter over, trying to see where it might have come from. What were they to do? She was glad that Daisy was alive and too far away for the authorities to find her. But what about her and Jake? With even *one* person knowing what had happened to Horace, it might not take long for the news to get around. Maybe it would be better for them to go west, too.

Ellie wrapped a heavy shawl around herself and left the boardinghouse. As she hurried toward the store to talk with Jake, the snow on the frozen ground crunched under her feet. Overhead, an old crow flew past, its raucous voice protesting at being shooed from the horses' corn at the livery stable. But Ellie barely noticed the sounds; for her mind was completely on the letter.

The writer said that Daisy had another little boy. But who was the father? Was he her husband's, or Horace's? Or maybe someone else? Ellie would not be surprised if it were someone else; for she'd been suspicious even before Daisy had married.

With the weather as bad as it was, and the mountains promising another snow before night, there were few customers in the store when she arrived.

"Afternoon, Ellie."

"Afternoon, Cora."

She nodded to the blacksmith's wife, but she didn't stop to talk. She went on to the back storeroom, where she waited for Jake. By the time his few customers had left and he had joined her, Ellie had already decided what to do. Now she only had to convince Jake.

* * *

Several days later Lulu, pleased with the way Ned had gotten along with Rebecca, gathered everyone into the parlor. It was Christmas Eve and she wanted to light the tree again.

"Who'd like to help?" she asked.

"I will," Tilda Mae said.

"And you, Julius? Will you help, too?"

"I reckon so."

Lulu smiled at her husband. "Did you think this time last year, when we got married, that you'd have another wedding in the family?"

"Well, this one ain't quite as hurried as ours. At least the preacher will know when he comes that he's goin' to do more than eat supper."

Lulu laughed. "Yes. You were an impatient man, Julius."

She looked out of the corner of her eye at Ned. Let Rebecca have her wedding night. After that, he wouldn't be quite so attentive. He'd be far too busy picking up where he and Lulu had left off—especially once her mama and papa had gone home.

Ignoring Rebecca, Lulu lit the first candle, watching it sputter and then take fire. Her eyes sparkled in excitement; for now all her wishes were coming true.

That same night, hundreds of miles away, another flame sputtered and then took hold. No Christmas tree, no warm hearth helped to alleviate the cold wind that touched the ice floes on the Ohio and stormed into camp on the eastern bank.

Laurel and the children, Agitsi′, Two Feathers, Night Hawk, and Tansee, with their blankets wrapped around them, sat huddled near one of the campfires that was visible for a few feet, then was swallowed up by the eerie fog rising from the river.

Laurel and Tansee had worked hard, making something special for each girl for Christmas. Carrying Duck held her new cornhusk doll, similar to Walini′s, while Walini′ struggled to dress her doll in its new clothes. Redbird and Kama′mă, too old for dolls, were busy putting the new ornaments in their hair.

The boys sat and examined the bird whistles that Two Feathers had carved for them. Then they put them to their mouths and began to vie with each other for the most beautiful bird sounds. Billy laughed aloud when his tentative call was answered by a bird farther down the river.

Looking around her, Laurel tried to keep her mind only on the moment—not on past Christmases, or even on what might be in store for them the next day. Her eyes reflected the love she felt for each one around the fire. She offered up a particular prayer of thanks because Redbird was almost well and none of the other children in their group had become ill.

She was sorry, though, that the old woman had been buried by the roadside with others several days before.

"All right, it's time to make a wish," Laurel said, handing a long stick to each child. "When the stick catches fire, then keep it burning as long as you can."

"The longer it burns," Black Moccasin said, "the easier it will be for the Great Spirit to see the smoke and give you your wish."

"But you're not supposed to tell anybody what the wish is," Redbird explained to Carrying Duck.

Night Hawk smiled and put on another piece of firewood so that the flames would flare up.

All of them were eager to light their sticks, to make a wish. Agitsi′ wanted to do it, too, but she knew that the game was just for the children.

"I wish, I wish—"

"No, Walini′," Ina′li cautioned. "Don't say it out loud."

The children were solemn and quiet as each lit a stick and, with help, stuck the stick into the ground, to watch it smoke and burn.

Night Hawk leaned over to Laurel. "What would you wish for, Laurel, if you were one of the children?" he teased.

She smiled a mischievous smile. "A Moravian sugar cookie."

Overhearing Laurel, Agitsi′ said, "I'd ask for a whole apple pie."

Night Hawk laughed. "Since you both told, your wishes have no hope of coming true. But how about some dried figs?" He opened a pouch and distributed the sweets to each child, each adult.

"Where did you get such a delicacy?" Laurel asked, popping a fig into her mouth.

Night Hawk hesitated. "From someone in another wagon."

Laurel knew immediately where he had gotten the dried figs. From Falling Star. But she didn't care. She was hungry enough for it not to matter.

"The wind blew out my stick," Kama´mă complained.

"But see?" Deer Stalker said. "It's still smoking."

Kama´mă felt better.

Soon all the sticks were snuffed out by the wind. But Laurel could see the hope burning in the children's eyes as they held their secret wishes in their hearts.

From the private talk with Two Feathers and Night Hawk earlier that day, Laurel knew that the journey ahead would be even more difficult. They would all need a strong hope if they were to survive.

That night they slept under the wagon while the horses, oxen, and ponies remained in a makeshift corral, hidden by the fog. But the next morning a large number of the animals were gone. They had been stolen while the people slept.

Now the journey took on new hazards. Some of the soldiers had deserted the detachment, and the only physician left was ill, himself. They had lost time, waiting for the high winds to subside so they could cross the river. And during this period of waiting, the food supply had dwindled, with little money for the commissary agent to purchase more.

The contractors along the overland route had charged exorbitant prices for their unpalatable meat and had been dishonest in measuring the corn. But the drought of the previous summer prevented the commissary agent from purchasing food from the settlers.

Farther behind, on the same overland trail, John Ross was finding it equally difficult. Added to his concerns were the weekly reports received from the detachments ahead—none of them good.

"We have a large number of sick and infirm persons in our detachment," wrote the Reverend Jesse Bushyhead. "They are being conveyed in the wagons, so we now have no wagons to haul the corn needed for the horses. Many of our oxen have died from eating poisonous weeds."

Another report said, "We had to pay forty dollars at the tollgate. Each day we are fleeced without the least abatement or thanks."

And Night Hawk had written, "John, there is no more game along the trail. So Two Feathers and I have decided to swing slightly north where we may find deer and turkey to help feed our detachment."

But for the principal chief, the most heartbreaking report simply read, "We pray every day that you will catch up with us. We need your presence among us; for we are all a dejected and downhearted people."

Allen stood beside his father and looked over the treacherous muddy morass ahead. He was aware of John's desire to catch up with the others. But staring at the impossible road, he asked, "What will you do now, Father?"

"One thing is certain, Allen. With the condition of the trail, we will never be able to catch up with even the last detachment."

"Why did we have to have such a cold, early winter?" Allen sounded frustrated.

"I don't know the answer to that, son, any more than I know why General Scott wouldn't let us all stay in our homes until spring." John stared again at the menacing road ahead.

"If we're lucky enough to get to Paducah, we'll take the water route as far as Little Rock. That should get us closer to the rest of the people traveling overland."

He looked again at his son. "Go and ride with your mother. She needs you."

"Yes, Father."

Night Hawk and Two Feathers continued on their westerly course, where they would cross the Mississippi at Cape Girardeau. But when they reached the river, the high winds and the ice kept them from crossing.

Not knowing how long it would take for the winds to abate and the ice floes to melt, Laurel, Agitsi´ and Tansee sought a suitable shelter for their group.

Night Hawk and Laurel's relationship had deteriorated, and he now spent much time in the evenings with Falling Star and her family as he did with Laurel. He had even taken Walini´ with him one evening, leaving Laurel in a strange, angry mood.

But if Falling Star wanted Night Hawk so much, she could have him. Laurel would not stoop to fighting over him, like some poor, destitute female.

That evening, when their meager meal was over and the children had settled in for the night, Laurel left the campsite to walk along the bluff of the river and to think. Overhead, the stars shone in a cold brilliance, with a thousand icicles surrounding each star. Even the moon looked frozen, pale, and anemic.

"What are you thinking, Laurel?"

Night Hawk's voice behind her caused her to jump. As she turned around, he said, "I'm sorry. I didn't mean to startle you."

"I suppose my mind was so far away that I wasn't paying attention."

"But it's not safe—your being out here alone. What if I'd

been some wild animal?"

Laurel smiled. "Then I'd have eaten you on the spot."

Rather than returning her smile, he remained serious. They were all hungry, and the days lost at the river only meant more hardships ahead.

But tonight, Night Hawk had other things on his mind, as well. Falling Star had made it clear that she would like to be his wife. He had waited for weeks for some sign from Laurel, some indication that her earlier rebuff had been a mistake, or that she had changed her mind now that she was older. Running Brook had made a good wife, and he had no doubt that Falling Star would also. But there was something in his heart that still whispered Laurel's name.

"What are you thinking, Laurel?" Night Hawk repeated.

"Oh, probably what everyone else is thinking—about finding my family, and then deciding what to do with my life."

Night Hawk hesitated. "What would you *like* to do?"

How could she answer that she'd like to be his wife, to make a home for Walini′ and the other children that would be born to them? How could she lower herself to make eyes at him the way Falling Star was doing, or beg for his love?

When she answered him, Laurel's voice was as cold and distant as the stars. "I hear that Samuel Worcester has opened another mission school. Perhaps he will offer me a teaching position."

Her answer made Night Hawk furious. Before she knew it, he had taken her into his arms. The kiss was no affectionate, playful kiss between friends. It contained all his pent-up desire for a woman out of his reach—the one he had dreamed about and, one night, had held in his arms.

Suddenly, he released her. "That is what I needed to know."

Shaken, Laurel watched him walk away. "Tskĭ-lĭ ," she whispered, too low for him to hear. "I love you."

Chapter 35

Nothing was the same. Black Moccasin and Deer Stalker had grown up under Laurel's very eyes. They looked more and more to Night Hawk and Two Feathers for guidance. And even Redbird had started her moon time.

They were no longer the children she had taught in the mission school and had taken care of for so long. They had been hardened by adversity and the knowledge that they must now make a life for themselves, apart from servants and the comforts they had been born to.

Laurel had lost Walini´, as well. For Night Hawk would be taking her with him once they reached the Territory. And Two Feathers had his own family. Only Tansee had remained the same, the loyal friend and servant.

"Your face is gonna fall into your shoes, if it gets much longer," Tansee said, watching her.

Laurel quickly came out of her reverie to look at the black woman. "Is it that obvious?"

Tansee nodded. "At least to me. You want to tell me what's troublin' you?"

"I'm afraid I've just destroyed my chance for happiness."

"You had an argument with Night Hawk."

"Worse than that, Tansee. I've pushed him into the arms

of Falling Star."

"I was afraid your pride was gonna do that to you."

Laurel looked down at her threadbare clothes, her muddy shoes. "Pride is the only thing I have left. I couldn't lose that, too."

"It's awful hard to go to bed at night with Mr. Pride by your side," Tansee commented. "Better to have a real man with the breath of life in 'im."

"Falling Star must think so, too."

Tansee did not pry further. It was obvious that Laurel was unhappy. But were they not all in a state of dejection? If they could only find more food, then everyone would have a different outlook.

The time passed slowly on the overland trail, with some of the detachments losing an entire month waiting for the weather to improve so that they could cross the Mississippi. But farther behind, John Ross finally reached Paducah, where he hired a boat, the *Victoria.*

After transferring his family and the sick and feeble in his care, he began the river portion of his journey, straining to make up for lost time so that he might catch up with the rest of the Nation.

The paddle wheeler set sail southward down the Mississippi, where the ice was less hazardous. But the wind and the rain reminded John that this, too, would be no easy journey. At times the boat had to anchor near the shore until the storms passed. Then the captain would lift anchor, start up the paddle wheel, and churn into the middle of the channel.

At Montgomery Point, where the White and Arkansas rivers join the Mississippi on its way southward to the Gulf, the paddle wheeler left the Father of Waters, navigated into the Arkansas, and headed for the port of Little Rock.

The gusting March winds, mixed with snow and sleet,

bombarded the paddle wheeler, with river water sweeping over the decks, threatening the sick and well alike, and drenching their few possessions. Only the trunk, holding the history of the Nation, remained impervious to the weather.

Finally, the river port came into sight, and the people looked to the overland journey once more. With John negotiating for wagons, horses, and food, additional blankets, and cotton cloth for makeshift tents, they camped on the bluffs overlooking the river that first night.

Quatie, already ill with a cold, as many of the others were, gave her blanket to a sick child that night. And by the time they started out several days later, with fresh supplies, her cold had become much worse.

As Allen drove their wagon Quatie sat up in front beside him. Hearing her cough, he said, "Mother, you sound terrible." Turning his head he spoke to his sister. "Jane, get Mother one of the new blankets to wrap around her."

"Do you remember the time when I had a terrible cough, too?"

"Yes, George," Quatie said, trying hard not to cough again. "I kept you in bed for several days."

"Maybe you should go to bed, too," Silas said.

"Yes, Mother," Jane agreed. "We could make a place for you to lie down in the wagon."

Quatie declined. Her husband, riding ahead on his horse, needed to see her. The people behind needed to see her, too. But later in the day, when she was too weak to remain in an upright position, she finally lay down in the back of the wagon.

Several miles ahead, the detachment led by Night Hawk and Two Feathers stopped for the night. They had given up the more northerly route and had swung south. Soon their campfires burned, lighting the countryside. John, leading his own small group, saw the fires, like beacons shining to guide him to them.

He continued the journey in their direction. And the people traveling with him also saw the fires and rejoiced.

The word spread quickly. "Gu′wisguwĭ′ has come into camp." The news continued to spread to every campfire, and suddenly the air of dejection disappeared. The camp took on new life, an atmosphere that vibrated with hope, with expectation.

Laurel, hearing the good news, forgot her sadness. "Tansee, I must go and speak to Quatie. Will you watch after the children and see that they get to bed?"

With Tansee's assurance that she would take care of them, Laurel left the campfire.

There was no doubt where John and Quatie were camped. Laurel followed the steady procession, smiling as she went. But as she drew closer she heard no hearty welcomes, no songs or chants of joy disturbing the quiet air. The people stood around in great silence, and from that, Laurel knew that something was terribly wrong.

Recognizing her cousin Jane by one of the wagons, she threaded her way past the crowd. "Jane, what's wrong?" she asked.

"Oh, Laurel, our mother is dying."

"Quatie? Quatie is dying?"

"Yes. Father is with her now. The doctor says she won't last the night."

Someone built a bonfire nearby. In silence the people sat, keeping vigil with their principal chief in his hour of sorrow. Silas and George, bewildered by their mother's illness, clung to their sister.

"I don't want Mother to die," Silas said, tears streaming down his cheeks.

"She *won't* die," little George announced. "I have promised the Great Spirit anything He wants, if He'll let my mother live."

With his announcement Jane could no longer keep back her own tears. She put her arms around him and said, "George, we cannot bargain with the Great Spirit. Mother is tired, and He's calling her to come where she'll never be tired, or sick, or cold."

"But I still want her to stay here," George said.

John motioned for his daughter. "Your mother is calling for you."

Jane turned to Laurel. "Will you watch after George and Silas for a moment?"

"Yes." Laurel took Jane's place beside the two little boys.

"Why can't we go, too, Laurel?" Silas asked.

"I expect you'll be going next," she said, holding them close.

Then, in a few moments, Jane returned and led Silas and George toward the wagon. "You must be very good," she warned them. "And remember, don't let Mother see you cry."

George wiped away a tear and bit his lip to stop it from quivering.

The people kept vigil all night. Even the soldier, relieved of his duty at eleven, remained nearby. Toward morning John left the wagon. His beloved Quatie was dead.

With the news a great wail arose among the people, their grief joining that of their revered principal chief.

Later that morning a grave was dug, and Quatie's body, uncoffined, was wrapped in a blanket with two long pieces of bark as her resting board and lowered into the frozen ground.

Then the two detachments joined and moved out, with a grieving John in front. With him he carried the history of the Nation, like an ark of the covenant, toward a strange and alien land.

* * *

John's cousin, Chief Joseph Vann, whose house at Spring Place had been confiscated by Bishop, had already settled in the west.

Bishop had not been able to acquire all of the Vann wealth. Fleeing over the Georgia line that day with his wife Jenny and their two children, Joseph had taken up residence in a dirt-floor cabin he owned in Tennessee.

He still had his steamboat, the *Lucy Walker,* and his best racehorse by the same name. But knowing that it was only a matter of time before Tennessee would go the way of Georgia, he had left voluntarily for the west.

Joseph was not a member of the protreaty party. Neither was he an idealist like his cousin John. He was an entrepreneur as his father before him, with the ability to make money in almost any endeavor. He was a pragmatist, who drank too much, raced too fast, but still had a great love for his people, and a loyalty to his family.

Hearing of the difficulties that besieged the detachments, their inability to replace the horses and oxen that had either died or been stolen, Joseph sent John a number of wagons and animals from the Territory, in the hope that they would alleviate some of the hardship.

"Look, Gu´wisguwĭ´," Night Hawk said to the man riding to his right. "Do you see what I see?"

"Yes. I wonder who has sent them."

John, along with Night Hawk and Two Feathers, galloped to meet the approaching wagons.

The driver of the first wagon held up his hand in greeting. As he stopped he spoke to John and handed over a letter addressed to him.

Opening it, John quickly looked at the signature. "The letter's from my kinsman Joseph Vann," he said. And reading further, he added, "He's sent these replacements for us."

"We can put them to good use," Night Hawk said.

In spite of the replacements, the rest of the way into the Territory was filled with hazards and more deaths. But the knowledge that their leader was sharing the same grief, the same loss and hardships, gave the people a strength of purpose that they so desperately needed.

The Old Settlers began to meet them along the way, looking for their close relatives. A few dropped out of the detachments, but the majority kept going until they finally reached their destination—the Indian Agency adjacent to Fort Gibson.

As the wagons came to a stop and the survivors looked over the vast frozen prairie, with "corpses of wood" for trees—the land the government felt no white man would ever want—the Cherokees, too, realized that this was no promised land.

"I wonder where the government agents who're supposed to meet us with good food are," Laurel said to Tansee as she looked around her.

Night Hawk, returning to the wagon for Walini′, overheard.

"I have seen the food, Laurel. It has an unpalatable smell—with crawling maggots in the meat and weevils in the flour."

"But they promised," a hungry Laurel cried.

"Have you not learned by now that the white man's promises are written on the wind?"

Almost as soon as he'd ridden off, Two Feathers came back to the wagon for his family. "We'll be getting in touch with you, Laurel," he said, "once we're settled."

Laurel kissed Agitsi′ and the boys good-bye and watched them disappear into the crowd.

The scene soon became one of frantic searching, as parents, long separated from their children, began to look for them, and children, some of whose parents had died before they had even left the east, looked eagerly into the crowd, as if their mothers and fathers might somehow miraculously appear.

Laurel stood with Carrying Duck, Kama′mă, and Deer Stalker, while Redbird and Black Moccasin waited to one side, their eyes searching just as wistfully as the others.

Seeing Carrying Duck, a woman in the crowd screamed and ran toward the child with open arms. "Nakwisi′! Nakwisi′!"

Noting that the little girl merely looked at the woman in a puzzled manner, Laurel stepped in front of Carrying Duck. She had cared for her too long to turn her over to a stranger who might not even be her mother. "Just a moment," she said. "How do I know that this is your child?"

Now it was the woman's turn to look puzzled. "But I recognize her. She is my little Nakwisi′."

"Is there someone who can vouch for you? Or something you can tell me about the child?"

The woman looked at Carrying Duck and begged, "Nakwisi′, do you remember the little duck I gave you—"

Laurel smiled and stepped aside. "Take your daughter. She carried her pet duck for over a month on the trail."

Kama′mă said, "Yes. Since she wouldn't tell us her name, we called her Carrying Duck."

They kissed the child good-bye and watched her disappear into the crowd with her joyful mother.

Deer Stalker left with his father. And then Kama′mă was reunited with her family. Only Laurel, Redbird, and Black Moccasin remained unclaimed.

"Look, Laurel," Tansee said. "Here come Chief Alex and Miss Trudie."

"Mother! Father!" Laurel rushed to greet her parents, but as she looked back she saw Redbird and Black Moccasin alone. "I hope you have room for two others," she said, kissing her parents. "The three of us are all together."

"Of course, Laurel," Trudie said. "We'll make room."

"I see that Tansee was as good as her word," Alex commented. "She found you. I'll have to thank her for that."

While he motioned for the black woman, Laurel walked back to the place where Redbird and Black Moccasin were standing. "Well, hurry and get your things out of the wagon," she said. "We're going home."

"But we don't have a home," Redbird said.

"Yes, you do. You and Black Moccasin are part of my family now."

They hurriedly took their few possessions out of the wagon and followed Laurel. Night Hawk and Walini′ had not returned. Walking through the crowd with Alex and Trudie, Laurel looked for them. But they had gone.

Feeling hurt, Laurel left, too. She had not realized that their alienation had been so complete. After all their months together Night Hawk should, at least, have allowed her to say good-bye to Walini′.

Chapter 36

John Ross was not allowed a suitable time to grieve for Quatie. The numerous problems of the Nation demanded his attention as never before.

Elias Boudinot, Stand Watie, John and Major Ridge, the principal members of the protreaty party, had ingratiated themselves with General Arbuckle, commander of Fort Gibson, and by their lies, had turned him and the rest of the government officials against John Ross.

Blending in with the Old Settlers who were loath to give up their own positions of leadership to the principal chief of the Nation, they began their utmost to drive a wedge in the unity of east and west.

Statesmanship, education, and religion, all important priorities of the eastern Cherokees, received little attention from their western brothers. The Old Settlers had been content to farm, trade with the Comanches near the Brazos River, race their horses, game, and dance.

Although settling claims against the government for property confiscated in the east, and reconciling the actual cost of removal against the unrealistic amount Congress had set aside for it, were top priorities, John realized that the most pressing problem of all lay in reuniting the Nation as soon as possible.

For this reason he approached the chiefs of the western group, who agreed to a joint meeting at Takatoka. Addressing the groups, the principal chief called for an amiable reunion for the welfare of the entire Nation. "Let us never forget this self-evident truth—that a house divided against itself cannot stand."

The western group, a small minority of the Cherokee Nation, listened to the protreaty men, intent on undermining anything John did. Convinced by them, the western delegates left before the meeting had ended, effectively undoing John's efforts.

Yet, John had been able to have a committee appointed to look further into the matter of a peaceable union. With Sequoyah elected as representative of the western group, and the Reverend Bushyhead, leader of one of the newly arrived detachments, to represent the east, an assembly was set for the next month at the Illinois Camp Ground.

But unknown to John, a clandestine meeting was also being held—one that had the potential to drive a permanent wedge between the two and destroy all hope of unity.

They came in the dark of night, said little, and stayed only a few minutes. But they followed the ancient blood law of the Cherokees, and the later law written into the Cherokee constitution by John Ridge, himself.

The woven basket contained as many slips of white paper as those who attended. Only a few slips had been marked with an X.

Silently, they came in an orderly manner, one by one, drawing out a slip and then looking at it to see if he had been selected as executioner. With no trace of emotion, each man folded his paper again, secreted it in a pocket until it could be destroyed, and then left.

The sound of ponies, the dust of the plains vanished,

leaving no evidence that the meeting in the night had ever occurred.

Not long afterward, John Ross sat on the porch of his newly completed home at Park Hill. It was late in the afternoon. Beside him sat his son Allen, who was paying undue attention to his father.

John had finally set aside the official papers that had taken so much of his time lately. And now, in silence, he sat and stared toward the sunset.

This was the house that he had sworn to build for Quatie. But not once since her death had he spoken her name. She had ceased to exist for him as *woman.* She was now the wind that swept over the vast prairie, the brilliance that touched the sun and trailed the sky in scarlet ribbons, the pulse in his throat that measured each heartbeat, each breath of sweet remembrance that kept him alive.

John stood up and started walking in the direction of the barn. "Where are you going, Father?" Allen asked.

"I thought I might check on Silas's pony. The animal seemed listless this morning."

"I'll go with you."

"Do you not have more important things to do?"

What was more important than making certain his father was not blamed by government agents for the events taking place? Despite all that had happened, Allen knew John was too forgiving to sanction the use of the ancient blood law. But the grievous injury to the principal chief and his people was too flagrant not to be avenged.

Allen's face remained bland as he answered, "I'd rather spend the evening with you."

* * *

John Ridge had built a formidable plantation house at Honey Hill. For his perfidy in betraying the Nation, he had been allowed to bring all his possessions with him to the west, including his slaves, and was repaid liberally for the ferry he had run, with government protection, until his emigration. He had also received a generous reimbursement for all other properties and goods he'd left behind in Georgia.

He was well liked by Arbuckle, too, and knew he could call upon him for a whole army to protect him if he felt himself in danger. But so far, no incidents had occurred. And although he had painted Ross as a dishonest scamp and drunkard, he knew better. Ross would do nothing to harm him. He had never enacted the ancient blood law of retribution.

He, too, watched the sunset from his palatial home. And later he went to bed with his wife—the white woman he'd met at Cornwall and married—beside him. He was secure in the knowledge that he was completely safe.

Twenty-five men, making no noise in the night, surrounded the house. A slight creak on the porch, an almost inaudible breaching of a window indicated that someone had gained entry to the house.

The moccasined feet of three men passed the children's rooms and stopped before the bedroom where John Ridge and his wife lay asleep.

Within seconds the man had been pulled from his bed. His wife awakened, screaming. She followed as her husband was dragged outside. She screamed again when the pale moonbeams caught the glint of the raised knives.

Moments later, the men had vanished. John Ridge lay dead in his own yard.

The next morning Major Ridge, unaware of what had happened to his son, left a friend's house on his way back from Arkansas to check on a number of his black slaves.

He was within a few miles of his home, on the old Arkansas road, when five shots rang out from a precipice above the road. He had been avenged by the same blood law that he, himself, had used earlier in dealing with Doublehead, who had also ceded lands without the sanction of the Nation.

For Elias Boudinot, the move west had been a good one. He had settled close to the new mission established by Samuel Worcester. He was now Samuel's translator, and a new printing press was in operation. Until he arrived, the only printing had been in Choctaw. But now, with a new set of type, a newspaper—as well as religious books—could once again be published in Cherokee, and Elias could write his editorials as he had done in the past.

On the same morning that Ridge was shot, three eastern Cherokees came to Elias's home, where he was busy drafting a letter to one of the northern newspaper editors with whom he corresponded.

"Yes? What is it that you want?" Elias asked, eager to return to his writing.

"Our families are very sick," one replied. "We have heard that the missionary Worcester might have medicine."

"Yes, that's true."

"Then would you direct us to the mission?"

Elias said, "I was planning on seeing Worcester myself a little later. But I could just as easily go now. You can follow me there."

Halfway between his home and the mission Boudinot was slashed to death with a tomahawk.

Near the small house belonging to Trudie and Alex MacDonald, Laurel, recovering from a long illness, sat on the banks of a stream with Redbird and Black Moccasin.

"You're looking a lot better today, Laurel," Redbird said.

"I'm feeling much better, too, despite the terrible news."

Black Moccasin's face became sober. "I'm just sorry that Stand Watie and the others escaped punishment. If I had known who to contact, I would have been part of the group, too."

"Now, Black Moccasin, you musn't be so bloodthirsty."

"But I blame them directly for our parents' death," he insisted.

Seeking to defuse his anger, Laurel commented, "If you want to be a chief one day, as your father was, then you'd better turn your mind to studying a little harder."

Redbird, reminded of school, said, "It will seem so strange going away in the fall to a boarding school where you're not teaching."

"I know. We've been together so long." Laurel smiled. "I remember the day you both came to New Echota—over seven years ago."

Tansee appeared, stopping Laurel's reminicence. "There's company at the house, and they're stayin' for supper," she announced. "Miss Trudie sent me to fetch you."

"Who is it?" Redbird asked.

The black woman smiled. "Somebody all three of you will be glad to see."

"That's not fair, Tansee. Tell us," Laurel said. "Is it Two Feathers?"

"My, aren't you curious! But you won't find out from me. You'll have to see for yourself."

Redbird and Black Moccasin eagerly rushed ahead while Tansee waited to walk with Laurel, who could not keep up with her two wards.

At Park Hill, John Ross, innocent of the conspiracy, sent his brother-in-law to the Boudinot house to find out what had happened. He returned, not only with confirmation of the deed, but with a letter from Elias's widow.

"John, I know you had no part in the tragedy. And that is why I'm sending this letter to warn you. Stand Watie, Elias's brother, has sworn to raise a company of men to kill you. I beg of you to leave your home and seek safety elsewhere."

But even as he read the letter, two hundred of the eastern Cherokees came and took their places around his house, guarding their principal chief from attack.

Realizing the military repercussions of the avenged deaths, John sat down at his desk and immediately wrote a report to General Arbuckle. "I trust that you deem it expedient to order an unbiased investigation in this tragic matter."

By the time he received the letter, General Arbuckle had already made up his mind; for he had gotten an earlier report that John was harboring all the culprits at Park Hill.

"I'll launch more than an investigation," he asserted. "I'll arrest every last one of them, including that scamp Ross."

But in the end the initial report he received from John's enemies proved to be untrue. If he could have found any excuse to arrest John Ross, he would have done so. But the U.S. government had no jurisdiction over the self-governing Cherokees. And John was astute enough not to accept Arbuckle's invitation to the fort. Instead, he invited Arbuckle to come to Park Hill to discuss the matter.

While Arbuckle and his dragoons were ranging over the countryside, questioning every Cherokee, the meeting to unite east and west was still scheduled for July 1.

A letter of entreaty to all the western Cherokees was sent by Sequoyah, the man who had united them earlier in a written language. "We, the Old Settlers, are here in council with the late emigrants. We want you to come without delay, to talk things over as friends and brothers."

But the dream of setting aside all differences and uniting east and west into one nation again was in serious jeopardy.

Chapter 37

As Laurel came within sight of the house she saw a child on the porch with Redbird and Black Moccasin. Recognizing her, she called out, "Walini'!"

Walini' heard the woman and saw her rushing toward her. She immediately left the porch and began running to meet Laurel. In moments the dark-haired child was in her arms.

"Oh, Walini', how I've missed you. I'm so glad you've come."

Clinging to her as she did on the trail, Walini' said, "I love you, Laurel."

"And I love you, too."

Walini' finally lifted her head and looked at Laurel. "Papa's in the house."

"Then I must go in and speak to him." Laurel smiled as she said it, but inwardly she struggled with her feelings. She must be cordial, no matter how difficult it would be for her, remembering the circumstances of their parting. Night Hawk was her father's friend, and it was only natural that he would seek out Alex once he'd gotten settled. It would be more difficult, though, to welcome Falling Star.

Holding Walini''s hand, Laurel walked toward the porch.

As they reached the steps Tansee suddenly intervened.

"Walini′, did you know that we have some little kittens in the barn?"

The child's eyes lit up with interest. "You do?"

"Yes. I'll bet Redbird and Black Moccasin would take you to see them if you asked."

"I want to see the kittens," Walini′ said, looking again at Redbird.

"And we have a new pony, too," Black Moccasin added.

Laurel stood and watched the happy child, holding on to Redbird and Black Moccasin's hands and skipping along the path toward the barn.

"Aren't you going inside?" Tansee prompted.

Laurel looked at the servant. "I suppose I'll have to."

Slowly Laurel opened the door. She walked toward the keeping room, but no voices, no laughter penetrated the air. She stopped on the threshold. The windows had been shuttered against the afternoon sun and the room was dark.

"Du-su-ka!"

She recognized the voice, and her eyes sought for its owner. She saw the man rise from the settle and begin to walk toward her.

"Tskĭ-lĭ″," Laurel said, her voice barely audible. Shaken at seeing him again, she frantically searched the shadows for some sign of Falling Star, or her mother and father. But only Night Hawk was in the room.

"I took Walini′ by the Worcester mission to see you, but you weren't there."

"No."

He reached out for her hand and led her back to the settle. "Alex tells me that you have been quite ill."

"Yes. It's strange, isn't it, that we walked through all the sleet and snow on the trail, and then I waited until I got to a comfortable, warm house before collapsing."

"Laurel, why didn't you wait to say good-bye? Walini′

was so upset."

"Do you mean you came back to the wagon?"

"Of course. I had to see—" He hesitated. "I had to see some other people."

Laurel nodded. "How is Falling Star? I'm surprised she didn't come with you today."

"She's fine. At least she was the last time I saw her."

It took a moment for the words to make sense. "What do you mean? Is she not your wife?"

"No, Laurel. She's the one I went to tell good-bye after our arrival. I haven't seen her since."

"But on the bluff that night—"

Night Hawk's voice sounded bitter. "You made it plain that you didn't want to marry me. So I turned to Falling Star for a while. But in the end I knew that I could never be happy with her."

Looking into Laurel's eyes with a fierceness she had seldom seen, he cried, "I've always loved you, Laurel. Walini′ loves you, too. Even if you don't care for me, I know you love her, almost as if she were your own. For her sake I'm asking you to make us a family again, as we were on the trail."

"Did you never guess, Tskĭ-lĭ′? I've loved you for such a long time. The night you gave me the shriveled peaches, I knew it. I knew it when you shared your blanket with me, and I went to sleep in your arms."

"Well, dammit, why didn't you tell me?"

"I don't know. It might have been because you taunted me so about—what was his name?"

"Edward Farraday."

"Yes. I—"

"You talk too much, Laurel." Night Hawk drew her closer, kissing her with an intensity that made her soul come alive.

Visibly shaken at their mutual need, he whispered, "Does

this mean that you'll marry me?"

"Yes, Tskĭ-lĭ´. You're my heart."

Later they drew apart; for the sounds of the children coming back inside the house interrupted them. Trudie and Alex suddenly appeared, too. And Tansee came in to light the candles.

"Well, Laurel," Trudie said. "The supper will be ready in a few minutes. Isn't it nice to have old friends come to visit."

"Old friends?" Laurel smiled. "Mother, you'll have to start speaking of this man as my husband."

Alex laughed and winked at Night Hawk.

That night at the table Walini´ sat beside Laurel— on a chair propped high with a pillow— with Night Hawk on the other side. Opposite them were Redbird and Black Moccasin, with Trudie and Alex at each end of the table.

"Have you and Night Hawk had a chance to discuss when you'll get married?" Trudie asked.

"No. Only that we want Samuel to perform the ceremony."

"Alex and I will be going to the meeting at Tahlequah in September," Night Hawk reminded Laurel.

"Then it might be better to wait until the meeting is over," Laurel said.

"But we'll be away at school," Redbird protested.

Night Hawk sided with Redbird. "You want them to be present, don't you?" he inquired, indicating the two across the table.

"Of course. They're part of our family."

"Then it will have to be earlier."

"Don't be impatient, Night Hawk," Laurel teased. "You've waited for—how long? Three years?"

"No. More like eleven. I first spoke to Alex about you when you were twelve."

Alex cleared his throat. "And as a party to this union

from the beginning, I believe Night Hawk will have to be patient a little longer."

"What do you mean, Father?"

"You seem to forget thay you're still recovering from your illness. Another few months will give you time to become strong again."

"Perhaps—perhaps we could have a Christmas wedding," Laurel suggested, "when everyone will be home for the winter holidays."

"And we could invite Billy and Ina´li ," Black Moccasin suggested.

"Yes. We've shared everything else with Two Feathers and Agitsi´. It will be nice to share our happiness with them, too," Laurel commented.

In the northeastern area of the Territory, next to the Arkansas border, Two Feathers had built a cabin near one of the smaller creeks. It didn't matter that it ran dry during certain times of the year; for after a rain it flowed swiftly, spilling over the rocks and reminding him of other singing streams.

It was far away from Tahlequah, the capital where the meeting was being held in an effort to bring east and west together. But Two Feathers had no need to be there. As a holy man, he had seen the signs that, despite political factions and the blood feud that would have to be dealt with for years, the Cherokee Nation would be reunited, at least on paper. And John Ross would be its principal chief for years to come.

"Papa, look," Billy called, reminding Two Feathers of the present again. "The nice lady at the new store gave me this sling."

"And what did you do to repay her kindness?"

"I brought in some extra wood for her cooking fire."

Two Feathers nodded. Billy had learned his lessons well.

Every kindness demanded repayment, no matter how small. If a plant were taken from the ground, a small gift must be left in its place—a kernel of corn, a bead, a pinch of sacred tobacco.

"I like Miss Ellie. And Mama likes her, too."

"And Ina′li?"

"Well, you know how Ina′li is. One day he likes somebody, and the next day he doesn't. Mama gets awful exasperated with him sometimes."

Billy forgot his brother for a moment. "Miss Ellie was interested when Mama told her I was going off to school soon. She said it would be so nice, especially since Mama didn't know how to read and write. How did Miss Ellie know that, Papa?"

"Maybe because Agitsi′ always has to remember what we need to buy. She never takes a list."

"Oh."

Two Feathers could never divulge what he knew. When Night Hawk had confided to him that he'd recognized Agitsi′, Two Feathers had sworn him to secrecy, to protect her. One day Agitsi′ would remember her past—but only after her husband was dead. By then Billy would be old enough to take care of her.

As darkness settled upon the land and a coyote howled in the distance, Ellie and Jake Dodge locked the front part of the store and walked to their living quarters in the back.

Their establishment was more like a trading post than the general store they had run back in Georgia at the Carter settlement. And the goods they kept for purchase reflected this change.

They had not needed the tools for gold mining—the picks and sieve pans that thousands had bought once the gold mines had been taken from the Cherokees. What they needed most were bridles and harnesses for the horses and mules, and good food. Corn meal, too. Only the white settlers bought flour.

"It hurts my soul, Jake, for Daisy not to recognize me," Ellie said as she put supper on the table.

"But it's safer, Ellie," Jake responded, "what with those lawless Starrs menacing the countryside and all the turmoil going on in the Nation. With feelings the way they are now, if word ever got out that we had a daughter living in Indian Territory, half of our white customers would stop trading with us, and we'd lose every cent we've invested."

Ellie sighed. "I suppose you're right. I guess we're lucky just to get to see her occasionally."

"She looks happy enough," Jake admitted. "And that Billy's growing up to be a fine boy."

"Yes. I wish I could say the same for that little Ina´li. But you know something? As dark as he is, he still don't look like an Indian to me. He looks more like—"

"Who, Ellie?"

"Never mind. Hold out your plate, Jake, for the stew."

Eight hundred miles away, in the Georgia mountains, Tilda Mae and Obadiah rushed down the icy road toward the Parker place. Julius had just sent word that Lulu's baby had been born.

"Can't you get the horses to go any faster, Obadiah?"

"They're goin' as fast as they'll go, Tilda Mae."

She closed her mouth. She should have known better than to show her impatience. Obadiah was getting more stubborn with each year. And it did more harm than good to complain about anything that he did. But the biggest change in him, she'd noticed, had come right after Ellie and Jake had pulled up stakes and gone west.

"I sure do miss Ellie and Jake," Tilda Mae commented.

Obadiah nodded. "The settlement's not the same without them."

The wind was blowing hard, scattering large white flakes of snow over the road as they finally approached the gate to the property.

In summer or winter Tilda Mae never got used to the beauty of the wide fields and orchards, or the fine house set like a jewel among the trees.

Seeing the property always gave her a sense of pride—to think that her own Lulu had come up so high in the world.

A few minutes more and then Obadiah stopped in the circular drive. The mountain laurels were already covered with snow.

Hearing the vehicle, a proud Julius met them at the door. "Well, Granny, are you ready to see our little boy?"

Tilda Mae wasn't so sure she wanted a man older than she to call her Granny. But in her eagerness to see the boy she smiled and said, "Lead the way, Mr. Parker."

"He's the spittin' image of me," Julius announced. "Except for the hair. He's got Louise's hair."

So he'd started calling her by that name, too. With her best friends, Derusha and Letha, calling her that, Tilda Mae guessed she and Obadiah were the only ones left who still called their daughter Lulu.

Julius tiptoed to the door of the bedroom and carefully opened it. "Louise don't like for me to be so loud. I might wake the little fellow," he confided. "And Obadiah, we'll have to go on the porch if we want to smoke. Louise says it ain't good for the baby."

When the door opened and Lulu saw her parents, she smiled in delight. "Mama! Papa! Come in and see Julius, Junior. He's awake."

Lulu looked like a queen, sitting in bed with the fine linen pillows at her back. Her dark, lustrous hair was tied in a blue ribbon to match the ribbons of her shift.

Tilda Mae tiptoed over to the bed to look down at the

baby in Lulu's arms. Speechless, she stared at him. The little boy was a replica of Ned Bates.

"Well, what do you think? Don't he look exactly like me?" Julius inquired.

Tilda Mae swallowed hard. "Exactly."

Chapter 38

The wedding dress lay on the bed.

Soon now Laurel would be leaving for the mission, where Samuel Worcester would perform the ceremony uniting her with Night Hawk.

As she bent over the dress her hands traced a Cherokee rose embroidered on the white wool by Tansee and her mother. It was a delicate dress, exquisite and ethereal looking—one made from the fabric of dreams and sewn with the threads of love.

How different it was from the ragged, threadbare dress she'd worn for so many months—first in the prison stockade and then later on the trail. Her hands, tracing the rich design, stopped at the embroidered crosses on each side of the rose—the crosses a symbol of the stars, an ideal beyond the reach of human hands.

This moment alone was a necessary one. For once Laurel put on the wedding dress and left for the mission, her old life, like the threadbare dress, would be left behind forever.

Laurel turned from the bedside and walked to the small dressing table, where she sat down. As she stared into the mirror, she automatically brushed her hair and began to pin it in the same manner as she had worn earlier, when she was a teacher at New Echota. But the mirror reflected much more than a woman arranging her hair.

The mirror suddenly became a labyrinth of reflections, with the present Laurel lost among the other faces, beckoning to her to remember them; for they were all a part of her— some acknowledged, some hidden in the deepest recesses where she had buried them with her pain.

"Father, look at me! Nacoochee and I can jump the fence now."

She was seven, and she wanted to show off her skill with her new pony, the one before Thistle.

"Be careful, Laurel," Alex called out. "Lift his head this time."

Knowing her father's eyes were upon her, and remembering her failed efforts earlier, she galloped down the lane, turned, and then headed for the fence.

She sailed over, with the pony's hooves clearing the tallest rail. A sense of elation and success enveloped her as she trotted proudly back to the place where her father waited.

Another face now demanded attention—its expression one of sadness and fear. It was a year after the pony episode, and she stood beside her mother, waiting for Two Feathers and the carriage. "I know you'll be homesick for a while, Laurel," her mother said, "but you must be brave. Remember that you are a chieftain's daughter and you must be educated as one."

"But I'll be so far away," Laurel said, trying to keep back the tears.

"Only in distance. When you're lonely, close your eyes and listen to your heart. We'll be there with you."

"Ya might think you've escaped, Indian gal. But we'll

git you yet!" An alien face, a threatening voice intruded, bringing a shortness of breath to Laurel.

"Please, Cloud Maker. We don't have much farther to go."

Others appeared, demanding equal attention. "I love you, Laurel." Will Podewell's face became Edward's face, with the same words echoing through the labyrinth. "I love you, Laurel. I love you, Laurel."

"No. If you did, you would never have deserted me," Laurel's intense voice shouted back.

"Pa, come quick....What are you doin' on my property?"

"This property is mine!"

"Ain't no more."

She stood at Ross's Landing and heard the military bugle. The martial sound, sending them into exile, was mixed with her own frantic voice, crying, "Walini′! Answer me. Where are you?"

"What's wrong?"

"Oh, Laurel. Our mother is dying."

"Quatie? Quatie is dying?"

The mirror became a prism, turning faster and faster to reflect the faces, the voices, the past that Laurel had never understood fully.

And then a voice—stronger and surer—the one she had not been perceptive enough to hear until it was almost too late, said simply, "I love you, Laurel."

"Tskĭ-lĭ′," she whispered.

The voices and faces disappeared. The mirror came into focus again, reflecting a woman who had finally put the past behind her.

Whatever the future held, she would share it with the man who had always been there for her. But like soul spirits searching for their own, she had not been able to recognize Night Hawk until she had found him in her heart.

When the tap at the door sounded, Laurel said, "Come in."

Trudie, dressed in her warm green woolen dress and cloak, said, "Your father has gone to get the carriage. It's time for you to put on your wedding dress, Laurel."

Tansee entered the room directly behind Trudie. Seeing her, Laurel could hardly believe her eyes. "Tansee, where is your old gray coat?"

"Chief Alex made me burn it," Tansee replied, prancing across the room and back to show off her new clothes.

"If you're not careful, you're going to steal the show."

"Well, now, a few heads might turn," Tansee admitted. She laughed at her own joke. Then she said, "We'd better get you in this pretty dress in a hurry. Chief Night Hawk is probably champing at the bit for you to arrive at the mission."

"We still have plenty of time, Tansee," Trudie said.

"Is Redbird ready?" Laurel inquired.

"Yes. She's waiting in the keeping room with Black Moccasin."

* * *

At the mission, Night Hawk was visibly nervous.

"Hold still," Jumping Rabbit cautioned him, trying to straighten his cravat.

"I think the old days were better," Night Hawk grumbled. "Give a gift to the father and then put your bride on your pony and ride away. None of this modern way."

"In the old days," Jumping Rabbit reminded him, "the women had charge of the judicial system, and control of half of the legislature."

Night Hawk smiled at his friend, whom he'd found shortly after arriving in the Indian territory. "They still have enormous power, Jumping Rabbit."

"You mean because they get to select the chiefs?"

"No. Because they turn a warrior's heart to a jumping trout, and his knees to corn mush."

"Tonight, your *knees* won't matter," Jumping Rabbit teased. "Your mind will, more than likely, be on another member of your body."

Night Hawk laughed. Then he became serious. "I've waited such a long time for Laurel."

Jumping Rabbit nodded. "A man has to be special for the Great Spirit to give him a second chance."

With the cravat retied and straightened, Night Hawk put on his long black coat. Beneath it, he wore an Indian shirt of rich calico, his wedding attire a combination of Indian and European, long ago adopted by his people.

At the MacDonald house, an admiring Redbird said, "Laurel, you're so beautiful."

"Thank you, Redbird."

"Here, the two of you wrap this around you so you won't get cold," Tansee insisted, unfolding another blanklet.

Tansee and Trudie sat opposite them in the carriage while Black Moccasin sat on the box with Alex.

"I wish Cousin John could have been here for my wedding," Laurel said.

"Yes, it's too bad he had to go back to Washington," Trudie agreed. "But Jane is bringing Silas and George."

They continued on their way, finally reaching the grounds of the mission.

Every space around the mission, for what seemed like miles, had been taken up with carriages, wagons, and horses tethered to the trees. People were everywhere, spilling into the square, lining the path to the chapel. They brought dishes of food and carried gifts.

"Look, there're Two Feathers and Agitsi′," Laurel said, peering from the carriage window. "They're going into the chapel now."

The news of the marriage between Laurel and Night Hawk had traveled by word of mouth. Now, on their wedding day, it seemed that all the people who had survived the trail of tears had come to share in their time of joy.

A few minutes later, Redbird walked down the aisle, proud that she had been chosen to stand with Laurel. She took her place beside Trudie. Jumping Rabbit and Alex stood beside Night Hawk.

As Laurel began to walk toward the altar where Samuel Worcester waited in his clerical robes, the people in the chapel began to sing a hymn that had long ago been translated into Cherokee. They had sung it on the trail of tears, asking for God's blessing in the time of their great travail. And now they sang it more joyfully. The people who stood outside the crowded chapel soon joined in, the sound lifting, like smoke to the heavens, sacred and sincere.

One of Arbuckle's dragoons, dispatched to check on such a large gathering of Cherokees, galloped to the edge of the crowd. "What's going on here?" he demanded.

The people ignored him, continuing to lift their voices to the heavens until the song was ended.

"It's the wedding of a chief and a chieftain's daughter," a man finally explained.

Still suspicious, the soldier left, but only as far as the nearest hill, where he sat on his horse and kept his eye on the vast crowd below.

Inside the chapel Night Hawk watched his bride walking to meet him. His heart quieted and his knees regained their strength.

When the two stood side by side, Samuel opened the prayer book and began the Christian service of marriage. Beside him stood Two Feathers, the Cherokee holy man, who translated Samuel's words for those who did not understand English.

Two Feathers had always been made aware of Laurel's destiny. That was why he had chosen to protect her as she traveled through the wilderness during her early years. One day she would be greatly revered and honored as a beloved woman by her people. The seeds had been sown on the road that cried. But today she was Night Hawk's bride. That was sufficient.

Samuel closed the prayer book. For the first time that day he smiled. Looking at Night Hawk and Laurel, he intoned, "You are now man and wife, flesh of one flesh, united in body and spirit as the sky and earth, the sun and moon, the trees and streams. Never forget that it is the Lord who made you, who gave you life, and will sustain you in all your trials. Amen."

The dragoon on the hill watched as a man and woman, in wedding attire, appeared outside the mission and, in the cold, they stood and received all those who had not been able to get a seat in the chapel. Then, when the couple finally turned to go back inside, the dragoon left, too, galloping in the direction of Fort Gibson.

* * *

That night, with Walini′ at the MacDonalds, Laurel and Night Hawk shared the small cabin that he had built by one of the streams. It was not a grand house; for he would still have to wait another year for his claims to be acknowledged.

As Laurel lay, content in Night Hawk's arms, he whispered, "I wish I could give you more than this, Laurel. A fine house, and books, and all the things you left behind—"

She reached out and lovingly traced the outline of his lips. "You've given me new dreams, Night Hawk. We're strong. Together we'll rebuild our lives in this strange, alien land."

In the night the wind, as if seeking out its lost children, blew from the east, sweeping over mountains and down icy rivers.

A spectral beating of drums and a great wailing joined with the wind. The voices cried, "Remember, remember."

And then, their grief spent, they became silent, vanishing into the rocks, the trees, and the flowers.

In the morning, as Laurel and Night Hawk awoke, the wind was gone. In its place was the sun, its brilliant rays promising a new day for lover and nation alike.

About the Author

Frances Patton Statham (Stay/tum) of metro-Atlanta, has received numerous awards in writing, music composition, art, lectures, and community service.

She graduated *magna cum laude* from Winthrop University with a double major in voice performance and music education. She holds an MFA degree from the University of Georgia, with further opera study.

Listed in such reference books as *World Who's Who of Women, the Dictionary of International Biography, International Who's Who of Intellectuals, International Who's Who of Authors and Writers, and Personalities of the South,* she is at work on her 17th novel.

CPSIA information can be obtained
at www.ICGtesting.com
Printed in the USA
FFHW011302011019
55347386-61073FF

9 780989 500715